Chasing A Butterfly

ᴬ Tiger Lily's Café® Mystery

By Kathleen Thompson

Kathleen Thompson

Chasing A Butterfly

Volume 7

A Tiger Lily's Café® Mystery

By Kathleen Thompson

ISBN-13: 978-0-9984023-6-9

ISBN-10: 0-9984023-6-2

© Registration # TX 8-309-108

Library of Congress Control Number: 2017904565

Kathleen Thompson

A List of Tiger Lily's Café® Mystery Series Books:

This cozy mystery series has everything you seek: an eclectic cast of characters, a mystery or two, and diligent detectives on duty. The detectives just happen to be feline.

Tiger Lily's Café is set in a Midwestern town nestled into the coast of a Great Lake. The setting itself acts as a character, bringing the reader into the sights, sounds and smells of the small resort community of Chelsea.

Read the series in order, or read any book alone. While characters grown and change, each volume stands alone with a clear beginning and a clear end.

- Turtle Soup (2014)
- Boo! (2015)
- Phishing (2015)
- Holiday (2016)
- A Rock And A Hard Place (2016)
- Splash (2016)
- Chasing A Butterfly (2017)
- Pumpkin Squash (2017)
- Snowblind (2017)
- Hearts On Fire (2018)
- Morel Of The Story (2018)
- Dragon Fire (2019)
- Beach Bunnies (2020)
- Shipwreck (2020)

Kathleen Thompson

Kathleen Thompson

Cast of Characters

Annie Mack, with the help of her "kids" and a talented staff, owns and manages a bed and breakfast, a cafe and other businesses on the south side of The Avenue. She has lived in Chelsea for only a few years, but her ancestral roots to the town date to the Civil War era.

Annie's SASHET Rainbow: (sa SHAY) a model that assigns color to each core feeling. **S**adness is blue; **A**nger red; **S**care green; **H**appiness yellow; **E**xcitement orange; and **T**enderness purple.

For more information, visit Liberation Psychotherapy: www.libpsych.com/articles/sashet/sashet.html.

Austin and Angela live in another state. They are the parents of Chris and have not been supportive of his career in the Coast Guard or his choice of a woman. Annie.

Ben and JoJo are college students. They work part-time all over town, including most of Annie's businesses.

Boone is the person to call if you need anything: mowing, snow removal, landscaping, maintenance, preventative maintenance, and just about anything else. He is married to **Harriet (Hilly),** who provides business cleaning services. His sons **Daryl** and **Donny** work for him. Their roots are in rural Appalachia, and they are so much more than people think.

Candice is the head waitress at Mo's Tap. A native of Chelsea, her long, thick, dark hair is the envy of most women who meet her.

Carlos is the manager and baker at Mr. Bean's Confectionary. He is a citizen of the US but was originally from Mexico. He supports his mother and younger sisters, who still live there. He is married to Isabel.

Cheryl inherited The Marina from her parents. It's a small deep water marina with basic amenities. Cheryl is married to Ray. She has known Annie since they were children.

Chris is Annie's special friend, although neither of them are ready to commit to a permanent relationship. He is the Officer in Charge of the Coast Guard Station. His stress relieving hobby is art. His sketches – in charcoal, pencil and pastel – are sold for charity.

Clara owns the flower and gift shop, Bloomin' Crazy. She is a citizen of the US, originally from Haiti, and has an ebullient personality. She keeps The Avenue decorated with fresh and silk flowers year-round.

Cookie probably has another name, but this is what he goes by. He cooks at Mo's Tap and learns what he can from Felicity at every opportunity. He's reticent at best, and he yearns to have his own restaurant. To keep him, Annie opened a fine dining restaurant, Bon Vivant Grille, on Fridays and Saturdays inside the Café.

Daniela is a former professional baker from Mexico. She has been a mother figure to Isabel, who is married to Carlos. She and her adult daughters, **Rosa** and **Valeria**, now live in Chelsea

Diana is the chief instructor at L'Socks' Virasana (Veer AHS ana). She is Mem's daughter. Diana left home right after high school and did not speak to her mother until her return ten years later. Their relationship, while tenuous, continues to grow stronger.

Felicity is the chef at Tiger Lily's Café. She is young, perky and extremely talented in the kitchen. She manages the Café, the upstairs catering facility and outside catering operations.

Frank recently moved to Chelsea to open an antique shop, Antiques On Main. He and Mem are in a relationship.

Gema recently moved to Chelsea to open Gema's Creations. There, she makes and sells unique jewelry pieces. She has space in the front corner of Antiques On Main.

George is the bartender and manager of Mo's Tap. He is a top-notch bartender and can be counted on to keep confidences. He is a volunteer with the local Coast Guard.

Georgia manages the kitchen at the Bon Vivant Grille on weekends, coordinates catering for the Café, and cooks part-time at Mo's Tap. Her father, **Fred Calendar**, comes to town on occasion to see her and her daughter Frederica **(Little Fred)**.

Geraldine was the leader of the "it" crowd in high school, and somehow, life didn't turn out quite as she expected. Everything Annie isn't – perfectly dressed, perfectly coiffed, and perfectly awful – Geraldine is more than a thorn in Annie's side. **Everett** is her on-again-off-again husband.

Ginger is the daughter of Pete, the Chief of Police, and Janet. She works part-time at L'Socks' Virasana. Because she moved to town as a teen (when her father retired from the Marine Corps), and because she is one of the few African American teens in town, she sometimes feels like an outsider.

Greg is a progressive realtor in Chelsea. His goal is to get the right property to the right owner, always moving Chelsea forward.

Gwen is Annie's accountant. A motherly figure, her financial acumen is hidden from all but those lucky enough to have her in their corner.

Hank is a former member of the Town Council. He opposes Annie in every way.

Harry is the regular driver for the rental company used almost exclusively by folks on The Avenue.

Henrie manages the KaliKo Inn in an elegant manner. He does not invite confidences and speaks little about himself. Always formal in tone, people have difficulty pegging his accent. Is it French? Cameroon? Rwandan?

Holly and Jolly, twins, own DoubleGood, an electronics and hardware store. Holly lives in a wheelchair. Natives of Chelsea, they used to hate the names given them by their parents. Now, they enjoy the novelty of it.

Ian is a childhood friend of George. He coordinates local sporting and team events. He is light-hearted and fancy-free.

Isabel is married to Carlos. She is attending classes to become a citizen. She works with Carlos in the bakery and at Bon Vivant as the hostess.

Janet is Pete's wife. She spent twenty years as a Marine officer's wife. She traveled the world and is now living in Chelsea. She is an outsider, not having grown up here like Pete. She is the ultimate community volunteer.

Jennifer and Marie, sisters and nurse practitioners, own The Drug Store and The Clinic. Folks call the sisters before calling nine-one-one. Chelsea natives, they know everyone. And their secrets.

Jenny is an attorney who focuses on family law. She enjoys taking on cases that will right an injustice. She is always ready to engage in battle with those who don't believe a woman, much less a woman of color, can dance with the big boys.

Jerry learned how to make candy in a minimum security federal prison. He was not an employee. Jerry works hard to overcome his shyness, particularly around women.

Jesus manages Sassy P's Wine & Cheese and also selects the wines. His family, famous vintners in the Napa Valley, owned, farmed and made wine for generations before California became a part of the United States.

Joan is a member of the Town Council. She opposes Hank in every way. Clara's pet name for her is "Joan of Chelsea."

Juanita is a reporter for the local newspaper. As every reporter on every small town paper, she also sells ads, develops and places the ads, does photography and…reports.

Laila owns Babar Foods. A traditional Pakistani, she is raising her children without the assistance of a husband. Her children are **James, Ava** and **Carl**, who lives with Autism.

Marco is a police officer in Chelsea. He is "second in command" because he was the only officer that didn't go off-kilter during a hostage situation. Marco prides himself on being one-hundred-percent-eye-talian-American.

Martha used to own a bed and breakfast. The cottage was renovated to add an apartment suite, now occupied by Georgia and Little Fred. Martha is retired and enjoys spending time at the Inn.

Mem owns the health food store and cyber café, CyberHealth. Her wisdom is reassuring to everyone, including her daughter, Diana. She teaches the safe use of social media to all ages and has equipment and technology that is helpful to the small-town police department.

Minnie chooses perfect cheeses to accompany the rotating wine selections at Sassy P's Wine & Cheese. She comes from several generations of cheese makers in Wisconsin.

Nancy and Sam are Annie's mother and step-father. They have been married since Annie was a child. They come for extended visits in Chelsea and have learned to call this town their second home.

Pete is a native of Chelsea. He retired from the Marine Corps and is now the Chief of Police. Like Annie, his ancestors arrived in the Civil War era. His, however, came up via the Underground Railroad. He and his wife Janet have three children, the eldest of whom is Ginger. Clarice and Tamara are in high school and junior high.

Ramon (ra MONE) is Clara's boyfriend. A Jamaican by ancestry, he plays saxophone with a jazz fusion band called Bergamasco (after the breed of his dog). He and Clara work hard to maintain their mostly long-distance relationship.

Ray owns and operates The Escape, a yacht fashioned into a cruiser for fishing, diving and pleasure. He is married to Cheryl; Chris is his best friend.

Teresa is a newcomer to the area. She came to this community to serve. She pastors a small church, Soul's Harbor, and pastors the community through her outreach.

Terrence & Jerald Timmer-Schmidt have just moved to town. Terrence is a heart surgeon; Jerald is a psychiatrist. They have opened a medical office building in town.

Trudie is the barista at Tiger Lily's Café. She is from Jamaica and ended up in Chelsea when a former boyfriend dumped her at the campground. Felicity saved her, and they have been the best of friends ever since.

WQVX Channel Two. "The Lake Region's good news station" is anchored by **Charles Veritone**. The "ace on-site reporter" is **Dan Tapper**. **Felix** does weather.

Annie's Cats

Annie has seven cats. Most people would call them "rescue kitties." From Annie's perspective, each of them rescued her.

Tiger Lily is a beautiful tabby cat with soft green eyes. She is the titular manager of Tiger Lily's Café, the main gathering place for Chelsea. She is generally calm and logical.

Little Socks is a bright-eyed black cat with white socks. She has a commanding personality and is small and sneaky enough to serve as a cat burglar. She spends time at the yoga studio, L'Socks' Virasana (Veer AHS ana).

Kali, Ko and Mo are litter mates. They shared a secret language as kittens; Kali and Ko now speak "cat," but Mo still speaks "secret." Kali and Ko can be found at the KaliKo Inn, a lakeside bed and breakfast. Mo spends time at Mo's Tap, an upscale blues bar.

Sassy Pants is aptly named; it's difficult to keep this little girl's attention. She is overly sensitive and will react out of emotion instead of reason. She entertains at Sassy P's Wine & Cheese.

Mr. Bean is the baby of the family and is mostly gray with traces of tiger. He has two speeds: fast and love me.

Other Companions

Brown Mousie finds Sassy Pants and makes a new friend. He lives in the long building and roams from the Café to the Wine & Cheese shop. He stays primarily at Sassy P's.

Claire is a blue point Himalayan cat whose human is Frank. She's beautiful and loves people. She is stand-offish with other cats.

Cyril is an English setter whose human is Pete, the Chief of Police. Cyril is friendly and calm. He is an excellent hunter.

Fiamma is a Bergamasco. Dreadlocks cover her face. In fact, her entire body is covered with a combination of long dreadlocks and mats of hair. She is an outrageous flirt.

Honey Bear is a large, golden, long-haired mutt of a cat who believes it is his perfect right to be anywhere. Other cats hate him.

Jock is a Portuguese water dog whose human is Ray, the captain of The Escape. Jock is spirited and affectionate; he loves children.

Oscar McMurphy was a stray, named Scaredy Cat by the kids. Despite the name, she is a girl who now lives with Holly and Jolly. She claims Holly as her very own. She is often in and out of the Inn and other places on The Avenue with her brother, Simon Finnegan.

Simon Finnegan was a stray, named Fat Cat by the kids, who now lives with Holly and Jolly. He claims Jolly to be his mom. He is often in and out of the Inn and other places on The Avenue with his sister, Oscar McMurphy.

Speckles is a tortoise shell cat, named for her orange speckles. She belongs to Georgia and is Little Fred's chief nanny.

Tillie came to live on The Avenue with her dreadful family from England. She is a Jack Russell Terrier and now lives with Carlos and Isabel above the Confectionary.

She has free run of The Avenue, including the Inn. She is small enough to squeeze in and out of the cat doors.

Guests at the Inn

Jeff Bennett is a Special Agent with the FBI and a regular guest of the KaliKo Inn. He told Henrie he was taking a vacation. Yeah, right.

Jessica, Paul, Jerome and Sally are Annie's niece (daughter of Patti), her husband and twin children. Jessica is doing the fifty-mile Lakeside Triathlon; Paul is doing the one hundred-mile.

Mark is introduced as a friend of Jeff, also on vacation, and staying at the Inn to participate in the Lakeside Triathlon. He happens to work for the DEA.

Patti, Fritz, Allen, Percy, Gracie, Ella and Ollie are Annie's half-sister, her husband, and five of her children.

Randy & Krissie are a couple in their thirties in town for the Lakeside Triathlon. Krissie is doing the one hundred-mile. Randy is doing Melanie.

Tim & Melanie are a couple in their thirties in town for the Lakeside Triathlon. Tim is doing the one hundred-mile. Melanie is doing Randy.

Others In Town

Chris's mother, **Angela**, arrives and stays in a nice hotel in Marsh Haven. Chris's father, **Austin**, comes to town later in the week.

Georgia's ex-husband **Ken** has come to town. He is staying at the campground.

Kathleen Thompson

1

Anyone other than Henrie would enjoy a Monday morning without complications. Henrie was bored. The guests from the week before were gone, the last having left Sunday morning. The rooms needed for today were ready; no one was on hand for breakfast.

The windows were open, letting the warm August breeze flow through the first floor of the house.

Henrie sat at the kitchen table and sipped a second cup of coffee. The kitchen smelled of cinnamon and apples. Breakfast was ready and stayed warm in a steam tray.

Perhaps he should call Annie and let her know it was ready. Perhaps he should let her sleep. After all, it was quite late when she got in the night before.

Henrie sighed. Then he started. Tiger Lily sat in the doorway to the kitchen. She could have been there for a while. She stared at Henrie, impassive, and he now stared back.

Finally, he said, "Good morning, Tiger Lily. Would you like a treat?"

Tiger Lily didn't move; she didn't blink. Had she blinked, Henrie would have gotten up to get a treat. A blink would have meant, "Yes, please." The stare meant, "Nothing good is happening here."

Henrie sighed again. This was going to be a hard Monday after all.

Henrie was the manager of the KaliKo Inn, a bed and breakfast in the resort town of Chelsea. Chelsea was nestled into a Great Lake on one side and a state park on two others. Cut off from the rest of the world with the exception of an access highway coming in from the east, it had the feel of a village, forgotten in time. Indeed, all of the buildings on Sunset Avenue were constructed post–Civil War when the lumber industry was booming.

Sunset Avenue derived its name from the brilliant sky visible every night over the lake. Known by the locals simply as The Avenue, it started at the town circle and ended, one long city block later, at the expanse of public parking lot and city park that led directly to the lake.

The KaliKo Inn sat at the corner of that expanse, situated on a plot of land that included its own white sand beach. A southern-style mansion from the 1880s, the Inn was the largest and most prominent of the B&Bs in town.

Henrie was a private man. He came to Chelsea from New York, having managed a five star hotel for several years, yet he was perfectly happy to be the chief cook, concierge, toilet bowl cleaner and baby sitter for this small town B&B.

He appeared to read minds; he was ready for anything that was needed before a request was actually made. His accent was untellable. Some thought French, some Rwandan, some Cameroon.

Henrie was ageless. He could be in his thirties, forties or fifties, depending on your perspective. Were you looking at that handsome, unlined face? Did the gray in his ultra-short hair or finely trimmed goatee and mustache catch your eye? Or was it the maturity, the presence, the intelligence that caught your attention? In any situation, it was a fine package, placed in the image of a tall, slim, muscular, coffee-colored man.

Henrie lived in a small apartment on the main level of the KaliKo Inn. Annie, the person to whom his mind turned, lived in the apartment that encompassed the third floor.

Annie owned the KaliKo Inn and the building to the east, a long, two-story brick building built to hold storefronts needed to keep the lumber industry going in the 1880s. Now it held five businesses that supported the tourist industry of the twenty-first century.

Henrie rose from the table. He pulled several small dishes from a cupboard; from the refrigerator he retrieved cooked bacon. He crumbled several pieces of bacon into each dish.

Tiger Lily, a pretty gray and brown tabby cat with soft green eyes, watched him, impassive, from the kitchen door.

Henrie carried the handful of dishes, seven in all, with a practiced efficiency. He walked from the kitchen to the dining room, leaned down to pull up a cloth covering a nearby table, and placed the dishes carefully on the floor underneath the table.

He stood, straightened the sign on the table – the sign that declared the covered table to be the domain of the Seven Cats Detective Agency – and looked back at Tiger Lily. She remained impassive but now sat facing the dining room, still looking at Henrie.

Henrie stared back but was polite enough to blink on occasion. He did not want her to think he was trying to win the staring contest.

"Where are your siblings this morning?"

Tiger Lily seemed to incline her head toward the stairway, but at that moment, several cats could be heard making their way into the dining room. Kali and Ko led the way, going straight to Henrie to demand attention. Henrie happily leaned down to give it.

"I missed you girls. It is so good to have you back."

Mo and Mr. Bean pushed Kali out of the way and rose to put their feet on Henrie's left leg. He leaned down to cup first Mo's head, then Mr. Bean's.

Sassy Pants dropped to the floor in front of him, requiring Henrie to lean further down to rub her stomach.

Little Socks jumped lightly to the top of the Seven Cats table, looked at Henrie with her bright green eyes and blinked once.

Henrie turned again as Annie walked into the dining room. At least it looked like Annie. Her straight, dark hair, probably at fifty percent gray, had the typical bounce. She wore her trademark capris and colorful flowing top. The sandals, practical, with a one-inch heel and good arch support, matched the outfit.

He wasn't sure Annie was actually inside the body. The spring in her step seemed to have sprung. Her walk was more like a trudge. Her face, beyond the cheekbones that hinted at American Indian ancestry, bore no expression.

Henrie, quite unlike Henrie, opened his arms, allowing Annie to walk into them. She leaned into his shoulder, arms around his waist, as he hugged her close for a brief moment. They parted, and he said, "You need coffee. Come."

Annie sat at the kitchen table, a butcher block with bar stools around it, and allowed Henrie to serve. He put the coffee in front of her and opened the steam tray to dish out what would pass for breakfast today, a French toast casserole made with crusty French bread and baked apple slices with cinnamon and brown sugar.

In spite of her demeanor, Annie smiled and took in a deep breath.

"It's good to be home, Henrie."

"It is good to have you here. I was lonely. I missed you, and I missed the darlings, Kali and Ko especially."

Kali and Ko purred and rubbed themselves on his ankles. They left cat hair on his pants legs in appreciation of his comments.

"Are the kids going to work this morning?"

Annie looked around the kitchen at the cats, all now on the floor, or on a counter top, or on top of the refrigerator. Sassy Pants sat at the kitchen sink and stared out the window, probably having caught sight of a chipmunk.

"I think not. I think we'll all take a break today. I'll probably go out later this morning, just to check in. Or maybe this afternoon."

Annie sipped her coffee and ate her casserole. She put her fork down and held the cup with both hands, staring deeply into it. Then around at the cats. Then down at her plate. Then into her cup. Everywhere, it seemed to Henrie, but at him.

Finally, he could take it no longer.

"Annie, something has been troubling you for a few months. I have tried not to read your mind, but I fear it is something not related to your angst this morning. So now, I have two things with which to be concerned on your behalf, and I do not know what those things are. It may not help you to talk about it, but it will certainly help me. Using your vernacular, spill!"

Annie couldn't help herself. She looked at Henrie and laughed, a bit of her natural sparkle returning. Henrie had actually used the word "spill."

"Henrie, I don't know if you want to know it all."

"I want to know all that you are willing to tell. For now, if it is difficult, a thumbnail sketch may suffice."

"I guess I was keeping a fairly big thing private from you, and from most of my friends. Chris, of course, knows, and some people, like Mem and Clara, have a bit of an idea, but it's all going to come out, so best you know now."

Henrie took a sip of coffee and glanced down at the table to lessen the intensity of the moment.

Annie continued. "In a nutshell, what I'll tell you more about later is that my life has been a complete lie."

Henrie couldn't help it. His head jerked up and he stared.

Annie stared back.

"All of this property, all of these businesses, everything I inherited from my father, were, um, I'm not sure how to say this."

They were silent for several seconds, her, getting her thoughts together and him, restraining himself to allow her the time.

Annie continued to look at Henrie as she started to speak. "According to Mom, Dad was aware of everything, and he still chose to, um," Annie looked down at her plate as she continued, "be my dad and leave all of this to me, but somehow I still think it was all based on a lie."

She stopped again and Henrie silently started to count – one, two, three – to keep from speaking.

Annie still stared at her plate. "My natural father is a man named Darrell Mayes. He died before I was born; he was a friend of both my father and my mother. Actually, Mom had an affair with him. She was married to Dad at the time. Dad found out, knew I wasn't his, but he loved me just the same. In the end, though, the affair is what broke up their marriage."

Henrie let the silence drift for several seconds. "But your father knew. He loved you. Never did he say or do anything to disavow you as a daughter. Why do you think your life has been a lie?"

"I don't know, Henrie. You're saying essentially the same things Mom says, and Chris, but I can't help it."

Henrie spoke slowly, praying he wasn't stepping into a minefield. "Have you considered talking to a professional?"

"I haven't, but that's not a bad idea."

Silently, Henrie breathed a sigh of relief. "Is something else bothering you about this?"

"Geraldine."

"Heavenly days. What does she have to do with it?"

Geraldine was, in both Annie and Henrie's opinions, a perfectly horrid woman. Currently, she was legally restrained from coming within five hundred yards of Annie's businesses. This order effectively prevented her from stepping onto Sunset Avenue.

"Well, I did some research into his – Darrell's – background with the help of the genealogist at the library. Turns out the genealogist is Geraldine's brother-in-law, and they talk all the time. I don't know if she knows everything, but she knows I was doing research into a man who is one quarter Cherokee and that he was from my home town. She's trying to score points with her crew with that information."

"I wonder if her point is your ancestry or your heritage."

"I think both. She is making a big deal with her friends, and, since they can come into my businesses and anywhere else on The Avenue, they're sniping and baiting whenever they can."

"Well, then, let us give them something to snipe about. Allow me to think on this for a time. We will, using another term I have heard, take a bull by the horn."

Annie smiled as she looked up. "Horns, Henrie. We'll take the bull by the horns."

"Well. Two, then. Better than one, certainly. And now, what is this new sadness that envelops you?"

Annie sighed and looked back at her plate. The telephone rang. Henrie rose from the table to answer it.

"Chris, good morning. How was your trip?" … "Oh, certainly, she is right here…"

As Henrie turned to give the phone to Annie, he looked at an empty table. "I am sorry, Chris, she seems to have gone back upstairs." He listened for several seconds. "Yes, I will relay the message."

As Henrie hung up the telephone, he put two and two together, coming up with five. Annie was sad; Chris did not answer a question about the trip; Annie avoided taking the call; Chris left a message rather than call Annie's cell. There was trouble in paradise.

On the other hand, the cats were home.

"Come, children. Let us go to the beach."

Kali, Ko and Mo walked sedately to the library and a nap in the sun. The rest scurried after Henrie as he made his way down the hallway to the all-season porch and out to the private beach. Three cats ran out to the sand, already warm with the morning sun. Tiger Lily stayed close to the Inn, in the garden area with tables and chairs.

She crouched in a hunter's stance. Her tail twitched slightly. Her prey was a late summer monarch, currently drinking from a flower.

Before she could pounce, the butterfly flew away, perhaps sensing the danger posed by the mighty hunter, the Tigress Lily.

Henrie, unaware of the hunter and her prey, called to her from the beach. "Tiger Lily, come on, now, we are going to walk up the beach."

Tiger Lily finally tore her eyes away from the monarch, now flitting around a bush, and joined her siblings at the edge of the water.

2

Two cars pulled into the parking lot at the Inn. One car had a bike rack that held what looked like a road bike. It was actually a triathlon bike, intended for road use but shaped for speed.

One man got out of each car. They stretched, as if the journey had been long, took bags out of the back seats and started toward the Inn. The man whose car held the bicycle said, "We're early. Think we can get in?"

"It won't be a problem. The front door is unlocked this time of day. We can at least put our bags down, and if Henrie isn't here, we'll go on to the Café for lunch."

"So you've been here a few times?"

"Yep. Normally I've been working on something. The first time, I was undercover to everyone, including the folks here at the Inn. That won't work anymore, though. At least not for me. You can stay under, though."

"Your contacts here are solid?"

By now, they were on the porch.

"Yes. We'll have good support when we need it."

The man familiar with the Inn opened the door. He didn't expect to see anyone at this time of day. He was wrong.

Annie, sitting at the computer on the second floor landing, glanced down and said, "Jeff!" She rose and trotted down the stairs to give him a hug.

Jeff hugged Annie quickly and turned to the other man. "Mark, meet Annie. She owns the Inn and all of the other places on this side of The Avenue."

Mark and Annie shook hands. Jeff continued to speak.

"Mark is a triathlete in his spare time. He's here for the fifty-mile this weekend. I'm here to try out some of the local wineries."

"Yeah, right. No other reason." Annie laughed.

"Sometimes I really do take vacation."

"Yeah. Vacation." Annie turned to Mark. "Did he tell you the Inn has been blessed with more than its fair share of murders and such?"

"He might have let that slip. That only added to the allure of the triathlon. I love a little mystery with my exercise."

"And I'm sure you know he's been involved in one or two. Or three."

"He might have let that slip, too."

"Do you work together?"

"No, actually, we don't. I've had the misfortune of becoming his friend. When he heard I was doing this triathlon, he invited himself along. Seems he likes this little town."

"We like him, too." Annie turned her attention back to Jeff. "Several people will meet you for dinner tonight at Mo's. Me, Chris, Pete and Janet, Ray and Cheryl, I think George has the night off and will be there, too."

"That's great. Hey, look, we're going to the Café for lunch. I expected to see you there, but…would you like to join us?"

"Thanks, Jeff, but I need to make my rounds. I'm getting a late start today."

"Okay. For now, we'll take our bags up to the second floor and come back to check in after we eat."

"I'll help."

Jeff and Annie took the bags and chatted as they went upstairs. Mark looked around. The Inn was clean, bright and modern, homey, but not as cluttered and kitschy as other B&Bs with which he was familiar. Large windows with minimal coverings allowed sunlight to stream through. The furniture looked comfortable but elegant, upholstered in shades of slate blue and gray. Tables and other wooden furniture were made of light walnut.

He walked into the library, a long room with a large-screen television at one end, several seating areas, and shelves filled with books and DVDs. Bow windows allowed plenty of windowsill room for three large cats napping in the sunshine. One cat, a long-haired gray, opened one eye to stare at him. Mark gave the cat a quick two-finger salute. The eye blinked, then closed.

The lavender walls of the library morphed into light blue in the entryway. Mark walked back through the foyer and into the dining room, painted rose. Fresh flower bouquets in the foyer and dining room were blue in hue, similar, but one was extra-large, the other smaller. Only "large."

Mark turned and walked around the foyer. He stuck his head into a small room with a refrigerator, cupboards, and a cabinet with a Keurig and several selections of coffee, tea and hot chocolate. He walked down the hallway that ended in what looked like a guest room at the end and the door to an all-season porch on the right. From the doorway to the porch, he saw the beach. A man and several cats walked toward the house.

Mark heard Jeff calling. He turned and walked back to the foyer. He was ready for lunch.

Annie left with them. Mark was happy to let Jeff and Annie chat while he looked around. The Inn was a beautiful example of southern charm on a midwestern Great Lake. A wrap-around porch was covered by a blue awning with pin stripes in a multitude of colors. Café tables and chairs were painted in the same color scheme, and wicker furniture had multi-colored cushions. A sign had two large dilute calico cats back-to-back. They looked suspiciously like two of the cats on the windowsill.

Across The Avenue was a long brick building, similar to the one they would soon walk past, but painted. Each storefront was set off from the next by a different color of pastel paint. Fun and funky logos were painted on the walls of the building, showing him a walk-in medical clinic, drug store, flower shop, hardware store, grocery store, a combination tea house and cyber café, and a church.

The Avenue itself was wide, deep enough for angle parking on each side and with a wide median. The median had a number of benches, small game tables, concrete flower pots filled with live summer flowers, midget trees, and a brick walkway up the center. Several walkers, a few gamers and teens with electronic devices filled the area.

While they walked forward, Mark turned his head to watch a camper. It drove down The Avenue toward the lake, turning in at the entrance to the state park camping area. Mark's gaze continued in that circle, causing him to turn and walk backward. He could see, now to his left, a small marina on what appeared to be a deep water harbor. A large boat painted in rainbow colors was headed out of the marina to the lake. He could make out the name on the side, The Escape.

Mark turned to walk forward and looked at the building they were passing. They had already passed a winery and confectionary, each with colorful awnings and café tables and chairs. Each had a sign like the one at the Inn. The winery's sign showed a playful cat of many colors and the confectionary's sign showed a strong gray kitten.

They were at Mo's Tap. Jeff was saying, "Mark, this is where we'll have supper tonight. You'll like my friends." The sign showed the long haired gray cat that had blinked at him from the windowsill.

Then they were at a yoga studio, and Annie said good-bye. In just a few steps, Jeff and Mark reached a door. Jeff opened it, and Mark was treated to the sights, sounds and smells of Tiger Lily's Café. Jeff had said everyone in town, either resident or tourist, ate here. This was the place to come for good gossip and great food.

The tabby cat that should have been at the hostess stand wasn't there. All of the cats must be taking the day off. Seems like they were on vacation, unlike he and Jeff.

Annie stepped inside the yoga studio. Her timing was perfect. Diana's class was just over.

Diana waved and gave Annie the just-a-minute sign. She showed a woman how to do a particular pose. It looked to Annie like she was giving the woman instructions on how to modify the pose for a knee that was less than one hundred percent.

Diana grew up in Chelsea. After several years' absence, she returned home. She now managed the yoga studio. She worked with a talented group of part-time trainers who could stand in if Diana was out of town or otherwise unable to be on hand.

Annie wanted to talk to Diana because Diana had recently visited the home of her long-distance boyfriend. Harrison Jones was filthy rich. He lived in one wing of a large home, one could say a mansion, and his mother lived in another. A third wing was used for housing guests and entertaining. The family wealth was similar to what Annie had just experienced.

First, Annie had to take care of a little business.

When Diana was free, she breezed over to the bench where Annie sat and said, "Where's my girl today?"

"We all took an extra day off, getting back into the swing of things, so to speak."

"Well, tell her I missed her. Not just me. The students have been disappointed not to see her."

Annie laughed. "I didn't think she interacted with the students that much."

"She doesn't, not much, but when she does, the experience is priceless."

"She'll be here tomorrow, I promise. Hey, I need to find out if any of your part-timers are available to babysit this week. My sister and her family, including several kids between the ages of almost two through teens, will be here for several days. I don't need anyone full-time, but two of the four adults will be doing the triathlon, so…a few times during the week and definitely on Saturday."

"Let me think. Ginger is working a lot, but she's trying to get as much money as she can for community college. You can call her. She won't be available Saturday. JoJo isn't working for me on Saturday, so she might be available, and Ben might be also. I'm not sure what I'm going to do when this crop of instructors starts to graduate from community college. I hope they all find something and stay here in Chelsea."

"I hope the same. We don't have a lot of possibilities, but maybe, just maybe, we can keep them happy here."

"Hey, how was your visit?"

"That's why I'm here, actually. I'd like to hear a little more from you, what it was like to visit Harrison at his home."

"Oh, what a nightmare!"

"You said. But tell me more. Why was it a nightmare?"

Diana looked thoughtfully at Annie. "Well, to start with, you remember I met Mrs. Jones before, when Harrison was in the hospital here."

Harrison came to Chelsea as a guest of the Inn, intending to ice fish when he had never fished before. Not on a riverbank, not in a boat, not deep-water. Never. The winter was brutal, but he persisted, in an effort to please his mother. The result was nearly a catastrophe, and it ended with an extended stay in the psychiatric wing of the regional hospital.

"I remember. It was a rude shock for her. It seemed to me that you helped her through that."

"I did. Then. This is now. She was back in control when I visited, and let me tell you, I did not measure up to her vision for appropriate wife material."

"Are you vying for wife?"

"Not really, but if you're the parent, that's what you think. I didn't measure up, in almost every metric."

"Tell me what the metrics were."

"Let's see. Ancestry."

"Ancestry?"

"Yes. My father abandoned my mother. My mother is a small business owner in a small, insignificant town. The blood in my veins runs red, not blue."

"As in politics?"

"No, as in the truly upper crust and their blue blood."

"Oh. What else?"

"Genes."

"Blue jeans? You wear them?"

"That, too, but basically my genes, DNA, bone structure, facial structure, less than perfect skin and hair, teeth not perfectly straight and pearly white, a few lumps here and there, even though I do yoga constantly, and nails. My nails are not picture perfect."

"All of that? She told you all of that?"

"In one way or another. She was awful."

"How did she say it?"

"Oh, in the beginning, it would be a subtle dig. And yes, let's start with the blue jean thing. That was the first dig." Diana raised her head, pointed her nose up and put on a haughty tone of voice. "Harrison must have forgotten to tell you we dress for dinner."

Annie and Diana laughed. "Did you have to change?"

"No. Harrison stood up and showed his mother that he, too, was wearing jeans. She put her nose in the air, but what was she really going to do? Send both of us to the other wing to change? It would have taken a half hour to get there, change and get back."

"That long?"

"I may have exaggerated. But certainly fifteen or twenty minutes. And her guests would not have wanted to wait."

"She did this in front of guests?"

"Yes. And that was an embarrassment for Harrison. After that, it got worse, until finally, she lost all subtlety. On the last day, she said," Diana once again assumed a haughty air, "'If you cannot afford to, Harrison can pay to have your teeth straightened and capped. I assume you know that will be a necessity if you are to join the family. And before you come again, we must find a good spa to work on your skin.'"

Annie didn't know whether to laugh or cry, but Diana was laughing.

"How important is this to Harrison?"

"Not."

"And to you?"

"Not. Well, maybe a little. Only because I think she will always make sure to embarrass me, and that has nothing to do with him, really. But she will make his life miserable."

"What are your plans?"

"Harrison and I plan to see one another as often as we want, either here or in another town. We won't put him or his mother through that again."

Annie and Diana lapsed into silence. Diana took in a deep breath and asked, "Why, Annie? Why did you want to know? What happened?"

"First of all, thank you for talking to me, but I'm not sure I'm ready to talk about it just yet. I just wanted to hear about your experience, to see if there were any similarities."

"Can you at least tell me that? Are there similarities?"

"Yes. Please don't say anything, Diana. I'll tell you when I figure it out myself."

"Don't worry. I won't say a word. But you know the best person to talk to about this, don't you?"

"Your mom."

"My mom. Talk to her." Diana's mother was Mem, the owner of the cyber café and tea shop across The Avenue. She was the woman that most women in Chelsea turned to when they needed sage advice. Annie made a mental note to chat with her as soon as possible.

As Annie got up to leave, Georgia, another employee, stopped in. "Hey, Annie. It's good to have you back. We've missed Mo at the Tap. Is he coming in today?"

"He'll be in tomorrow, and thanks. It's good to be back."

"I'm sorry to interrupt, but I have a bit of an emergency. Diana, which of your part-timers is available to babysit for the rest of the week? Little Fred's daycare has to close for a family emergency."

Annie and Diana looked at one another.

"Oops."

"Oops?"

"I was here to get the same information. My sister and her family is coming. We are in need of some babysitters, too. The twins are just a little older than Fred."

"Oh, no. I don't know what else to do."

"You will do exactly what you were going to do. My sister won't be here until the day after tomorrow. You make arrangements for tomorrow, then I'll make arrangements for the rest of the week. Drop Fred off at the Inn starting Wednesday. On those days, it's my treat."

"Annie, thank you!"

"You're welcome. Ladies, I'll see you later." Annie left, feeling a little better. Diana seemed to have survived her nightmare with panache. Perhaps she could do the same.

Annie stopped at the Café, just to look in, and she saw Mem leaving her table. She waited at the hostess stand for Mem to get to the door, opened it for her and walked out with her. The warm breeze lifted their hair and ruffled a scarf on Mem's shoulder. "Do you have time for tea, or are you busy?"

"I always have time for tea. Come on over."

Annie followed Mem across The Avenue, and they went into Mem's tea shop, health food store and cyber café, CyberHealth. A part-time clerk was in the back, taking care of a gamer. Mem put her purse on a chair in the tea room and invited Annie to do the same. "I just received an order with a tea I've been dying to try. Sit. I'll put the water on."

Mem brewed tea the old fashioned way. Always heated water on the stove. Always used loose tea in a tea ball or round teabags without staples or strings. Always steeped it in a china teapot. Always served it in china tea cups with saucers. Of course, nothing matched. The teapot didn't match any of the cups and the cups didn't match any of the saucers. And often, the teapot was in a colorful cosy resembling a ladybug or squirrel or a nut of one kind or another. This August day was warm enough, the cosy was not required.

Annie browsed the kitchen gadget section until Mem returned. She wondered if she would be a better or more creative cook if she purchased all of the colorful items that promised kitchen wizardry. Or even just one. She picked up a cherry red pie plate with a bright white center and read the description.

"Rose's Perfect Pie Plate with deep-fluted edge for beautifully scalloped pie crusts and more secure handling into and out of the oven. High-fired ceramic pie plate with scratch-free glaze is decorative and durable; resists staining, odors and cracking. Deep-fluted edge supports more substantial pies and elaborate, decorative crusts, for apple pie, pumpkin pie, shepherd's pie, and more. Transitions beautifully from oven or broiler to the table; doubles as a baking dish for quiche or serving plate for vegetables, and more. Four cup capacity; dishwasher safe for easy cleanup; award-winning design from Rose Levy Beranbaum."

She took the pie plate to the table and returned to look again. This time she picked up a set of ceramic pie plates, fluted, and wouldn't you know it. In all of her feeling rainbow colors. Blue, red, green, yellow, orange and purple. Those went to the table as well.

She had to go back. She had seen colorful place settings. Dinner and dessert plates, soup bowls that could serve as huge hot chocolate cups, and mugs. They were a mass of orange, blue, green and yellow, the bottoms and outsides in one solid color, rims in another solid color, and the tops and insides in yet another color, with swirls of white outlining flowers, leaves and hummingbirds. Annie selected two place settings of four.

She returned to the glass section. She had spied rainbow colored glasses. Sets of six, again, one each in her signature colors, but with unique designs on the outside of each, textured, colorful and tasteful. Annie needed to purchase two sets.

Mem was coming toward the table with a tray carrying the tea and the cups.

"What are you doing, Annie?"

"Feeding a fever. I don't know. I just need to buy something! Can you tell me why dinner plates come in sets of four and glasses come in sets of six? It's like hot dogs! Hot dogs come in tens and twelves. Buns come in sixes and eights."

Mem set the tea down on the counter and took the glasses from Annie's hands. She turned. The table was full. Seven pie pans, eight dinner sets, now twelve glasses, and...

Annie walked past her and placed two more sets of glasses at the table. Wine glasses. Hand-painted in different patterns with slim, curvy stems that would frustrate anyone with arthritis. "At least wine glasses come in fours."

Mem was still holding the water glasses as she turned to watch Annie go back one more time. She picked up two stainless steel pie servers with colorful glass bead handles and two sets of stainless flatware with her rainbow colors enameled on the handles. "Sixes again."

"Are you done?"

"No. I saw tablecloths in the corner." Annie picked up two packages of linen and cotton blend tablecloths and napkins. Each package contained four tablecloths and eight napkins, in red, green, blue and yellow.

"Those will fit your kitchen table, Annie, but not your dining room…"

"I'll use more than one, I might need three. It will be a part of a rainbow. And now I have sixteen napkins."

Before she sat down, she grabbed a set of ten wooden serving spoons and forks in a variety of sizes, handles painted, again, in rainbow colors.

Mem finally found room on the table for the glasses she held. She stood back, hands on her hips, and took stock. She took a deep breath. "Do you really need seven pie pans?"

"No. But I want that bright red one. It will be perfect for my tomato tarts."

"You make tomato tarts?"

"Well, I have. I mean, it's been a while. But I do. And pear pie. If I make a tomato tart and a pear pie at the same time, I'll need another pie pan."

"So you got six."

"They're in my colors."

"And one of them is red. But it's not red enough for…"

"That single red one is beautiful. The others are cute."

"Okay. Well, let's sit at another table, and I'll, um… Mark, could you come here, please?"

Mem's part-timer walked from the back.

"Could you please get one of our carts, put these things in, ring it up, then deliver it to the KaliKo Inn?"

"Sure."

Mark turned to get a cart and Mem turned back to Annie. Do you want to take another look before he gets started?"

Annie closed her eyes, angled her head up and to the left and thought. Plates, bowls, mugs, glasses, wine glasses, silverware, tablecloths, napkins, pie pans – you can serve anything in a pie pan, even fruits and vegetables – and serving utensils. "Nope. I'm done. No! I need a soup tureen! And a pitcher for water."

Annie went back to the pots and pans section and found a stove-top-to-table-top ceramic pot, orange. Perfect. Now she needed a soup ladle, and something to set the ladle on at the dinner table…. She found a set of three upright ladles, orange, yellow and green, that would stand on the table after use, and a set of six acrylic counter savers that could also act as trivets, clear, with colorful designs swirled into them. Nearly forgetting, she doubled back to a shelf that had several hand-painted Polish ceramic pitchers. She chose a white one with a blue handle, a flower garden painted from the bottom to almost the top third.

"Now I'm done." Annie added the last items to the cart Mark had brought. Hmmm. Quite a shopping trip.

"Do you want us to charge this to the Inn, or is it a personal expense?"

"Personal. Oh. I don't have my billfold." Annie pulled out her cellphone and clicked on her contacts. She went to the counter and wrote down the number, expiration date and other pertinent information. "Charge it to this, Mark, then please put a match to that paper."

Mem poured tea and Annie sat.

"So, tell me what's going on, and why all the interest in kitchen items all of a sudden?"

"The kitchen items don't have anything to do with anything, I don't think. I just felt like…"

"Burning through several hundred dollars?"

"Well, maybe…"

"How often do you think you'll use those things?"

"I'm going to start cooking."

"For Chris?"

"For me. And the kids."

"I'm sure the kids will love a good tomato tart. That's always on the top of any cat food list. Along with pear pie."

Mem drank tea. She took long, slow swallows, breathing in the aroma as she did so. Annie followed suit.

As she breathed in, she could smell chamomile, lavender and lemon. It was very relaxing. As always, Mem had chosen the correct tea for the moment.

"So tell me, Annie, what did you want to talk about?"

3

Chris arrived at the Inn about an hour earlier than expected. He walked through to the kitchen to find Henrie doing prep work for the next day's breakfast.

"Henrie, what's for breakfast?"

Henrie turned with a smile. "Chris, it is good to see you. Would you like something to eat?"

"No, thanks. I ate all weekend, and, well, you know the kind of food we'll be eating at Mo's tonight."

"Coffee? It's fresh."

"I'll take a cup. No, don't bother, Henrie, I can get it myself."

Chris got a cup from the cupboard and poured coffee from the always-fresh pot. Henrie turned back to his work while Chris leaned against the counter. Neither spoke. Both wanted to ask a million questions, but both knew the person to ask was Annie.

Even with the unasked questions, Chris and Henrie were close enough the silence was companionable.

Chris and Annie had been friends since Annie moved to Chelsea and special friends for close to a year. He was the Officer in Charge of the local Coast Guard Station and, because of the growing relationship with Annie, had given up an opportunity for promotion that would have taken him away.

Annie, Chris and the cats returned the night before from a several-day trip to the home of Chris's parents. Chris grew up in an old-money family on the coast of another of the Great Lakes. Growing up in privilege, he attended private schools and an Ivy League college. He chose a career in the Coast Guard, much to the consternation of his parents.

Chris recalled a particularly awful conversation over the weekend in which his parents blamed Annie for that decision, made years before they had even met.

Finally, Chris asked if Annie was home for the day or still out.

"I believe she is in the apartment. The children have had their afternoon snack and are anxiously awaiting the arrival of Cyril and Jock."

"Do you think it's okay if I go up?"

Henrie turned to look at Chris. "I am not even going to make note of the last time you had a need to ask that question."

"That obvious, huh?"

"Yes. But I will not ask. It is not my business."

"Will you give advice?"

"Yes. Go upstairs. Give Annie a hug. I do not know what the issue is, but by all means, apologize."

"But…"

"Apologize."

"Yes, sir." Chris put the empty cup on the cupboard and walked, as if to his own funeral, to the stairway.

He walked slowly, savoring what would possibly be the last minutes of life as he knew it. He went up the first flight of stairs, stopped and looked down at the foyer. He made note of the fresh flowers, the arrangement of furniture, the cleanliness of the first and second floors. He sighed.

He went up the second flight of stairs, stopped outside the apartment door, took out his key, looked at it, put it back in his pocket, turned around, started back to the stairwell, stopped, thought, turned around, went to the door and knocked.

He could hear the cats on the other side. They knew the minute he hit the hallway, so they were already at the door when he knocked.

Sassy Pants came halfway through the cat door. She looked at him as if to say, *"Are you comin' in?"* Chris heard the other cats behind her. One of the cats, he couldn't see which one, pushed Sassy Pants, but the little girl held her ground.

Annie did not answer the door.

He knocked again.

He heard footsteps, heard Annie say, "Come in or go out, Sassy."

Sassy Pants turned and went back in. Chris was alone in the hallway again.

He heard the lock turn. The door opened. Annie appeared. Her eyes were red, her makeup streaked.

Chris opened his arms and said, "Annie, I'm sorry." When she moved into his embrace and sobbed onto his shoulder, he held her tight and whispered over and over again, "I'm sorry, I'm sorry."

Annie and Chris would have liked to spend the evening alone, but, as Annie thought about it, being surrounded by friends after a tense several days was probably a good thing.

She and Chris waited in the apartment for their friends to arrive. Two large dogs, Cyril and Jock, would remain at the Inn for the evening. Sometimes the dogs were given free run of the Inn, but they couldn't follow the cats everywhere.

The cat doors that allowed the cats to roam all over The Avenue and inside the Inn were large enough for big cats and small dogs. Cyril, an English setter, and Jock, a Portuguese water dog, were big. They could stick their noses through the doors. If they put their faces on the ground, they could see through. There was no way they could squeeze through.

Closing them in the apartment was a better option for them. They could get into every room on the third floor, and depending on the season and the weather, Annie left the deck doors open so they could enjoy fresh air as well.

Cyril was the companion of Pete, the Chief of Police, and his wife Janet. Their oldest daughter, Ginger, would start attending the community college in Marsh Haven later this month. She worked part-time for Annie at the yoga studio. Their middle daughter, Clarice, survived a swimming scare two months ago. She had nearly been pulled under in a rip current and was saved by a woman who…well, Annie hated to think about it.

The woman and her friend, who had participated in the rescue, were murdered that night. Pete and Janet were not able to properly thank her. Pete returned the favor the best he could, by discovering who murdered her and arresting him.

Pete and Annie's ancestors arrived in Chelsea in the same era, around the time of the Civil War. Annie's ancestors arrived in style and became lumber and commerce barons. Pete's arrived via the Underground Railroad. After the war, Pete's ancestors took jobs in the lumber industry.

Janet was not a native. She came to Chelsea when Pete retired from the Marine Corps military police. As an outsider in a small town, she had some bridges to build. But, she was Pete's wife. That gave her some status to begin with. She was a prized volunteer for many community organizations.

Jock was the companion of Ray and Cheryl. Annie had known Cheryl since she was a child. Annie grew up in another state, but she spent every summer with her father here in Chelsea. Cheryl's parents owned the Marina; as teens, Annie and Cheryl spent many a day on the water.

Cheryl now owned the marina, called, oddly enough, The Marina.

Ray, a retired Naval officer and a little older than Cheryl, moved to Chelsea for love. Now married to Cheryl and aching to be on the water, he used money from an inheritance to purchase an old yacht. He refurbished it, named it The Escape, and started a cruise and fishing business. His boat was much in demand for both day trips and multi-day cruises. Recently, after severe damage, he repainted The Escape using Annie's rainbow color scheme.

Pete and Janet arrived first. After the initial hellos and the flurry of Cyril greeting the cats, Janet asked, "How was your trip?"

Chris looked at Annie. Annie looked at Chris. Neither knew how to answer. Chris finally said, "It was an adventure." Annie smiled and nodded. Pete and Janet wisely remained silent.

Annie opened the deck doors to allow the warm, pre-storm breeze into the kitchen. Seven cats and one big dog almost knocked her over in their haste to get out. At the same time, Chris opened the door to Ray, Cheryl and Jock. Jock went from zero to forty in two seconds and slid onto the deck behind the rest.

Annie, used to the activity, turned at Cheryl's greeting.

"Annie, it's good to have you back. How was the trip?"

"It was an adventure, thanks for asking."

Chris's voice rose above the human and companion greetings to say, "Henrie has a couple bottles of wine chilling on the back porch. Why don't we go down, and you all can say hey to Jeff and meet his friend."

"What's his name again?" asked Janet.

"Mark."

"And does he work for the FBI as well?"

Annie answered. "DEA. They say they're on vacation and that Mark is doing the triathlon."

Everyone laughed, even Pete, who had a great deal of experience with Jeff. Chris and Ray looked at one another as they laughed, a meaningful I-don't-think-so glance passing between them.

The night was beautiful. A storm brewed over the lake, and the clouds and sunset made a happy kaleidoscope.

Seven cats and two dogs settled on the upstairs deck. They watched the approaching sunset and smelled the storm as it drew closer. For a while, they listened to their humans, now on the all-season porch two floors down. Their voices carried up on the breeze.

Cyril and Jock listened closely for a while, ever vigilant for hints of adventure, but Tiger Lily and her siblings wanted to share the visit to meet Chris's parents.

Mr. Bean said, *"Let me! Let me! I want to tell the first story!"*

Mr. Bean told Cyril and Jock about their arrival at the estate. *"That's what they call it, an estate. I tried to ask Mommy what that meant, but she didn't know what I was saying."*

Cyril had police experience in several countries before coming home to Chelsea with Pete. His wisdom served them well. *"An estate is a large piece of property, usually with a very big house, or more than one house, and it passes from generation to generation. It probably belonged to Chris's grandfather or great-grandfather."*

"Wow. You're right. There was a lot of property, and one really, really big house, and a couple of other houses that were bigger than the Inn. Anyway, we got there, and Chris's Mommy, her name is Angela, she was real polite to Mommy and Chris. His Daddy, his name is Austin, was polite, too. Then they weren't."

Jock said, *"What happened?"*

"We all jumped out of the car. Angela, she said she knew Mommy had cats but she didn't know how many cats we were. She thought maybe two."

Sassy Pants jumped in, *"An den we hadded to wait whiles dat woman callded some person and said, 'you gonna has to puts more food an stuff in da partment cuz dere's too many cats.'"*

Mr. Bean laughed at the memory. *"Mommy was doing her deep breathing exercises, and Chris was smiling really stiff-like, and he said, 'Mother, I told you there were seven.' And she said, 'It must have been in an email. I was certain you meant to say two, or perhaps my eyesight is going.'"*

Everyone chuckled appreciatively. Little Socks then said, *"I don't normally tell stories, but this one is good. The apartment we stayed in – us and Mommy, Chris had to stay on the other side of the house – was fine, but the house looked so fun. So after Mommy went to dinner, we decided to explore."*

Jock put his paws over his eyes and said, *"This isn't going to end well."*

The cats laughed. Little Socks continued. *"We found the dining room. It wasn't hard, really, because we just followed the smells. And then, well, it wasn't really our fault."*

Cyril and Jock looked at Little Socks. Little Socks sat still while everyone else chimed in – at the same time – with something that wasn't their fault.

"Da littal chickens tasted really good." "We didn't know we weren't supposed to get on the table." "The women had really short skirts and really high heels; it was funny when they fell." "Trill!!!!" "The tablecloth was white and the wine was red, and, well, it looked really pretty when the glasses spilled." "I didn't mean to run between their legs. I was just trying to get away."

Little Socks finished the story. *"Angela stood in the corner of the room and screamed, then she cried."*

Tiger Lily wiped the tears from her eyes. It was still very funny. Then she sobered up. *"Mommy apologized for us. I don't know why she had to do that, but she did, and Chris said that once we got used to the house, we wouldn't do stuff like that, and why did she have guests on our first night there."*

Kali added her two cents. *"And then Angela said something about this big important man that was at the dinner, some senator or something, and that it was important for Chris to make a good impression."*

"Oh," added Ko, *"and then, after everyone left, Angela said Chris never did the stuff he was supposed to do, and he picked a woman that would never allow him to go places."*

Cyril cocked his head. *"What places will Annie not let Chris go?"*

"We didn't understand that either. Chris can go wherever he wants to go."

"Well certainly not all the exciting stuff happened on the first night."

"Oh, no. We went outside the next day, and Mo decided to dig up some really pretty flowers. He had all the best intentions. He needed to get to the roots to take them to Mommy because the stems had pointy things."

Mo sat up and preened. *"Trill!"*

Kali and Ko both translated. As litter mates, they understood Mo when he spoke their secret language. While the girls progressed to speaking cat, Mo did not mature in that way. Together, they said, *"Mommy deserved to get the prettiest flowers." "Mommy was sad and Mo wanted to cheer her up."*

"Apparently, they were some roses that won some kind of a prize, and Angela said Mo ruined them beyond all redemption."

"No one's tolded me yet wot's redemption."

Jock answered. *"Redemption is some sort of rescue, so apparently, there was no way the roses could be saved."*

"So why has da roses if you can't see dem in da house?"

"Who knows why Angela does anything?"

"She's mean."

The cats continued to tell stories until they ran dry, then Tiger Lily said, *"Mommy was really mad at Chris, but I think they finally made up this evening."*

Cyril and Jock asked together, *"What did Chris do?"*

"I'm not sure. It's confusing. Something about him not standing up for her, or expecting her to be a different person, or something."

"She must have been right. He said he was sorry."

"Trill!"

Sassy Pants was the only cat in the family to have a loose grasp of the English language, but for some reason, she could read minds. She translated for Mo. *"He sez Chris was being gallant."*

"Really?"

They all looked at Mo.

Sassy Pants translated without Mo saying a word. *"Mo's a Romeo, an he knew wot he talks about."*

The friends lapsed into silence. They looked at the night sky and took deep breaths of the rain in the air.

When everyone else had fallen asleep, Tiger Lily told Cyril and Jock about the butterfly. She went on to explain why it was still here. *"Mommy told me about the late monarchs."*

"What are late monarchs?"

"They're the ones that come out all grown up at the end of summer. It's really late for them; they can't stay here in the winter or they'll die. So they don't have babies like other butterflies. They have to use all their energy to fly south. Then they'll come back in the spring and lay eggs. But now, they have to drink lots of what she called nectar."

"What's nectar?"

"Something in the flowers. So they drink a lot of that, then they have to fly two thousand miles. Mommy says that's a really long way."

"It is a long way. Do you know where they go?"

"Some mountain range in Mexico. Because it's so late, they catch some warm air and soar. That's easier than beating their wings all the way."

Cyril sighed. *"I'd like to soar somewhere one day."*

Jock sighed. *"Being on the boat in the middle of the lake feels like flying, but sometimes, I'd like to soar, too."*

They fell asleep, Tiger Lily's head on Cyril's belly, her back feet on Jock's shoulder.

4

On the all-season porch, the group of friends met Jeff and Mark, already seated. Mark had a glass of white wine; Jeff had a red. Jeff made introductions while Chris and Annie poured wine for their guests.

Pete said, "Jeff, before the night is over, I expect you to tell me about this 'vacation' of yours."

Jeff laughed as he said, "I'm checking into a couple of local wineries while Mark does the triathlon."

"Really? You're a triathlete, Mark?"

"I am. Well, this will be my first. But I've been practicing. I've done some bike racing and I've done the Indianapolis 500 Mini-Marathon."

"So this will be a stretch for you."

"Isn't that what everyone wants? A stretch?"

"I guess. You probably won't find any of us out there. But then again, we probably are nowhere near as healthy as the two of you."

"The only thing Jeff will exercise is his right arm."

"Not true! I'm an ambidextrous drinker. See?" Jeff demonstrated by moving the glass to his left hand. As he took a sip, some red wine dribbled down his chin. "Well, I'm going to work on it. Stretching myself."

And so the evening started. After wine, they walked up The Avenue to Mo's Tap. At the Tap, they took a large table and were joined by George and Candice, both of whom had taken the evening off.

George was the manager and bartender of Mo's; tonight the bar was managed by Georgia, who worked at three of Annie's businesses. Candice, the head server and floor manager, was also married to George. The reality of the sudden marriage, now a few months old, was still sinking in with Candice. And George. And, well, everyone else.

Mark allowed Jeff to carry the conversation. He spent most of his time looking around at the guests of Mo's Tap. He masked his review of the guests by focusing every now and then on the details of Mo's itself.

He was drawn to the month's special menu. He heard Annie explain that all four of her food-serving businesses had northern Italian specialties this month. The focus would not be pasta and marinara sauce; some guests would not be able to tell the fare was Italian.

Mark ordered one of the specials, rosemary grilled sirloin steak with red skin mashed potatoes, grilled onions, peppers, mushrooms and pepperoncini's with a side of burro sauce, a sauce made with butter and grated Parmesan cheese.

After he placed the order, he asked the server about the special menu. "Who chose the specials?"

Sara, the server, replied, "Our lead cook. He likes to experiment."

"Please tell him I'm familiar with the cuisine, and if it tastes half as good as explained on the menu, we're all in for a treat. Please give him my compliments."

"Cookie will be happy to hear it. If you are in town over the weekend, check out his fine dining restaurant. It opens in the Café Friday and Saturday nights."

"Thanks, I will." Mark smiled at the server and continued his look around the room, listening to the conversation and participating enough to be polite.

He watched the servers as they went about their business, noting who appeared to be regular customers and who were tourists or otherwise unknown to the staff.

He watched the bar traffic, customers coming and going or coming and staying.

He watched people who appeared to do what he was doing, watching the crowd.

Mark excelled at people-watching. He was able to form an opinion about most of the guests in two or three covert glances.

He liked the bar. Mo's Tap was an upscale blues bar. It was casual but set a high standard for behavior. Blues music played in the background, loud enough to hear but soft enough to allow for conversation. The walls were soft yellow with a taupe accent wall. The tables and chairs were of burnished oak; the booths were cushioned; several private areas with overstuffed chairs and accent tables were scattered around the back of the room.

Pendant lights set to a low level were over each table, and each table had a candle inside a holder with roof-shaped lids. Mark reached over to bring the candle from their table closer and he examined the lid.

Jeff explained. "Mo, the long-haired gray cat that is often here, likes the candles. He likes them so well he can catch his tail on fire."

"Ouch."

"Yeah. Instead of kicking Mo out, Annie got lids for the candle holders."

"One can always find another way to look at a thing."

Throughout the evening, Jeff would make eye contact with Mark and Mark would respond with a slight shake of his head. Nothing yet.

The group was preparing to leave when the table was approached by a man who had just entered.

Chris said, "Ian, another exciting week for you."

"Yeah. We've got a record number of triathletes this year. It will be great!"

"With this weather coming in, it's possible you may have to forego the lake this year."

"I hope not, but we're ready if we have to."

Chris made introductions. "Ian, this is Jeff, and this is Mark, friends staying at the Inn. Mark will be doing the triathlon. Ian is Chelsea's event coordinator. Well, at least the coordinator of our sporting events. And some other things."

"It's a pleasure. Have you taken a look at the course yet?"

"Not really. We walked to the beach today and saw the buoy markers. So what happens if we can't do the swim?"

"That happens on occasion. We have a deal with the state park to add some walking trails for an additional run before the bike ride."

"How long are the trails?"

"Are you doing the fifty mile or the one hundred mile?"

"I'm a beginner, so I'm doing the fifty."

"Well, actually, either way, the run is the same length as the swim, so for the fifty, it's one and a half miles. The walking trails are rough. They go up and down some small hills, and there are tree roots to get over and some brush to duck away from."

"Can we take a look at it?"

"Sure. If you're registered, show the confirmation at the park gate and get in for free. They'll give you the route map."

"Tell me about the lake laps."

"For the fifty mile lap, you'll get your mile and a half in by starting at the buoy close to shore and swimming to the buoy we choose that morning. You make a turn, then swim parallel to the shore to the other buoy on the lake, make the turn, and swim back to the first. People on the one hundred mile do that twice."

"Why do you wait until that morning to choose a direction?"

Ian looked at Mark closely. "You really are a novice."

"Yep."

"And you're starting with an open water swim? You've either got guts or you really don't know about open water swimming. Spend much time on a big lake?"

Mark looked at Jeff, then back to Ian. "Not really. I, well, this just caught my eye."

Ian laughed. "Are you a runner?"

"Yes. I am a runner. Usually streets or trails, though, not on what I can imagine the state park trails are like."

"Pray for a rip current warning. You'll do better on the run. But to answer your question, open water swimming will sap your strength. We gauge the direction of the surface current on the morning of the event and try to make sure you swim against it at the beginning, not the end."

As Ian chatted with the group, Mark stood to leave. He turned his back on the group and watched Jeff walk past him. Jeff looked at him with a smile. Mark tried to keep his temper in check.

Throughout the evening, Annie had looked off and on at a male guest, seated in the back of the room. He wore a hat and appeared to purposely blend into the background. He watched the bar for most of the evening.

As Annie watched, it appeared to her that he turned away every time Georgia turned to face the room. She couldn't be sure.

Mark had noticed the man as well. He couldn't tell who at the bar would cause the man to turn away, but, like Annie, he noticed the surreptitious nature. He committed the man's face to memory.

5

Henrie awoke to a morning fresh from a quick summer storm. The storm came in from the lake overnight and moved on to the south before sunrise. The storm had moved on, but rain would begin in earnest within the hour.

It was Tuesday morning, and, according to the weather prophets, yesterday was the last nice day until Friday. Perhaps Saturday. Mother Nature did not care that the triathlon was scheduled.

The rain did not dampen Henrie's spirits. Finally, guests were on hand for whom to prepare breakfast. When he thought about it, he realized only one morning had passed without guests. That was one too many.

As he did every morning, Henrie made bacon, as much for Annie and the cats as for the guests, and other breakfast meats. Today he cooked Canadian ham and sausage links.

He scooped out the inside of a loaf of Italian bread and poured in a sausage and egg mixture. As it baked in the oven, he answered a knock on the Inn's back door, the one that entered into the kitchen.

Isabel, recently married to Carlos, the baker and manager of Mr. Bean's Confectionary, stood at the stoop with a basket. Her Jack Russel terrier, Tillie, stood politely at her heels.

"Isabel, since when do you knock? Come in."

As Isabel walked in, Tillie ditched her decorum and ran into the kitchen, through the dining room and out to the stairs. She was out of earshot and probably on the third floor before Isabel finished her first paragraph, spoken in a soft Mexican lilt. "I'm not here to visit. I'm making a delivery from the bakery. I think this will be something I do from now on."

"Walk in as you always do. Do you have time for coffee? We can chat while I finish breakfast."

Isabel stepped in and took a deep breath. "That smells Italian. What are you making, Henrie?"

"It is an egg casserole, a standard breakfast item, but in honor of the Italian theme of the month, this is made inside a loaf of Italian bread and has Italian sausage, basil, mozzarella and parmesan. What did Carlos send?"

"He sent an Italian breakfast bread." Isabel turned back a towel to show Henrie the yeasty bread made with lemon and dried cranberries.

"Marvelous. And what is this?"

"Scones. I don't know if they meet with the Italian theme, but they are good. They have roasted pears and chocolate chunks."

"Today, pears and chocolate are Italian."

Isabel helped herself to a cup of coffee as Henrie finished putting together tomato breakfast cups. He scooped the insides out of the tomatoes, mixed the tomato with cooked, crumbled Italian sausage, Italian spices and grated parmesan. This mixture was spooned into the tomato shells. They went into the small upper oven.

"I cannot decide if I should make blueberry pancakes."

"How many people are you feeding?"

"Well, let me see. There would be two guests, possibly Annie, possibly Chris if he pops in, possibly you, anyone else that decides to show up. A slow morning, actually."

Isabel laughed. "I remember your breakfasts, and I loved them dearly, Henrie. I think you'll have enough without the pancakes. I would stay, but I promised Carlos I would manage the ovens this morning. Tillie will probably come home when Mr. Bean comes to work."

After Isabel left, Henrie finished plating items into warming dishes on the dining room buffet. He walked to the foyer and listened intently. Hearing no movement from the guest rooms, he went down the hall to the all-season porch and out to the beach. There, he stood and breathed in the lake air. The rain was coming. He could smell it, feel it, and he thought he could even see it over the lake.

As he turned to go in, he noticed Tiger Lily on top of a picnic table. She stared in rapt attention at one of the flowering bushes. Henrie took two soft steps, enough to see what had enthralled her. It was a butterfly.

The butterfly sat on the bush, apparently staring at Tiger Lily. Then it suddenly flew up. Tiger Lily's head jerked to follow the motion of flight. Her head turned to and fro while the butterfly moved about on the wind. Finally, the butterfly flew away. Tiger Lily's eyes followed the flight until she could see it no longer.

Body still motionless, Tiger Lily turned her head to gaze at Henrie. She blinked once and jumped from the table. Like a queen, she walked past Henrie, head and tail held high.

Henrie followed her in. She went down the hallway and up the stairs. Henrie, passing through the foyer, heard Jeff and Mark talking on the second floor landing. He looked up. They were looking at the computer situated there for guests. Jeff noticed Henrie and said, "Hey, Henrie. We're on our way down. Just checking the weather."

"Did you find it interesting?"

"You bet. Rain, rain, some spotty showers, then more rain. And then tomorrow, we can expect more of the same. Even the sand will have mud puddles by Saturday."

"It will start soon. If you want to watch the rain come in over the lake, I suggest you take breakfast onto the porch."

Henrie got trays for Jeff and Mark. As they filled their plates in the dining room, he carried a carafe of coffee and another of juice to the porch. He opened cupboards to reveal cups, glasses, napkins and condiments.

Kali and Ko sauntered in. They knew Jeff could be counted on to drop some food on the floor.

Jeff entered as Henrie turned to go. "I shall leave breakfast on the dining room buffet until I know you are done or that you have left. Can I get anything else for you?"

"No, thanks, Henrie. Our plans for the day are set."

"As you wish. It is good to have you as a guest again, Jeff."

After Henrie left, Jeff got his cellphone and called the Coast Guard station. "Could I speak to Chris, please?"

Mark settled at a table with a view of the lake. He listened to Jeff's side of the conversation.

"Morning, Chris. It's Jeff. Will you have time to see Mark and me this morning? .... We're eating breakfast now, watching the rain come over the lake. .... Yes, it's beautiful, and the smell is, I don't know, a fresh that I can't quite explain. .... That would be great. We'll be there then. .... Why don't I tell you when I get there? .... You're right. Not quite a vacation. I think we'll be able to use you. .... Channels? If I went through channels, but, hey, this is a cell. We'll talk in a bit. .... Okay."

As if by magic, food managed to fall to the floor, sometimes from Jeff's plate and sometimes from Mark's. When Kali and Ko were full, they jumped to the sofa to watch the rain. They looked at one another as they got comfortable. That was an interesting telephone conversation.

Jeff and Mark marveled at the sheet of water that came across the lake. It came closer and closer until it finally became a mixture of sight and sound, rain hitting water. It hit the beach and moved like a waterfall on wheels toward the Inn, over it and on, covering all of Chelsea with the soft patter of a long-lasting summer rain.

6

While Jeff and Mark ate breakfast, Annie hurried five cats and a dog out the door to get to work before the rain hit. She grabbed an umbrella on her way out and yelled, "Henrie, I'm leaving!"

Henrie got to the foyer just as she was ready to shut the door. "How will the little ones get home this afternoon?"

"I'm going to borrow Clara's covered wagon. Why don't I just get one for myself?"

"Do not do it. I did not have an idea for Christmas, but if you will wait until then, I will get the deluxe model with the heater built in."

Annie laughed as she closed the door. She opened it again and said, "Hey, Mom called. They'll be here in a couple of hours."

The companions congregated at the end of the sidewalk, looking over the expanse of public parking lot to the lake and the rain, beginning to bear down.

"Scoot, kids! Get to work before the rain hits!"

Five cats and a Jack Russell terrier looked at Annie, looked back at the coming rain, turned and ran. One or two peeled off at a time, first Sassy Pants, then Mr. Bean and Tillie, Mo, Little Socks, and finally, Tiger Lily ducked into the Café just before the rain hit the sidewalk behind her. Annie stood, half in and half out of the door of the Winery to watch her just make it. By the time Tiger Lily made it to the Café, Annie's umbrella and the part of her body not inside the door or under the umbrella were soaked.

She squeezed the umbrella into the door and shook the rain off both the umbrella and herself. Minnie, stocking the cheese counter, laughed.

Sassy Pants, who had not been at work for several days, ran around, looking, smelling and poking, to make sure all was as it should be. She finally cleared the front of the winery and ran to the garden dining area.

She checked out the back, then jumped into a concrete urn with a potted flowering bush. It was close to the edge of the covered portion of the dining area, barely out of reach of the rain.

She settled down to watch the rain. And a mouse.

There was a mouse!

Where had the mouse come from?

It was a small brown mouse, and it crouched under the curved base of a concrete urn, shivering either from the cold of the rain hitting it or from the fright of seeing Sassy Pants. Frightened or brave, the mouse stared at Sassy Pants and didn't move.

Sassy Pants stared back. Finally, she said, *"Ize Sassy Pants. Who iz you?"*

The mouse continued to shiver but didn't answer.

"Duz you speaks human? Or cat? I duzn't tink I unnerstands mouse."

The mouse shivered and stared.

"How bouts I juss tawk an you lissens? Ize Sassy Pants. O. I say dat already. Ize a cat. Ize apposed to catch mices. Dat's you. Youze a mice."

The mouse looked carefully around to see if anyone else watched, then looked back at Sassy Pants.

"So, okay, I duzn't really wants to catch you. You juss run out to da rain and I duzn't want to go dere. So, wot are you called?"

The mouse stared, still shivering.

"Okay. Iza gonna call you Brown Mousie. Okay?"

The mouse looked at Sassy Pants and slowly nodded its head.

"Okay. Now weze talkin'. Duz you unnerstand me?"

The mouse nodded, shivered again.

"How you gets here? Duz you live here somewhere?"

The mouse nodded.

"Where?"

The mouse didn't say anything.

"Is you cold? Duz you want to come to my flower pot? Ize dry here."

The mouse, still shivering, took one small step, then another. Minnie and Annie, talking, walked past the door to the garden dining area. The mouse skittered back to the wet urn.

Sassy Pants looked at the door. *"It's okay now. Daze not comin'."*

The mouse looked furtively at the door, then scurried to the urn. Sassy Pants looked down at the mouse, huddled at the base. *"Come on ups. I duzn't bite."*

The mouse scurried up and settled under the bush on the side opposite of Sassy Pants. Sassy Pants curved her head around the base of the bush and said, *"Duzn't be scairt.*

Weze gonna be friends. If you lets me gets to know you, I will learn to read your mind. Den we can really talk."

Minnie, the cheese expert for Sassy P's Wine and Cheese, showed Annie the monthly cheeses. "They're Italian, of course."

"Of course. Tell me about them."

"Well, we always have mozzarella, provolone and asiago, so you don't need to hear about them. But here's one."

Minnie pulled out a wedge of white cheese and cut a slice for Annie. "This is Pecorino Toscano, made from the milk of sheep and originating in Tuscany. This would be good with a salad, and I'd give you a good Chianti."

Annie took a bite. "Rich."

"Yes. Cheese made from sheep's milk is always rich. Here's another." Minnie pulled a container out with a soft, fragrant cheese. She used a spoon to capture some cheese and smear it on a cracker.

"Wow. This tastes better than it smells. Is it always this, um, ripe?"

"If it is served at room temperature, which is how it should be served. Or you can melt it. But I like it like this, on a cracker or crusty bread and with a fruity wine. Maybe Soave."

"What's it called?"

"Oh, forgot to tell you! Taleggio. I have one more for you. Fontina."

"Ah. I know this one! This you serve with fruit, right?"

"Yes. Fruit or melted on a Panini or for grilled cheese."

"What small plate specials do you have?"

"One we call Crema di Formaggio. It's a combination of feta cheese, thyme, dried cranberries and dried cherries, and it's topped with spiced pecans. We serve it warm over crostini, toasted slices of Italian bread. And another we call Poutine. Fried gnocchi covered with marinara sauce and fresh mozzarella, giardiniera and basil."

"Why the fancy names?"

"Believe it or not, people like the fancy names. The names make them stop and read the description, and after that, they're sold."

"I'll be in later this week to try them. Now, I guess I'd better get the umbrella and go next door." She sighed.

Once inside Mr. Bean's Confectionary, Annie once again shook off the water. "It's supposed to rain like this for three days. Do you think we should build an ark?"

Jerry, the candy maker, laughed. "No. We'll just get on The Escape. Hey, do you want to try my new truffles?"

"You have to ask? Tell me about them, but put them in a box for later."

"Sure. I'll have them ready for you to pick up this afternoon. I have two new ones."

Jerry reached into the candy case and pulled out two truffles. "This one, you can see it's rolled in cocoa, is dark chocolate, your favorite, and the filling is a soft crème with almond and orange flavoring. It's supposed to have almond and orange liquor, but I made them safe for everyone."

"Is that going to be my favorite?"

"Hard to say. This one is also dark chocolate, topped with crushed hazelnuts. It has a soft roasted hazelnut crème. There is a hint of coffee."

Annie looked at Jerry, then looked at the truffles. "I have to try it. Can we share?"

"Sure." Jerry pulled out a knife and cut into the hazelnut truffle. The soft cream threatened to burst from the confines of the dark chocolate shell.

Annie tasted it and immediately felt her feet leave the ground. She sighed. "This one will be my favorite, but put a few of both in the box."

Annie took her time eating the remainder of the half truffle. "I guess I should ask about the lunch specials."

"We have two salads, a traditional Caesar and a barbabietola."

"What?"

"We thought the same. That's the Italian word for 'beet salad, so we're just going to call it Italian beet salad.

"What is it?"

"Mixed greens, roasted beets, pine nuts, dried cherries, and fried feta cheese, topped with a balsamic vinaigrette."

"Yum. Anything other than salads?"

"We have a muffaletta, that's ham and salami with provolone cheese and olives, and for the midwestern palate, we have a hot Italian sub."

"You know what the problem is with having specials all the time?"

"What?"

"You can't decide what to order. Then you order everything. Then you eat too much."

"You're supposed to share."

"I do. Bummer. I'd rather eat it all by myself. Where's Carlos?"

"He needed to take his mother and sisters to the federal office in Marsh Haven."

"Problems?"

"No. Just taking care of business. Still. It takes time."

"It does, and he should remember. It took him a while to finish the paperwork and classes in order to become a citizen. Do you need anything?"

"No, but thanks. Isabel is baking now, and Ben or JoJo, whichever one is free, will be over to help during the lunch rush."

Annie took hold of her umbrella, getting ready to leave, then asked, "Where are Mr. Bean and Tillie?"

"They're interested in something in the back of the kitchen. They have their snouts up against that sink that connects to the winery's back garden. I hope we don't have a mouse."

"Eek. And tell me, what are they doing in the kitchen? That's kind of against the rules."

"I know, but I can't get them to leave. That's why I'm afraid we might have a mouse."

Annie arrived next, wetter still, at Mo's Tap. They were not open yet, so George was not at the bar. Mo was. He opened one sleepy eye from his prone position on the bar next to the once-clean-now-embellished-with-long-gray-hair glasses.

Annie walked to the kitchen where Georgia prepped for lunch. She leaned against a counter and watched while Georgia cut potatoes and sweet potatoes into strips.

"You sure put in a lot of hours, Georgia. By the way, did you get a babysitter?"

"Yes. JoJo and Ben tossed a coin. Ben is sitting; JoJo is going to Mr. Bean's."

"Did they have a preference?"

"Sadly, they did. Neither of them care to change the poopy diapers."

Annie laughed, then turned serious. "Georgia, did you notice a guy here last night, he sat in the back, had a hat on, seemed to spend a lot of time looking at the bar?"

"I saw a guy in the back that wore a hat. I noticed him, because most people take their hats off in here. But I didn't see him looking at the bar. Every time I looked that way, he was looking down or in another direction. To be honest, I was a little worried that I never saw his face."

"Know anything about him?"

"I asked Sara, his server, about him. She said he was just a quiet guy. She didn't get a name. He paid cash. She wondered why I was asking."

"What did you say?"

"I may be young, but I know this business, so I used it as a training moment. I told her it was the bartender's responsibility to make sure no one was overserved, and since I couldn't see him clearly, I just wanted to know."

"I knew there was a reason we wanted you to work here."

Georgia laughed.

Annie asked, "What are your Italian specials?"

"Oh, Cookie chose some great things for lunch. There's a chicken pesto Panini, but my two favorites are the burgers. One is made with a combination of ground beef and pork and is served with mulled pears and goat cheese. The other is a grilled ground duck burger. It's topped with dried cherries, red onion and honey mustard."

"Sounds great. A guest from the Inn ordered the Italian steak from the dinner menu last night. There was something else. What was it?"

"Grilled salmon with pears, fried Brussels sprouts and butternut squash puree."

"Oh, yeah. I almost ordered that, but just got a burger and fries instead. And why are you getting ready for lunch alone?"

"George and Candice just ran upstairs for, well, they just ran upstairs. They'll be down before we open. Want me to give either of them a message?"

Annie smiled. "No. No message. I trust everything is going well with them."

Mo thought about the man they discussed, the one with the hat. He would have to keep an eye open for him.

The man with the hat walked up and down a residential street. In the middle of a residential area, there were no benches upon which to sit, no place to rest that would be unobtrusive. He altered his path from time to time, but never enough to take him out of sight of the house for more than five minutes.

Ben walked to Martha's former bed and breakfast, now a home that included an apartment for Georgia and her daughter. He noticed the stranger with a hat as he got close to the house. A few minutes later, he carried Little Fred to the front porch as Georgia left for work.

The rain had not yet begun, and Georgia would walk to work. She turned to give Fred a hug, and Ben noticed the man for the second time.

Ben watched Georgia walk up the street and didn't go into the house until he saw the man leave, walking in another direction.

Someone else watched the man. Speckles, the nanny kitty, sensed a disturbance in the atmosphere. She jumped to the porch rail and kept an eye on him until he was out of sight.

Nancy and Sam arrived shortly before noon. Henrie, always on top of things, was ready with a rolling cart to take their luggage to the carriage house.

Annie's mother and step-father stayed a few weeks at a time at the Inn throughout the year. This was a great arrangement for everyone. Nancy and Sam got a vacation home without the worries of owning a second house or condo, and Annie was assured of a tenant for extended periods of time.

They paid a figure somewhat less than others who rented the carriage house, but Henrie and their cleaner, Hilly, spent less time on the room when they were in residence. Another benefit, since the carriage house was separate from the main house, was that Annie maintained a semblance of separation and privacy when her mother made extended visits.

As Henrie and Sam emptied the luggage cart, Nancy looked around the first floor suite. Everything seemed to be in order and ready for them. The first floor was decorated in Victorian style. Completely accessible, the suite had every amenity of the main rooms plus a walk-out deck with a hot tub large enough for four people. The deck was enclosed by a six-foot fence for privacy. This room was used often by honeymooners.

The kitchenette was stocked with staple items, including coffee and tea for the Keurig. Nancy opened the refrigerator and noticed Henrie had added some snack and meal items.

"Henrie, you always go three steps beyond what everyone expects. Thank you."

"My pleasure. Shall I assume you plan to lunch at the Café?"

Nancy laughed at Henrie's formal tone. While normal for Henrie, it took some getting used to when they first arrived. "Yes, we will lunch at the Café. And how is everything with you, Henrie?"

"Perfect. We have a full house scheduled, including you and the rest of the family, so I will be, as you say, in my element."

Sam came out of the bathroom, having placed their toiletries in the cabinets. "Say, Henrie, how long do you expect this rain to last?"

"Most of the week, through Friday, perhaps Saturday."

"Well, that won't sit well with all the folks coming for the triathlon."

Nancy looked at her watch. "The Café will still be in their rush. I'm going to take a short nap. Wake me at one o'clock, Sam."

"Sure thing. I'll go over with Henrie and help myself to some of that fresh coffee I know he's got brewing."

Henrie removed the last item from the cart. He placed it carefully on the floor. "I have taken the liberty to lock all the cat doors for you."

"Thanks, Henrie." Nancy leaned over and opened the door to a large cat carrier. After a suitable moment of reflection, The Dreaded Uncle Honey Bear strode out, imperious. He gazed at Henrie, dismissed him as useless for the moment, and, with two steps and a hop, jumped to an easy chair and readied it for a nap.

Henrie looked at the large, honey-colored long-haired cat. "Welcome to the KaliKo Inn, Honey Bear. It is nice to have you in residence once again. I am certain your nieces and nephews are ecstatic you have arrived."

Sam chuckled as he took an umbrella and left the carriage house with Henrie.

Jeff and Mark, without hurry, because they were already soaked to the skin, entered Mr. Bean's Confectionary for lunch.

"We'll eat at the Café another day, when we're not going during a rush. I swear, not even a rainstorm will keep people from coming out to lunch on The Avenue."

Mark tried to get some of the water from his hair and face. "You know I have to get some practice time in, for two reasons."

Jeff laughed.

"This isn't funny. One, I'm completely unprepared for this, and I have to make it believable. Two, I have to get a handle on the route and the possible, let's say points of interest."

"Well, at least we have the water covered."

"Yeah. Chris is pretty cool. I'm surprised he's going to give us a hand on that lake without going through his channels."

"He owes me. I knew he would do it."

Mark looked down. A muscular gray kitten wrapped himself around both ankles at once, even though the ankles were drenched with rain water. A little dog – maybe a Jack Russell Terrier – investigated Jeff's legs.

With the impediment to his legs, Jeff had to talk to the pretty Hispanic woman at the counter from a distance. He managed without difficulty.

"It's good to see you, Isabel."

"Jeff, it's good to see you as well. Are you and your friend having lunch?"

"If we can get free of the kids long enough to sit at a table, yes. I see you have some specials. Why don't you get us an Italian beet salad and a muffaletta with a couple of plates? We'll share."

Mark finally freed one leg and took a step toward a table. Once the first step was taken, the kitten allowed him to walk toward it without "help."

As he sat, he looked at Jeff. "Mr. Bean, I presume."

"Yep. And the little lady at my feet is Tillie. You'll see her all over The Avenue, but she lives upstairs here."

Mark looked around. Another attractive space, bright, with lime green walls. Lime green and sunburst orange shapes were scattered on the bright white accent wall. The day was dreary; little natural light came through the large front windows. Pendant lights added some light to the room, making it cheerful, regardless of the gray day. A live flower arrangement was on the countertop, low and arty with green flowers.

Before long, the salad and sandwich arrived. "I don't know if this will be enough for me, Jeff."

"It will be. You're in training, and you have to save room for dessert."

Mark looked at the display cases for the first time. Cookies, cakes, pies, breads, truffles, even animal treats beckoned.

"You're right. Lots of room. And let's talk about that training." Mark's smile turned to daggers, aimed directly at Jeff. "Why is it that I'm the one doing the triathlon?"

"They know me here. They know it's not something I would do. And let's face it, you have the ability. And, well, we're doing this on our own time. I still can't believe we are taking this risk. And yes, I'm taking a risk, too."

"I know. But, man, Jeff, you are stretching the limits of our friendship. Not with this little investigation, but do you realize I might have to get in that lake and swim?"

"Not much chance of that, trust me."

"But you didn't know that when we…"

"I know, I know. Jeff chuckled. "Eat up. We have a police station to visit."

Mr. Bean and Tillie, sticking close to the men, looked at one another. They would have something to share when they got back to the Inn.

The lunch rush was ending. Annie, filling in at the coffee bar, looked up to see Nancy and Sam enter.

Tiger Lily, napping at the hostess stand, roused herself to sit up straight. Nancy walked to the stand, wrapped both her hands around Tiger Lily's head, then gave the purrfect back rub, still using two hands. She leaned in to kiss Tiger Lily on the top of her head.

Annie came from behind the counter to give Sam a hug. "It's good to see you, Sam. Sorry you had to come on the rainiest day of the year."

"Ah, it will dry out soon enough."

Nancy moved over for a hug as well. "One hug, then I have to have some lunch. I am starving."

Annie showed Nancy and Sam to a table. Unfortunately, they had to walk past Everett, Geraldine's husband. Nancy looked down at Everett as they walked by, smiled and nodded a hello. Everett, in return, sniffed and turned away. The group of friends with whom he sat responded in a similar manner.

Tiger Lily, following Annie to the table, gave a low hiss on her way by.

Annie sat down as Tiger Lily jumped to one of her ledges, the one in between Annie and Nancy. Annie put a hand on Tiger Lily's back and turned to Nancy. "I've waited for you to eat lunch. I'm starving, too. I ordered for us already. Lunch will be served fairly quickly."

"Wonderful. Tell me, why is that horrid man here? I thought there was a restraining order."

"The order is against his wife and Hank and a couple of their cronies, but Everett and most of their friends are free to come to The Avenue whenever they want."

"Well, why do they keep coming? I thought they hated you, but here they are, still, patronizing the Café, and probably every other place."

"They'll spend money here in the hope they can go away with good gossip."

"Unfortunately, at some point that order will probably end. Do you have a court date?"

"A hearing is scheduled for tomorrow, actually. The judge will probably end the order, but he isn't going to be pleasant. As a matter of fact, the judge has a couple of additional issues, and he will probably give her a serious lecture."

"What other issues, dear?"

"Well, shortly after the original order was issued, he added a stipulation that she couldn't go to places that I typically volunteer – that will probably be vacated also – and he also has a problem with Geraldine's use of relatives to harass me."

"Really? He knows about the library's genealogist?"

"The Judge is on the library's board."

"Well, you've always come out on top in these situations. You probably will again. It's unfortunate you will have to deal with her in your own places of business again."

Tiger Lily soaked up the constant massage to her back and everything that was said.

7

During a break in the rain, Tiger Lily decided to leave the Café for the Inn. On her way home, she trotted across the street to DoubleGood, hitting every puddle on the way. She walked through the cat door and nodded politely to Holly, who sat at the front counter. Holly, also politely, didn't mention the water that dripped from Tiger Lily's legs and belly.

Tiger Lily trotted and dripped her way to the back of the store and was pleased to see she had guessed correctly. Simon Finnegan and Oscar McMurphy, known by the cats as Fat Cat and Scaredy Cat, were napping in the store. Usually out and about, they eschewed their wandering ways today for a dry bed.

Fat Cat yawned and stretched while Scaredy Cat continued to nap. Tiger Lily, anxious to get home before the rain started again, was brief.

"Henrie asked me to invite you over this afternoon."

This roused even Scaredy Cat. *"What?"*

"I know. Odd. But there it is. This morning, Henrie asked me if I would please invite the two of you to come over. It's not raining. Do you want to come now?"

The two cats looked at one another, looked at Tiger Lily, and said, at the same time, *"Sure."*

They followed Tiger Lily out of the store, nodding to Holly as they left.

When they arrived at the Inn, Tiger Lily discovered her siblings were of the same mind. They noticed a break in the rain and ran home. Everyone, including Tillie, gathered under the Seven Cats Detective table.

Henrie came into the dining room with a tray. On the tray were ten small dishes, each with a little bit of the day's afternoon snack.

Guests at the Inn were always treated to something special to get them through the long afternoon. Today, in keeping with the Italian theme of the week, Henrie served calamari, lightly breaded – guests received the calamari with a balsamic glaze – and breadsticks brushed with garlic butter and parmesan cheese.

Tiger Lily was vociferous in her praise of the snack. She ate quickly, then sat back, waiting to see why Henrie wanted Fat Cat and Scaredy Cat to come over.

Henrie cleared his throat. Nine cats and a little dog looked up. Henrie only knew their guests by their human-given names, because no matter how nice and, actually, intelligent, he was, Henrie could not speak cat.

"Simon Finnegan and Oscar McMurphy, I requested your presence today because you recently performed admirably. Your protection of our guest went unnoticed by almost, but not quite, everyone."

Earlier in the summer, a guest, Kim, was targeted for death by her brother and cousins. When the cats discovered the plot, Fat Cat and Scaredy Cat volunteered to take the long trek to the far side of the inland lake, Lake Scott. There, the men intended to simulate an accident during a bicycling event. The cats bravely fought them, allowing Kim to remain safe until other bikers came along.

As Henrie alluded, only a few humans in Chelsea knew the skills of the neighborhood cats. Chief Pete, arriving at the scene of the supposed accident to investigate, saw Fat Cat and Scaredy Cat at the scene. He put two and two together, offered the cats a ride back to Chelsea, and reported his suspicions to the only other humans in Chelsea that would understand. He tried to tell Holly and Jolly, their humans, but they told Pete he needed to take a vacation.

As Henrie spoke, Simon Finnegan (Fat Cat) and Oscar McMurphy (Scaredy Cat) sat tall and proud, smiling and looking around at their friends.

Henrie continued, pulling a small envelope from his pocket. "To acknowledge this effort on your part, I want to make the following change to this beautiful sign."

Henrie picked up the sign that read "Seven Cats Detective Agency." From the envelope, he pulled a page of adhesive markings. One at a time, he pulled two straight lines, both red, from the page and made an "X" over the word "seven." He then pulled the word "nine," also red, from the page. He placed that word at an angle over the x'ed-out seven.

The sign now read "Nine Cats Detective Agency." Henrie, knowing that the cats, no matter how intelligent, were not able to read, cleared his throat again and began.

"I now place this sign, reading 'Nine Cats Detective Agency,' over the door of the afore-mentioned agency, this table. The two of you are now ranked among them."

Fat Cat and Scaredy Cat, momentarily flummoxed, sat in stunned silence as the other cats congratulated them. Tillie sat where she was, an expression of sadness on her sweet little dog face.

Henrie waited for the commotion to die down, and he looked at Tillie. "My good girl, Tillie, please do not think you have been forgotten."

Tillie licked her lips and watched Henrie closely. Maybe it would get better.

"There was not room on the sign to say 'Nine Cats And A Dog Detective Agency.' Instead, I have this."

Henrie reached behind the flower vase and pulled out a small sign. "It says, 'Tillie, A Hero With Paws.' What do you think about that?"

Tillie wagged a cautious tail.

Tiger Lily stepped up to say, *"You're special. Your name is on the sign."*

Tillie looked up again, wagged her tail with more animation, and gave a 'yip!'

Henrie hung the sign on the table beside the larger one. He then stood, folded his hands, looked down at the ten companions and said, "I am honored to know you all."

Henrie left to take care of human matters and the friends huddled under the table. The companions were so excited, they didn't notice that Henrie's human tasks included locking the exterior cat doors. He would unlock them when Nancy took Honey Bear "home," and hoped the cats would not notice.

Tiger Lily took charge.

"I think we're going to have an exciting week."

"Yes!" said Sassy Pants. *"I metted somebody!"*

"We have something, too!" said Kali. Ko nodded agreement.

"Us, too," added Mr. Bean, with a nod to Tillie.

"Trill!"

"*Okay, Mo, we'll get to you, too,*" said Tiger Lily. She glanced at Little Socks, who looked around the room and down at the floor.

At that moment, Nancy and Sam came into the Inn. Nancy carried her cat carrier into the dining room. "I thought I would find you here. Look who came to visit!"

She opened the carrier and out came Honey Bear. The room was silent. Honey Bear glanced over the group, sniffed, and climbed upon the most inviting cushion, pushing both Mo and Mr. Bean out of his way. Mo jumped to the right; Mr. Bean jumped to the left. Neither said a thing. Honey Bear went to sleep.

Nancy beamed. "Look, Sam. They're getting along just fine this time."

Sam shook his head and said, "Come on, dear, let's go to the kitchen. Coffee's on."

"Just a minute, dear. Girls and boys, you'll be happy to know that I'm going to unlock the cat doors at the carriage house and let Honey Bear come and go as he pleases. In a few days. After the rain stops. What do you think about that?"

Tiger Lily looked up at Grandmommy. She knew this was a bad idea, but she didn't know how to explain it in a way that Grandmommy would understand.

Nancy, continually clueless about Honey Bear's status with the rest of the cats, said, "I knew you would like it. See you all later."

Nancy and Sam left as Tiger Lily turned to look at Honey Bear. Honey Bear smirked and went back to sleep.

Tiger Lily looked around at her fellow detectives again and said, *"Wonderful. Oh, well. Who will go first?"*

"Me! Me!" Said Sassy Pants. *"I metted a mouse! I named him Brown Mousie. He lives at da Winery. Weze gonna be best friends."*

Little Socks gave an inward groan. Would this cat never learn to speak correctly? Tiger Lily stepped on her tail.

"We saw," said Mr. Bean. *"Tillie and I watched you from the hole under the sink. We tried to get your attention, but you were busy talking to him. He looks like a nice mouse."*

"I tink he can help us. Heze a tiny little guy, an he can get into small places. I tink he can be a tective too."

Little Socks, incredulous, said, *"We don't play with mice. We don't work with mice. We eat mice. It's like a prime directive."*

Sassy Pants glared. *"Heze a nice mousie. We duzn't eats him!"*

Mr. Bean added, *"We saw him. He's a nice mouse, and he seems really smart."*

Tiger Lily moved, this time to stand on the black tail of Little Socks. *"This sounds promising. It'll be nice to have someone small enough to spy for us. We'll all have to go meet him sometime."*

"He can come to everybody dat works in da long bilding, but Kali and Ko will has to finds anudder way."

"Send him around. Tell him we won't bite or anything. He'll just have to tell us he's Brown Mousie."

"I duzn't tink he can talk."

"*Well, send him anyway, and we will introduce ourselves to him.*"

"*Okay. I tells him tomorrow.*"

Fat Cat asked, "*Can he come across the street?*"

"*Probly not. It's not safe. But you come over to da winery. You meets him dere.*"

Fat Cat and Scaredy Cat nodded to one another.

Honey Bear, only pretending to be asleep, licked his lips. Tiger Lily noticed, but she didn't say anything. Instead, she looked at Mo.

"*Mo, what do you have?*"

"*Trill, trill, trill.*"

Kali and Ko said, at the same time, "*Mo says there's a mystery guy in town.*" "*Some strange guy wears a hat.*"

Sassy Pants translated further. "*He sez da guy wuz watchin' somebody at da bar.*"

"*Hmmm. Okay. We'll keep an eye out for him. Kali, Ko, what do you have?*"

Again, the two talked together. "*Jeff called Chris.*" "*Chris is going to help Jeff.*"

They looked at one another and Kali continued. "*Jeff called Chris and it sounds like Chris is going to help him with some FBI investigation.*"

"*Wow. What are they investigating?*"

Kali and Ko shook their heads and Ko answered. "*They didn't say, just that Jeff and that friend of his, Mark, were going to see Chris about it.*"

"Why can't we get all the information at one time?" lamented Tiger Lily. *"We always have to piece things together."*

Mr. Bean said, *"Well, we have something about that, too."*

Tillie was excited to be a recognized member of the team. *"They were going to talk to Pete this afternoon. I'll bet Cyril will be able to tell us something."*

"Interesting," said Tiger Lily. *"We need to get Chris a dog so we can hear what goes on at the Coast Guard Station."*

Once again, Tiger Lily looked at Little Socks. She had curled into a ball and pretended to be asleep. Tiger Lily continued, *"Well, my information is about Geraldine. Mommy said there will be a court hearing tomorrow, and maybe Geraldine and that awful Hank will be able to come back to The Avenue."*

"No!" "What?" "It can't be!" "Trill!" "They're awful!" "How can this happen?" "Dat's not fair!"

"Mommy and Grandmommy seem to think this is what will happen."

"Weze gonna keep ize on her. We make life mizerble for her."

"Good idea, Sassy Pants. Let's do this. Whenever she is in any of our places, let's bug her."

"Good idea." "Yeah." "I gots good ideas bout wots to do to her." "Me too!"

Little Socks appeared to sleep on, but she had some ideas as well.

8

Nancy and Sam met their good friends Mem and Frank for dinner. Frank owned an antique shop on Main Street. He and Mem had discussed living together, even getting married, but for now, they were content to date. Mem lived in the apartment above her store, CyberHealth, with her daughter Diana. Frank lived on the third floor of his antique shop.

Tonight they dined at Frank's place. He was becoming something of a gourmet cook, and he wanted to practice on his good friends.

Nancy looked around the apartment. While the antique store on the ground floor was done in cherry and oak, this apartment gleamed with glass and chrome. The walls were a neutral eggshell, but around the rooms were splashes of color. Modern art and colorful metal wall sculptures, colorful pillows, throws and lamps, pieces of art.

Frank served the first course, prosciutto-wrapped brie bites with rosemary walnuts. "I'm sorry we can't go to the roof to see the sunset tonight."

"We'll be here for a few weeks. There will be plenty of time."

Frank's roof was, undoubtedly, one of the best places to watch the sunset in all of Chelsea. The roof of the three-story building, one long city block from the lakefront, had an unobstructed view of the sky over the lake. It was comfortably furnished with tables and chairs to accommodate several people. Tonight, however, they looked toward the lake and the rainy sunset from the

French doors that led from the kitchen to the third floor balcony.

As Frank served the second course, white gazpacho, with almonds, cucumber, garlic and lemon, Mem thought about Annie. "Nancy, did you know Annie purchased several kitchen items? Bakeware, table service, that kind of thing?"

"No. I didn't know she needed anything. When did she do this?"

"Yesterday."

"I'll have to go up to her apartment. If she just purchased it, it's still sitting around somewhere in boxes. It will sit like that for weeks."

"She said she was going to start cooking."

"And my mother was the Queen of Egypt."

Frank served the third course, spicy chicken thighs with tangy honey glaze and a side of quinoa salad with peaches, arugula and red onions. Nancy shared Annie's news about the upcoming court hearing.

Mem's response was typical. "Geraldine will get what's due her eventually. For some reason, she has decided that Annie is the worst thing that could have happened to her. I've thought about it often. Annie took nothing from her and did not oppose her in any way. Geraldine took an instant dislike to her and has martialed all of her friends to oppose her in the most, well, let's just say the most rude fashion imaginable."

Nancy said, "Well, Mem, you are aware of Annie's, um, parentage, and I assume you shared this with Frank?" Mem and Frank nodded. "Well, I don't know if you are aware that Geraldine became aware of it through a dreadful brother-in-law, the one that works at the library, and, well, I think she is going to try to hurt Annie with it."

Mem and Frank chuckled. Frank said, "Geraldine grew up in Chelsea, but she doesn't have a pulse of the community. She grew up in privilege, and it's not surprising she didn't get to know the heart of the town, the folks that support the tourist industry. The people of Chelsea, the real people of Chelsea, will see Annie's Native American heritage for what it is. A piece of history. Something that was never Annie's fault. And they will admire Victor for loving Annie as if she were his own."

Mem, tactfully, did not add her thoughts about other ways in which Geraldine might get her revenge. Those ways involved Nancy, not Annie.

By now, Frank had risen to bring in the last course. Dessert. He carried a tray with four plates. Each plate had several slices of fresh apples, peaches and pears and a ramekin of hot marshmallow caramel sauce for dipping.

Nancy had one final thought about Annie. "I wonder if that trip to see Chris's parents had anything to do with that big purchase?"

"She told me something about that."

"Really? She's said nothing to me."

"Let's just assume that she'll tell you when it's time. She needed a shoulder, so I'll hold her confidence. But I can't quite see how kitchen supplies would fit."

Chris and Annie stayed in as well. Annie, never the best cook, and not ready to try out her new purchases, served take out small plates from the Café, Mr. Bean's and Sassy P's. The rain kept them off the deck. They sat at the small kitchen table that looked out on the lake.

Chris sighed. "No sunset tonight."

Their silence together, usually companionable, was tense tonight. Annie was glad for a little relief when the rain broke. She walked to the balcony and breathed in the fresh summer air. A movement below caught her attention.

Tiger Lily had also taken advantage of the break in the rain. She was in the garden below. She watched something closely. Annie concentrated on the area in which Tiger Lily gazed and saw a summer monarch.

As Chris joined her on the deck, she quoted from one of her favorite authors, Henry David Thoreau. "Happiness is like a butterfly: the more you chase it, the more it will elude you; but if you turn your attention to other things, it will come and sit softly on your shoulder."

Chris didn't notice Tiger Lily and didn't realize Annie's quote was specific to Tiger Lily's interaction. He thought Annie referred to their relationship.

"Annie, I don't know how to make this any better. I love my parents. I will always respect and honor them. But I will not allow my mother's narrow views of life define who I am. And I will never ask you to go through that again."

He hugged Annie's shoulders from behind. "If you think you need time away, to think about us, I understand."

Annie grasped his hands and turned her head to look up at him. "Are you saying you want to walk away?"

"No. Not at all. I thought…"

"You thought I wanted to?"

"You said you wanted to turn your attention to other things. What other things?"

"Oh, that! That was a quote from Thoreau. Tiger Lily has a butterfly cornered down there."

"What?"

"Look."

By now, Tiger Lily was looking up at Annie and Chris, but the butterfly remained.

"See it? On that bush? Tiger Lily has been watching her."

"Say it again."

"Happiness is like a butterfly: the more you chase it, the more it will elude you; but if you turn your attention to other things, it will come and sit softly on your shoulder."

Tiger Lily looked at the butterfly again. It didn't come to sit on her shoulder. If flew away.

Chris didn't notice. He buried his head in Annie's hair. He held her close for several minutes until the rain started again.

9

After another glorious breakfast, Mark looked at Jeff. "It's Wednesday. I have to be fit on Saturday, and yet again, it's raining. It's time to go to the yoga studio."

"What?"

"You don't do yoga?"

"No. You?"

"Sometimes it's the only alternative to keeping your body limber. Come on, let's go."

"Can we wear street clothes?"

Mark laughed. "Sure. Come on."

By the time they arrived at the studio, Annie had already dropped the cats off at their places of business using Clara's covered wagon.

Little Socks, sleeping on a black cushion, opened one eye to look at the new yoga students. Jeff. Huh. This should be fun to watch.

Diana moved to the head of the room to begin instructions. Luckily for Jeff, this was a beginning level session. Little Socks sat up, stretched, yawned, and focused on Mark and Jeff.

As Diana took the group through limbering up exercises, Mark looked around the room. Like all of the other places of business on this side of The Avenue, one wall was filled with windows. The window wall was painted bright orange. Colorful benches lined the wall in front of the windows and black cushions sat on each windowsill, obviously for the small tuxedo cat.

The wall opposite was mirrored; a ballet bar was fastened along the length. The side walls were painted eggshell, and yoga poses of every sort were painted in primary colors. He could see a small locker area in the back, large enough for showers and changing rooms.

His gaze turned to Jeff. Jeff concentrated on the instructions given by Diana. Mark didn't recall ever seeing Jeff look clumsy. Until now. He chuckled under his breath.

Then he noticed the cat. She had moved from the windowsill to stand at Jeff's feet. Well, the word "stand" was certainly a misnomer. At the moment, she was on her hind legs, to be sure, but her body moved in lithe concert to Diana's instructions.

She stretched, turned, dipped, lifted one back leg, then the other. Her tail even moved with the instructions, sometimes like an arm and sometimes like a leg.

She was graceful beyond his imagination.

Jeff was too busy following instructions to notice Little Socks. She noticed him. He strained, lost his balance, caught it again, strained some more, and started the process over again.

Before the session was over, Jeff fell over, narrowly missing Little Socks as she jumped out of his way. She decided life would be easier on the windowsill and jumped back to the pillow.

After the session, Mark refrained from making fun of his friend and instead said, "Your friend Ray just walked into the Confectionary. No time like the present."

Jeff nodded, happy not to have to relive the yoga experience. On their way out the door, Mark picked up a schedule that included all of the exercise classes offered by the studio. He was pleased to see several types of exercise classes that weren't yoga-based.

Little Socks followed. She wanted to make up for not having anything to share the day before. She stepped around rather than walk through the rain puddles on the sidewalk.

Inside the door, Little Socks watched as the men greeted one another, picked out baked goods and sat down. Mr. Bean and Tillie were not in sight. Probably back at that sink, watching that infernal mouse, she thought. Jock lay at Ray's feet, rain still glistening on his fur. He looked up at Little Socks, huffed a hello and went back to sleep.

Mark watched with amusement as the cat followed them from the yoga studio to the Confectionary. He hoped she would come to him, but she didn't. She jumped to Ray's lap, stretched out on his right leg and settled in to listen.

Mark looked up in time to see Annie enter. She looked at the table and said, "Wow, Ray. What did you do to deserve this?"

"Not sure, but I'm enjoying it. This is the first time she's come to me or let me touch her."

Annie walked through to the kitchen. Isabel and Carlos worked at the ovens. Daniela sat at a table in the back of the kitchen with Rosa and Valeria, the younger sisters of Carlos. They were hunched over what looked to be a mountain of paperwork, brows knitted in concentration, pens working from time to time on the forms in front of them.

Annie sat with them. "How's it going?" Then her attention was caught by the cat and dog in the kitchen. In the kitchen! For the second day in a row! They concentrated on the floorboard underneath the sink.

"Mr. Bean! Tillie! Get out of this kitchen! The health department will have my head on a platter!"

Tillie jumped and ran from the room. Mr. Bean looked at his mommy, looked back at the wall, pawed it a couple of times, then turned. He sat for a few seconds, gazed at Annie with an unreadable Beanie expression, then rose and trotted from the room.

Annie and the three women watched his progression from the room. Even Carlos stood from his work and watched. He shook his head. "Sorry, Annie. I didn't notice them. I think we have a mouse."

Annie made a face and sat with the women. Rosa had a grimace on her face. "English is not my first language. Sometimes the questions are hard to understand."

Valeria, back to work on her forms, said, "Like this one. I just read it three times and came up with three interpretations."

"Sometimes the English language can be hard to decipher. Vowels and consonants don't always behave the way you think they should. Do you want me to read them to you?"

"No. We have to figure it out ourselves."

Daniela said, "I was just about to say yes, I want your help, but since the girls declined, I guess I will also. I can't be shown up by my own children."

Annie sat with them a while longer until she heard her mother in the shop. Today they were going to the library. Mindful that Geraldine's brother-in-law would share everything he learned, Annie and Nancy had decided this couldn't stop them. They were on a mission.

Annie learned recently that her biological father's family – the ancestors of Darrell Mayes, who was of Cherokee origin – were "old settlers." They left the Cherokee territory before the clans were forcibly removed during the Trail of Tears era.

As they walked to the library, umbrellas at the ready, Annie recapped that information for her mother. "I didn't want to think about them on that Trail. It doesn't lessen the horror, but at least we know that Darrell's ancestors moved of their own free will."

"I'm glad we don't have to look into that further. I want to be blissfully ignorant of the atrocities we committed in the name of progress."

Annie checked in with the genealogist, picked up the folder he held for her, and they went to the computer section. As they looked through the records, Annie and Nancy learned that not only was her Mayes ancestor an "old settler," he was also a slave owner, and he served in the Army of the Confederacy.

"I just continue to add to my resume, Mom. Think we should let this information slip as we walk out?"

"Why not?"

They chatted about those very items as Annie handed the folder over on their way out. Annie looked over her shoulder and smiled to herself when she saw him on his cell phone.

Geraldine put the cell phone in her purse. So Annie was not only an Indian, she was a descendent of slave owners and a Confederate! This would add fire to the furnace. She glanced back at her friend with a smile.

Geraldine sat in the courtroom with her attorney. They waited for the arrival of the Judge. At the next table was that horrid woman, Jenny Howe. Some kind of a rabble-rousing justice-loving jungle heathen hired by Her. Annie. By the way, where was Annie? Surely she left the library to come here.

Geraldine looked around again. None of her simpering friends were here today. No one to watch but this...this...jungle bunny.

"All rise."

Geraldine rose and looked to her own attorney. When they were seated again, she barely listened to the proceedings. The Judge droned on, and sometimes her attorney said things, sometimes the jungle bunny did. Geraldine tried – and failed – to not look bored. She sat straight. She didn't move her head. Much. She tried to keep her eyes forward. It wasn't her fault they continued to roll first one way, then another, in response to the inane things the jungle bunny said.

Finally, her attorney touched her elbow, and they rose again. The Judge said some things. Something about despicable behavior. Too bad he couldn't keep the order going indefinitely. A civil case was still pending. Well, she was aware of that. He didn't need to tell her.

What was that? Something about volunteering. Meddling in personal affairs that were none of her business. What had he heard? And from whom did he hear it?

Well, of course I know Chelsea is a tourist town. Who doesn't? I do not involve my family in…what did he say? Personal vendettas? What a choice of words! You'd think I was a member of the Mafia!

After an interminable time, the Judge banged his gavel – Geraldine jumped – and he said, "With great misgivings and with a strong admonishment that the defendant grow up, I vacate this order."

When Geraldine turned to leave, she saw a flash and heard a click. That reporter! Juanita! Where had she been hiding?

10

Jeff and Mark walked to Sassy P's. Mark said, "It's a good thing we did some yoga today. We've done nothing but eat. Breakfast at the Inn, pastry at Mr. Bean's, now lunch. How soon do you think we can have a snack this afternoon?"

Jeff laughed. "We'll go back to the yoga studio after lunch, then we'll be ready to eat again."

Even though Mark could feel his muscles turning to mush, he reflected on the last two days. They had been productive. They had secured the cooperation of the Coast Guard, the local police department and the owner of a yacht that would provide support on the lakefront on the day of the triathlon.

Now, they were eating in a new place, Sassy P's Wine & Cheese. When they walked through the front room, Mark saw a bright room with light walnut finishes, including a bar with delicate hand-carved trim. The wall behind the bar was cranberry red; the other walls were lavender. Another color combination that worked.

And two new cats. Two large tabby cats walked from the back dining room, through the tasting room and out the cat door.

"Do all the cats in town come in and out of here?"

"Maybe," answered Jeff. "Maybe they come in here looking for mice. There is an outside patio here."

Jeff led Mark to a table in the back garden area, open in the back to face the woods of the state park. Potted plants, miniature trees and flowering shrubs filled concrete urns that sat near load-bearing beams. The foliage lent an air of privacy to most of the tables.

As they looked at menus, Mark decided this would be the perfect vacation town. He ordered the Crema di Formaggio small plate and settled in for another delightful meal.

At the Inn, Henrie, Nancy and Annie finished setting up a light buffet lunch just as a modified school bus pulled in. Nancy rushed to the porch in time to run into the arms of Patti, Annie's half-sister.

They arrived in a relatively dry period of time; the sky merely sprinkled water for a few minutes. This allowed Patti's husband, Fritz, to be a ringleader, pulling children and bags out of the front and back doors and directing them appropriately. He directed their younger children, Allen, eighteen, Percy, fourteen, Gracie, twelve, Ella, ten, and Ollie, six, with varying sizes of bags and bundles, to the carriage house. "Go upstairs, kids, and put the bags on the beds."

"Daaad!" came a wail from Percy. He had the teenaged ability to make the word three syllables long.

"Now, Percy. Henrie has lunch ready. We don't want him to wait forever, and it's not raining for a minute."

"Oh, alright." Percy followed his siblings up the stairs.

Their eldest daughter, Jessica, carried bags and herded her twins, Jerome and Sally, well into their terrible twos, into the Inn and down the hallway to the back bedroom on the ground floor. Paul, her husband, took two large bags and a backpack. Since he wasn't herding children, he stopped to give Nancy a kiss on the cheek on his way by.

Henrie and Annie did the wise thing. They sat at the kitchen table and waited for the cacophony to die down. Soon enough, the noise would come back to the dining room table.

Annie held a coffee cup in both hands. "I still have trouble getting used to the noise on arrival. At least it levels out after they're here for a while, after the kids find things to do."

"I added new board games to the library. I thought the twins might be old enough to try their hand at Candyland."

"I love that game. I'll teach them. Oh. It's changed over the years. Did you get a modern one?"

Henrie smiled. "I knew you would care. I procured the sixty-fifth anniversary edition. It is supposed to have the classic graphics."

The decibel level rose again. Henrie and Annie rose to serve lunch to their growing family. Conversation ebbed and flowed. Adults talked to other adults and talked to children. Children talked in raised voices to adults and at higher levels to other children. A hum of normal levels of adult voices persisted, punctuated with a raised tone on occasion.

"No, you cannot have dessert first." "Please try it; you may like it." "Ollie, you can't stand in the chair. Here, use this cushion." "Sally, the food goes into your mouth, not on the floor." "Mom, I'm so glad we could do this." "Paul, try this pasta. It is outstanding." "MOM, MAKE HIM

STOP!" "Percy, stop teasing your sister." "Aunt Annie, when can we go to the beach?"

Jessica and Paul competed in triathlon events as often as possible. For a few years, they had discussed running in the Chelsea event, only to be waylaid by the birth of their children and, well, having two young children. This year, they planned their participation with Patti and Fritz and Nancy and Sam. Built-in babysitters. Plus a few that Annie could hire.

As they ate lunch, and around other conversations, they discussed plans for the week, which included child care.

Annie said, "Ginger, one of our local teens, is in the apartment right now with Little Fred. She's younger than the twins and will be included in child care plans for the week."

Patti and Annie were about as different as sisters could be, which probably helped them to get along as well as they did. Patti, while picking up a fallen fork and spoon from Ollie's place, said, "I can't tell you how much we appreciate being able to vacation here, Annie. There are so few places we can all get together, besides my house, and that seems to get smaller as the years go on."

"Or the kids get bigger."

"And more numerous," added Nancy. She raised her voice. "Henrie, come in here and sit down with us. It's a family lunch, and you're family, after all."

Henrie came to the doorway. "Thank you, Nancy, but I have already eaten."

Annie turned to face him and rolled her eyes. Henrie's facial expression didn't change, but he looked at Jessica to say, "Please check out the game section in the library. I believe you will find some new games for the little ones."

"Thanks, Henrie. You think of everything!"

Fritz said, "Jess, why are you only doing the fifty? Why not join Paul in the one hundred?"

"Paul's had more opportunity to get into shape. I'm just now getting there, and I didn't want to overdo it."

"Mommy said she's fat!"

"Mommy's fat! Big fat butt!"

"Children!" Paul's voice had a strangled quality to it.

Nancy and Sam laughed while Patti did her best to keep her own young children out of the fat-calling. Annie smiled and thought to herself that cats were the better option for her, after all. She had no need to worry about not having children.

The crowded dining room at Mo's was helpful for the stranger who wore a hat. He took a table in the back and looked toward the bar. Today, the bar manager was there. No sign of the woman.

Sara, his server, remembered him. "Hi. Welcome back."

Her familiarity surprised him. "Oh. Thanks. Didn't think you would remember me."

"It's a small town. What would you like to drink?"

"Oh. Just get me a draft, whatever craft beer you have on draft, and, hey, there was a lady bartender the other day. Where's she?"

"She's cooking today. Want me to get her?"

"No. I was just curious. Bring me the black and bleu burger and sweet potato fries."

Sara remembered the little lecture from Georgia. Well, it wasn't a lecture, exactly. She merely used a conversation as a learning experience. When she went to the bar to place the man's lunch and drink order, she motioned for George to come closer.

"There's a guy in the back. He was here Monday. I remember because he didn't take his hat off, and Georgia couldn't get a look at his face. He sat in the back that day, too."

"Is there a problem?"

"No, just, I don't know, I have a funny feeling about him. Georgia asked me about him because she couldn't see him, and, well, he seems to want to keep his face hidden. And he asked about her."

"Georgia? By name?"

"He asked about the woman who was behind the bar Monday."

"Okay. Thanks, Sara."

George took the lunch order back to the kitchen to hand it to Georgia personally. "Hey, there's a guy out there, a guy you asked Sara about the other day. He was asking for you."

"The one that didn't take off his hat?"

"That's the one."

"Where is he?"

"Back of the room."

"Thanks. I'll deliver his order personally."

When Georgia made her way through the crowded room to the table in the back, black and bleu burger in hand, she saw a half empty pilsner glass and a ten dollar bill on the table. He was gone.

Speckles the nanny kitty stirred from a nap. Martha answered a knock at the door. Speckles crept to the hallway door. It was that man!

"Yes, can I help you?"

"I wanna see my baby."

"Your baby? You must have the wrong house."

"My baby's here. Pretty sure I heard it was a girl. Name of Fred."

"Oh. Well, Fred isn't here, and I'm sure, if you want to see her, you'll have to get her mother's permission."

"It's my baby. I can come in if I want."

"No, I don't think so."

"I have a right."

Martha tried to shut the door, but the man put his foot into the doorway and pushed against the door with both arms.

Speckles did the only thing she could think to do. She howled like someone was trying to kill her. The sound shocked the man enough to give Martha the seconds she needed to give the door a mighty shove and get it shut.

The man stood at the door and pounded it with his forearms. "I got a right! That's my baby in there!"

"Go away! I'm dialing nine-one-one right now!" Martha grabbed the telephone from the hallway table.

"I got a right!"

"Yes. Emergency." Martha gave the emergency operator the address of the house as she stood at the door, ready to put herself in harm's way if he somehow got through.

The man continued to shout that he had a right to see his baby.

Martha pleaded on the phone, "Hurry! He's breaking in!"

Chelsea was a small town. In less than a minute, Martha heard police sirens headed in their direction. The man glared at the door, pounded one more time with his forearms, and turned to run away. He ran across the street, between some houses, and was out of sight before the police car pulled to a stop.

11

Tension was high at the Inn when the cats got home from work. One by one, they ran home between rain showers and found Mommy and Henrie, Nancy and Sam, The Dreaded Uncle Honey Bear, Aunt Patti and Uncle Fritz, cousin Jessica and Paul, all of Patti and Jessica's children, Pete and Cyril, Martha and Speckles the nanny kitty, Georgia and Little Fred. Ginger and JoJo tried to corral the younger cousins to keep them out of the way. Even Fat Cat and Scaredy Cat were there, drawn by the police car sitting outside.

It was difficult to figure out what was happening. Finally, the cats, Cyril and Tillie headed for the dining room. The little ones crowded under the table while Cyril lay on the floor and stuck his head under the tablecloth.

The excitement concerned Little Fred and the unwelcome appearance of the man. Kali and Ko's concerns about Little Fred were more personal than the rest. They had acted as nanny kitties to the little girl for several weeks and had, in fact, trained Speckles to take over. The two big girls sat in a corner under the table, huddled together for comfort.

Everyone listened respectfully, even Little Socks and Honey Bear, as Speckles and Cyril outlined the danger to Little Fred.

Speckles finished with, *"It's a man with a hat."*

"Trill!"

Kali and Ko translated. *"He said that man was at the bar."* *"He's been watching Georgia."*

Kali continued. *"If he said Little Fred was his baby, then he has to be Georgia's husband."*

"Ex-husband," corrected Little Socks.

Speckles looked directly at Tiger Lily. *"I've been watching how things are done. Georgia hires babysitters. Martha hired people to make the apartment for Georgia. I was thinking that maybe I could hire you."*

"Hire me?"

"Hire you. You and the detectives. Can you help protect Little Fred from this man?"

Tiger Lily looked around at all of the faces staring at her. This was a new twist. She had never considered that they could be hired by someone to actually be detectives. Or bodyguards.

She looked back at Speckles, who mistook the confusion about roles for something else.

"I don't know how I can pay you, or what you charge, but whatever it takes, I'll do it. I can save up treats, or hide cat food, maybe catch a mouse or something. Anything."

Tiger Lily shook her head. *"It's not that, Speckles. We would do it for free. We've just never been hired before. I…we…well, I'm sure we would do anything we could, but we're never there, at your house."*

"I think Little Fred will be here while Georgia works for the rest of the week, at least through Saturday, but you're right. I don't know how to keep her safe when she's at home."

Sassy Pants entered the conversation. *"Wot skills you gots?"*

"Huh?"

Cyril said, *"I think she was asking if you have any particular skills that could help you protect Little Fred."*

"Oh," said Speckles. A thoughtful look appeared on her face as she considered her answer. She looked around at all of her friends. *"I'm pretty good at catching my tail. I can get it on the second try."*

Mr. Bean said, *"That's a good skill."*

Little heads nodded assent, then several cats talked at once. *"But that won't help." "She needs some other skill." "Trill." "Maybe she can dazzle him."*

Tiger Lily brought some order to the conversation. *"That's a good skill, Speckles, but do you know how to do anything else?"*

Speckles thought again. Then she brightened. *"Georgia says I'm a ninja kitty. I can do ninja."*

"What's ninja?"

"I don't know how to explain it, but I can show you. We need more room."

The cats and dogs moved into the dining room proper.

"Is this enough room?" asked Tiger Lily.

"I think so. Let me try."

Speckles took a deep breath, then took a leap. And several more. She leapt to the table top, ran to the end, leapt toward the buffet, turned in mid-air to land again on the table. She did this several times in the course of just a few seconds and seemed to touch every table top, every floor surface.

She whizzed by Tiger Lily, who ducked. Kali and Ko hid their heads under their arms. Mo and Mr. Bean jumped out of the way as she sailed close. Sassy Pants and Tillie dove under the tablecloth to the detective agency.

Cyril got as low as he could. Fat Cat ran for the kitchen and sat in that doorway while Scaredy Cat ran in the other direction, turning to watch from the foyer door.

Only Little Socks and Honey Bear seemed unfazed. Honey Bear licked his paws and cleaned his ears. Little Socks watched, following with her eyes as Speckles sailed from one part of the room to another.

As Speckles stopped, coming to rest on the top of the detective agency table, Little Socks said, *"Now that's a skill worth having."*

Everyone crept from their hiding places and they discussed the best ways they could keep an eye on Little Fred for the rest of the week.

Tiger Lily looked at Speckles. *"You know, if he comes for her, it will probably be when she's at your house. There are fewer people there. You'll have to do your ninja best. Don't be afraid. Get in there and do as much damage as you can."*

Pete called for Cyril as they finished their discussion. Cyril gave a bark to let Pete know he had heard, then turned back to the group.

"Pete will be helping Jeff and Mark with a drug investigation. I have to go now, but I'll try to stop in at the Café tomorrow and tell you what I know. I think Chris will help, and Ray. So Jock may know what's going on, too."

"A drug investigation? Really?"

"It has something to do with the triathlon. They think someone will be here that weekend and…"

"Cyril! Come on, big guy!"

"I've got to go. I'll tell you tomorrow."

Henrie walked from the library to the kitchen. He looked at the cats and dogs gathered in the room. Eventually, his eyes rested on Honey Bear. Egad! He had completely forgotten to lock the cat doors!

12

At supper, Patti heard about Geraldine's court order for the first time. Also for the first time, she heard that Annie's biological father wasn't who she thought. Annie was talking, and Patti had to back her up for clarification.

"Tell me again what you meant by the genealogist, and looking for information about your father?"

After the clarification, Patti's only comment to Annie was, "Hmm. Darrell Mayes. Vic's still your dad, right? I mean, he's still the one you call 'dad,' right?"

To her mother, who had the out-of-wedlock affair, Patti said, "You never cease to amaze me." She looked at Sam and added, "No surprises for me, right, Dad?"

Sam and Nancy stared at Patti, who laughed. They all heard a loud crash from the dining room and then the sound of a sudden silence. Patti rose from the table to investigate.

Jenny, Annie's attorney, had given Annie a blow-by-blow description of the courtroom proceedings that day. Annie had been in the process of telling her family and Chris what she learned.

Annie continued the conversation. "So, anyway, the judge gave her a lecture, and he allowed press into the hearing, so we'll read all about it tomorrow."

Chris asked, "What did he include in the lecture?"

"Oh, don't do this again, be a better person, don't involve your family and others in your personal vendettas, this is a small town, we're a tourist town and we can't have scenes like this in front of our guests. The usual."

"So, we can look forward to Geraldine everywhere we go."

"Right."

"Is the civil suit still going on?"

"Yes. I still might get some cash from her for defamation, but really, you can't get blood from a turnip. She and Everett have gone through everything they have ever made or inherited."

"You can't tell it from the lifestyle they lead."

"Why is it that the ones that started out on top still seem to have money, even after it's gone?"

"They must have something hidden somewhere, something that they can get to and convert to cash."

"It's magic."

Annie looked at her mother. "You know, she's going to throw this hatred your way, too."

"Oh, I know, dear. I already heard one of her little friends telling another of her little friends, in a loud whisper, that I was the 'one that had the affair.' And the other one said, 'Her? Really?' And then there was some laughter and a few other choice words."

"And they didn't say it was with a red-skinned savage?"

"They didn't say the words. You could hear that unstated fact in the tone of their voices."

Sam took Nancy's hand and gave it a squeeze. "When they go low…"

"I know, dear, I know. We'll go high."

"Henrie had an idea. He thought we should take the bull by the horns."

"Really? He said that?"

"He tried. He didn't get it right, but that's what he meant. Anyway, this was his plan."

Annie leaned in and told them Henrie's idea. "He's already shared it with everyone that works for me and everyone on the other side of The Avenue. It feels better than just letting her have her way."

Nancy and Sam laughed. Chris smiled. "This sounds easy. So easy it will probably work."

Chris didn't know Geraldine's spite would come to him as well. Easy? Not so much.

13

Henrie laughed so hard, tears ran down his cheeks. He read the article, then read it again. He looked once again at the photograph. Juanita caught Geraldine just as she turned to leave her attorney. Her expression was priceless: angry, cruel, startled, and vain. Her mouth was partly open, moving into or out of a snarl, and the image of her recently-tucked eyes was an embarrassment. One hand moved toward her face while the other clutched at what had to be a knock-off Hermes handbag.

Henrie reached for the handheld receiver. He called The Drug Store and asked, "Could you please put back at least ten copies of…"

Holly interrupted him with a howl. "I already put thirty back for you!"

Once again, Henrie read the article. Juanita had captured the hearing to perfection. The article was outstanding in its attention to detail, particularly the details of the Judge's long-winded lecture.

She should win a Pulitzer for this one.

Angela cursed under her breath. She stared at her feet. This rain was ruining her shoes. She sat in a rental car outside Chris's condominium. The condo was in an upscale lakefront community just north of the historic lighthouse museum.

She thought about calling him before flying in, but realized he would discourage her visit. Her flight arrived in Marsh Haven the evening before. After checking in – Marsh Haven had one hotel that minimally met her requirements – she tried to call Chris at his home. He didn't answer. She did not call his cell phone, because she assumed he would be with that horrid woman.

And now, after knocking on his door and getting wet in this wretched rain, she realized he did not come home the night before. Angela couldn't bear to think what he had been doing.

Well, there was nothing to be done.

Angela started the car, drove back toward the middle of town and parked on The Avenue, on the side opposite the Café. Well, at least the Café looked like a pleasant, albeit a touristy, place to eat. As she looked at the other businesses on that side of The Avenue, she had to admit, grudgingly, they looked like decent places. Even that Inn. It was an attractive building.

And there was Chris! He walked with that beast of a woman and another couple, older, toward the Café. Under umbrellas, she couldn't get a good look at the couple. What was today? Thursday? Still the middle of the week and there he was. Coming out of her house. In front of God and everybody. Thank goodness the Senator was not here to see it.

And she pulled a covered wagon of some sort behind her! They stopped at every place of business on the way down. That perfectly dreadful woman pulled the wagon to each door. And something happened each time. What was it?

By the time the wagon got to the place just across from her, the yoga place, she realized what it was. She was letting those infernal cats out of the wagon!

Angela looked around. She was parked in front of a tea shop. She would go in, hopefully get a table at a window, and watch.

Inside the building, she shook rain from her umbrella. The only table near a window was taken by a well-dressed woman. Her kind of woman. Perhaps she would be sympathetic.

"Pardon me, but I was hoping to sit at this table. I need to watch for someone. Would you mind allowing me to have it?"

The woman looked up and seemed to assess Angela, perhaps to see if she was worthy of consideration. The woman looked around the tearoom. "It seems all the other tables are taken, but I am alone. Please. Join me. My name is Geraldine."

As the group entered the Café, Annie was called over to the coffee bar. Trudie held the morning paper in her hands and couldn't stop laughing. "Did you see it?"

Annie smiled, working hard to keep the laughter from bubbling up. Again. "I did. I'm trying to be an adult about it."

Trudie laughed again. "Felicity called The Drug Store and had her hold back forty copies."

"Henrie got thirty."

"Holly said the delivery man – just because he knew we would want them – dropped two extra stacks today. There will be plenty to go around."

Annie looked around the room. "Do you think we need some wall art? We could put something next to that framed article Juanita did…you know, the one that focused on the good aspects of our open house…"

"Are you serious? I'll ask Clara…"

"No! Just joking. But I want this paper to accidently appear all around the room today. All day long. And tomorrow…and the next day…."

Chris, Nancy and Sam sat at a table in the window facing across The Avenue. They were joined in short order by Pete and Ray. Annie was busy at the moment, but she would join them shortly.

Tiger Lily, perfectly dry, jumped out of the way as Cyril and Jock shook the rain from their coats. At least they weren't close to a table or any of the guests.

Trudie, the barista, always had treats behind the coffee bar. She brought out bowls with dog biscuits and a few cat treats, set them behind the hostess stand and received their grateful thanks.

Cyril asked the most obvious question. *"Why is Annie having breakfast here?"*

"She and Chris said something about a decibel level. I think that means noise. Grandmommy agreed with them. The rest of the family is having breakfast with Henrie."

Tiger Lily looked closely at her friends. *"Okay. Tell me what you know about Jeff and Mark."*

"Well, like I said yesterday, Pete will be helping them on Saturday. We have our eyes open for strange folks in town already."

"Strange, how?"

"Well, new and suspicious, even people we know that start acting in ways we don't expect."

"Us, too," said Jock. *"We already planned to help at the triathlon. We were going to sit just past the swimming buoys in The Escape. Now we're going to spend as much time looking out toward the lake as in toward the swimmers."*

"What if a swimmer gets into trouble and you're busy looking out at the lake?"

"Cheryl is coming with us. She'll watch the swimmers; Ray and I will watch the lake."

"What are you looking for?"

"Boats coming into the harbor with out-of-state or Canadian registration. If we see some that we don't know, or that look a little off, we'll let Chris know."

"We thought Chris might be helping, too. Where will he be?"

"He'll be a little further out. He'll be watching as well, but since he has a wider patrol area, he may miss something."

"What do they think is going to happen?"

"They think a drug supplier is setting up a new distribution and collection point. They got a tip, but it was not something their bosses wanted to follow up. They thought a little place like Chelsea couldn't be important."

"But Jeff thought it was?"

"Jeff likes us. A lot. He didn't want to think something could get set up here."

"So why now? Why during the triathlon?"

"Jeff and Mark don't think the new contact will be an athlete. They think this weekend was chosen because of the large

number of people that are here, and the larger-than-usual number of boats that will be in the harbor."

"So, a boat is coming here to meet someone. Is it someone from town?"

"It could be. Or it could be a stranger. They don't know. They just know that the connection is supposed to be made this weekend, and after it's set, the drug runners will be familiar to us."

"So it wouldn't be unusual for the person or people to be here, and they can go about their business without anyone knowing."

"Right."

"So we have to watch everybody."

The three friends turned as a guest entered. Ian stopped just inside the door. He looked around until he saw Tiger Lily and the dogs. He walked behind the hostess stand to give each companion his trademark two-handed pet, and walked to the table where their special humans sat.

They looked at one another.

"Even Ian's a suspect," said Tiger Lily.

"Bummer."

It was time to get to work. On days like this, Georgia drove the car given to her by her father. It was old, but reliable.

She took a few bags to the front porch then went to the back yard, where the car was parked. She was happy that Annie was taking care of child care for the week, but that meant she had to get Little Fred, her diaper bag and some extra items into the car.

Georgia drove the car down the alley and turned to park in front of the house. As she got out of the car, she saw a man with a hat rush from the house to the porch. He stopped and looked straight at her. It was Ken. Her ex-husband. He really was in town. And now he had Little Fred.

He ran.

She jumped into the car to give chase, but he ran between houses, up an alley, and between other houses. Georgia got out of the car to give chase on foot, but he was too far ahead.

She dropped to her knees and cried out in grief, the rain pouring down upon her. Shortly, she was roused by the sound of police sirens. Martha must have called them.

Slowly, Georgia pushed herself up from the ground and trudged back to the car. She drove back to the house. Dazed and confused, the oddest thought occurred to her. Why was Ken's face covered in red paint?

Annie watched as Martha, sobbing and almost delirious with grief, finally accepted a cup of hot tea from Henrie. He checked the ice bag on her face and determined it was still cold enough.

"There, there. The police will find him and will bring our child home to us soon." Henrie looked at Annie over Martha's head. Neither of them believed his soothing words. The man, apparently Georgia's ex-husband, probably had a getaway plan.

Annie sat with Georgia. George and Cookie made plans to get through the day without her, but Georgia would have nothing to do with that plan. "I have to work, Annie. There's nothing I can do here. I've told Pete everything I know."

"Are you sure?"

"Yes. I promised Cookie I would help him get ready for the weekend. He's letting me do the soup and appetizer courses. I don't want to let him down. And I can't just sit here. I'll go crazy."

"Alright. I'll call George and let him know. But understand this: when Little Fred is found, you are going to take some time off, even if it's only a few hours, to make sure she's okay."

"Thanks, Annie." Georgia turned away from Annie to blow her nose. She noticed Tiger Lily for the first time.

"You brought Tiger Lily?"

"She refused to be left at the Café. Cyril ran out with Pete, and, well, she started to howl and didn't stop until I picked her up. There's just no telling what they know and what they don't."

"It looks like she's actually commiserating with Speckles."

Annie looked over. "Yes, it does."

Tiger Lily crouched next to the kitten, who cuddled into her side. *"Tell me again, Speckles. Tell me what happened."*

"It happened so fast. Georgia said I could go with Little Fred to the Inn today, so I was lying next to the carrier. Georgia

went out to get the car. She went out the front, because she had several things to take, and she wanted to put them on the porch. Anyway, the front door was unlocked for just a couple of minutes, and he came in."

"*Tell me again about him.*"

"*He was like a wild man. He ran in, looked in the dining room, then here in the living room. We were in here. He unhooked her safety belt, and that's when I did it. I did the ninja kitty thing. I got him good. I scratched him all up on his arms and hands. He screamed real loud, and that's when Martha came in.*"

"*And he hit her?*"

"*Yeah. He hit her in the face with his fist. That blood on her was his own. I made Martha bloody.*"

"*Don't worry about that. Go ahead; tell me the rest again.*"

Speckles sighed. "*Well, after Martha fell down, he turned to get Fred, and I got him again. This time, I jumped on his back. I scratched his neck and when he turned, I got his face, then I got the other side of his face. And then he grabbed me and threw me over there.*"

"*Thank goodness you landed on the sofa.*"

"*Yeah.*" Speckles looked down at the floor. "*But I didn't save Little Fred. He got her.*"

"*There was nothing more you could do, Speckles. But if Cyril finds him, they'll know they have the right guy. He'll have those marks for several days. Maybe he'll get infected. That would be even better.*"

130

Speckles cuddled deeper into Tiger Lily's side. Tiger Lily licked the top of her head as she said, *"You're a very brave kitty."*

Pete and Cyril returned from searching the neighborhood. "Cyril followed the scent to the back end of the state park. I left Marco there; he's coordinating a search effort. Maybe our guy is staying there. We might get lucky."

Pete went back to the front door. "We need to get back there. I just came back to get the car. Cyril! Come!"

Cyril, adding his tongue to the washing effort, gave a final lick to Speckles and trotted to the door. He looked back at Tiger Lily as he left. They would have much to discuss.

14

Jeff and Mark were bored beyond belief. They had done everything they could to prepare themselves and their partners for Saturday. They had done nothing to prepare Mark for Saturday.

They sat in the foyer of the Inn, stuffed from breakfast, even after a yoga session followed by Pilates. Mark insisted they wait until at least two o'clock to eat lunch. The plan was to go to the Café.

Their umbrellas sat in the umbrella tray, wet. Their shoes were beside the door, wet. Their clothes were wet.

The clock crept toward the appointed lunch hour.

Just before leaving, they heard a commotion on the porch. Four people opened the door and stamped their feet as they shook wet umbrellas on the porch.

One of the men looked at Jeff and Mark. He said, "Hi. Nice weather you have here. We're here to check in."

"Uh…" Jeff was happy to point to Henrie as he entered the foyer.

Henrie was always calm. The guests couldn't tell he was rattled about Little Fred. What they noticed were the two cats who materialized to sit like bookends on either side of him.

"Good afternoon. I am Henrie. Welcome to the KaliKo Inn."

Jeff and Mark gave a brief wave to Henrie as they donned wet shoes and picked up their umbrellas. Mark, on his way out, said, "You're gonna like it here. See you later."

Henrie went through the routine, happy to have a full house once again. This would keep him too busy to worry about Little Fred. Perhaps. He gave them a tour of the Inn, pointing out the amenities such as the coffee corner and the computers to which they had access.

Kali and Ko, after sniffing the luggage carefully, followed.

Randy and Krissie were in their thirties, as were Tim and Melanie. Two of the four were entered in the triathlon; Krissie and Tim planned to compete in the one hundred mile course.

Henrie showed Randy and Krissie to the room facing the lake. "I regret the weather will not allow you to enjoy the deck today, and I fear you will not be able to see the sunset tonight. However, as the week draws on, please enjoy this view. You will find the deck furniture comfortable."

Henrie shooed Kali and Ko off the bed and pointed out the television set and remote control. "You may access the internet using the television or use your password for any devise." When Henrie offered the key to the locking armoire, Randy reached out his hand to accept it.

Tim and Melanie, having participated in the tour of the lakeside room, waved Henrie off when he showed them to the room facing the garden and the winery. Kali had already moved through the room to the deck doors; she turned around. She wanted to pose for the handsome man while Henrie finished the tour. Ko went around her and nudged her toward the hallway.

Henrie turned to leave, then turned back to address the group. "Might I suggest, especially to the two of you competing in the triathlon, that you make use of the yoga studio next to the Café as long as the rain persists. Saturday should be clear, but by then, your muscles may have gotten a bit, shall we say, soft. In the foyer, you will find a schedule of all of the yoga and exercise classes available. Show the instructor your room key for free use of the studio and attendance at the classes."

Henrie returned to the kitchen to make the afternoon snack. Today it would be pear quarters with bleu cheese and walnuts spritzed with Italian vinaigrette dressing, and bruschetta topped with marinated artichoke hearts, parmesan and sun-dried tomatoes.

Henrie thought about his newest guests. An undercurrent existed that was, well, not quite right. He wondered if the attraction between Randy and Melanie had consummated into a relationship or if it was unrequited. He believed the relationship had probably crossed the line.

He hoped the explosion – sure to occur at some point – did not come while they remained at the Inn. They had enough excitement on their plate.

Jeff and Mark entered the Café as the rain stopped for a few minutes. Mark looked around for Annie but didn't see her. Trudie came from behind the coffee bar to show them to a chair. He noticed Tiger Lily was not at the hostess stand.

Mark looked at Jeff. "Where's Annie? Didn't you say she's usually here during lunch?"

Trudie heard the question. She looked at Mark and Jeff closely. "I thought you two were some kind of law enforcement. You don't know?"

Jeff answered. "We're actually on vacation. What's happening?"

"There was a kidnapping in town this morning. One of our staff. Well, not one of our staff, but her baby."

"No. Can we help in any way?"

"Pete's on it. If he needs you, I'm sure he'll ask."

"Who's the staff?"

"Georgia. She works at Mo's, and here, and, well, in most of the places here. Mostly at Mo's. And here. I'm just rattling on."

"That's okay. Look, we don't have to eat here if it's too much…"

"No, please. We need to keep busy."

As Mark sat, taking a menu from Trudie, he looked around. The first time he was here, the Café was busy. Now he could look around at the details.

This was a pretty place. If he had to choose a favorite of Annie's businesses, this would be it.

Their table's top was ceramic, painted with a scene of two cats under a willow tree; they played with a ball of yarn. He noticed each table was the same, but with different scenes. The chairs were colorful, and playful pendant lights hung around the room, suspended from what appeared to be the original tin ceiling.

Then his hand bumped something attached to the underside of the table. He looked. Then he looked again around the room. "What are these?"

Jeff smiled. "This is Tiger Lily's Café. These are for her. She can jump up and talk to the guests or make suggestions for their order."

Mark shook his head and looked at the menu. A server came to explain the specials and take their order.

"We have an Italian theme right now. Well, a northern Italian theme. We have two soups on special. One is Italian peasant soup, made with chicken, two kinds of sausage and beans, and the other is Tuscan sausage and kale. It's made with sausage and kale."

Mark smiled, trying not to laugh.

"I'm sorry. I'm a little rattled today. Um, we have a sandwich special, too. We have vegetarian grilled Panini bites, those are small sandwiches with mozzarella, tomato and pesto, a salami and provolone Panini, and a Mediterranean turkey sandwich, made with the bread of your choice."

"I think that sounds good. Give me the turkey sandwich on whole wheat toast and a bowl of the Tuscan sausage and kale soup."

Jeff said, "I'll have the same, but put that sandwich on a baguette. Tell me, do you know anything about the kidnapping? Do they know who did it?"

"Yeah. Apparently it was Georgia's ex-husband. He's been in town a couple of days, and he went to her house yesterday, demanding to see the baby. A few people have seen him at Mo's, too."

"Did Georgia know he was going to do this?"

"She didn't see him until he had Little Fred – that's her baby – and she didn't know he was in town until yesterday. She didn't know he knew she lived here."

Mark looked at Jeff then back at their server. "Did anyone describe him? Just in case, you know, we may run into him?"

"Not really, just a guy with a hat. Everyone noticed the hat because he never took it off. Probably so Georgia wouldn't recognize him."

As the server left, Mark leaned in, "Well, that's one guy from the bar that's off our list of drug suspects, but, well, I know what he looks like. Did you see him the other night? He sat at the back of Mo's."

"Yeah. I saw him, but from where I sat, I couldn't see his face. You did?"

"Yeah. I could pick him out of a crowd. I'll keep my eyes open, but you know he's left town."

Mark's attention was drawn to a beautiful dark-skinned woman. She took the fresh flower arrangement from the hostess stand, placed it into a covered wagon, and pulled out a new one. Like the one it replaced, it was a riot of purples and lavenders. The woman turned and smiled. She walked toward their table.

"Jeff, it's so good to see you. I understand you're supposed to be on vacation. And you must be Mark." The woman turned to offer her hand.

"Yes. Pleased to meet you…."

"Clara. I have the flower shop across the street. This is my day to replace all of Annie's fresh arrangements."

"I think Annie has a wagon just like this, for her cats."

"No. Annie has my wagon for her cats. She forgot to bring it to me today, with all the excitement. I had to come over here to get it."

The woman had a soft laugh, and her voice had a lilt to it. She was from, Mark wasn't sure, perhaps Haiti. Perhaps some other island in that vicinity.

"I have to go, but I hope to see you both later, maybe you can join Ramon and me for dinner Saturday night? After the triathlon?" Her laughter followed her out the door.

Mark looked at Jeff. "What? Does everyone on this street already know everything about me?"

Jeff laughed as he said, "Pretty much. This is Chelsea. Get used to it." He turned serious. "And this is our problem. If someone gets in here and becomes familiar with the townspeople, then it's all over. And that someone could already be here."

15

Sam entered the carriage house with a tray. He carried snacks from Henrie's kitchen. A jewelry box was safely hidden in his back pocket.

"Well, Sam," said Nancy, "what do you have?"

"Henrie's snack. Pears with some good stuff and artichoke bruschetta."

"Thank you! Did you hear?"

"That kidnapping is all anyone is talking about. I wish there was something I could do."

"We have to trust that Pete will be able to find her. What do you have in your pocket, dear?"

"I can't hide anything from you, can I?"

Sam, anxious to keep his sanity on a rainy day with all of the children in close proximity, had chosen to spend the day at Frank's antique store. There, he had puttered around, helping Frank rearrange small displays. He played with Claire, the resident cat, and hoped Honey Bear would not begrudge him the long white cat hairs he was sure to bring home.

He also spent time at Gema's jewelry counter.

Gema was a new resident and new small business owner in Chelsea. Her unique jewelry was showcased in a front corner of the antique shop. The shop, Gema's Creations, featured several pieces, both to sell and to be used as examples of what could be made.

Sam, after looking at her display, found a simple opal on a silver chain. Perfect for Nancy.

"It's just a gift for you, Nancy."

"For me? Let me see!"

Sam took the box from his pocket and handed it tenderly to Nancy. As she opened it and looked inside, tears came to her eyes.

"What's the occasion? It's so lovely."

"I just wanted to give you a little something."

"For no reason?"

"There is a small reason. I know that a lot of people are focusing on Annie's issues with Geraldine, but I can see it coming, and I can see it in your eyes every time this situation is mentioned. I want you to know how much I love you."

Nancy's tears and her heartfelt hug were thanks enough.

Patti and Jessica were at wits end. Would this rain never end? The kids wanted to go swimming. They wanted to ride bikes. They wanted to take their outdoor games – volleyball, badminton and ring-toss – out to the beach.

They had to content themselves with video games and movies. Books were spread around the library, some open, some closed. All touched, looked at and thrown down out of boredom.

Finally, the twins up from their afternoon naps, they sat down to a game of Candyland. Jerome and Sally were too young to understand it, really, and they had to make sure the gingerbread men pieces didn't go from hands to mouths, but the game board was colorful and inviting.

Gracie and the older boys weren't interested. They turned on another video game. Ella and Ollie huddled with Patti. Ella, excited, said, "I'll help the babies learn how to play!"

Tiger Lily moved close. She lay on her stomach on top of the game table, her front paws barely touching the edge of the game board. She watched and listened carefully.

Jessica pointed to the box; her finger traced the words. "This says Candyland. See? This says can-dee, and this says land. Can-dee-land"

Tiger Lily watched as she traced her finger. She glanced up quickly to look at Jessica. Her eyes were on the twins and her finger. She didn't notice the cat. Tiger Lily looked back at the box.

Jessica looked at her mother. "It's hard to teach reading when the words are used differently. Look at this. On the side it's two words, but on the top and on the game it's one."

"That's minor, dear. It didn't seem to affect you."

"I've never seen this kind of a board before."

"This is the kind of board I learned on. It's the classic."

Jessica turned back to the children. Keeping it simple, she traced her finger along the colorful paved road. "See? We start here, where the children are playing. This sign says 'start.' Then, using the cards that we'll draw, we'll make our way all the way here, to this gingerbread house. This sign says 'home sweet home.'" Jessica's finger followed the trail all the way home.

The game began. Jessica let the children choose their color of gingerbread man game pieces and shuffled the cards.

"The older children will go first, so you can see how it's done."

Ella pulled a card. One blue. She moved her blue piece to the correct space.

Ollie went next. One orange. The red gingerbread man went one space beyond Ella's. Ella stuck her tongue out at her brother.

"Now you, Jerome. Did you see what they did? Pull the top card from the pile." Jerome did. He looked at it and looked up at his mother with a question. "You got one green. Take a look at the board and show me the first green space."

Jerome put his index finger on the gingerbread plum tree.

"That's green, but let's look at the spaces. Watch my finger."

Jerome and Tiger Lily watched as Jessica moved her finger from the starting point to the first green spot.

"Here it is. Your gingerbread man is yellow. Put it right here." With a little coaxing, Jerome placed his piece on the correct space.

"Now look at this. This green space is at the base of the rainbow trail. See?" Moving her finger on the words, she again sounded it out. "Rain-bow-trail. You get to move your piece all the way here." Jessica took his piece and moved it ahead.

Ella, remembering that she was supposed to be in training mode, said, "That's really good, Jerome!"

Sally said, "Me! Me!"

"Yes, it's your turn. What does your card say?"

Sally pulled the top card from the deck. One purple. Jessica went through the routine again, and eventually Sally's green piece went to the first purple space.

"I wanna go wainbow twail!" "That's not the card you drew, honey. Let's just keep playing."

Ella drew one purple and placed her piece beside Sally's. Ollie landed on the gold after the candyland hearts. Once again, Jessica pointed with her finger and sounded out the words. "Can-dee-land-harts." Jerome advanced one space; Sally passed candyland hearts. "I wanted to hit dat one!" She pointed to the two candy hearts on the road.

After one more round, the only notable move was that Ollie moved beyond the peppermint stick forest. "Pep-per-mint-stick-fore-est." Little progress was made during the next round. Sally was now right behind Ollie past the peppermint stick forest.

The next round was even less progressive. Patti looked at Jessica. "They've drawn only one space cards so far. Those doubles and the picture cards have to be coming up."

The next round was more exciting. Ella and Ollie were still just past the peppermint stick forest, but Jerome got two orange spaces, putting him past the crooked old peanut brittle house. After another sounding-out lesson, Sally picked the ice cream float card. "Ice-cream-float."

"Ize winning!" "Not yet, honey, but that was a great move."

In the next round, Ella passed the gumdrop mountains – "gum-drop-moun-tons" – and Ollie moved past the mountain pass. Jerome and Sally progressed without incident.

Ella reached the outer edge of the gumdrop mountains; Ollie landed on the blue cherry pitfall. "Chair-ree-pit-fall. Again, Jessica pointed it out with her finger. You're going to have to stay here until you draw a blue card." "No!" Jerome and Sally trudged on a few spaces.

Ella was now at the crooked peanut brittle house. Jessica sounded it out again, pointing with her finger. Ollie drew an orange card and had to stay on the cherry pitfall. "No!" Jerome pulled the lollypops, advancing him to the outer edge of the lollypop woods – "loll-li-pop-woods" – and Sally drew the gumdrops.

Jessica pointed to the gumdrops on the playing board. "You have to move here." "But that's backards!" "The word is backward, and yes, that's where you go." After some discussion, the green piece was moved to the lollypops.

Ella had to move back, all the way to the gingerbread man. "Gin-ger-bred-man." Ollie picked the hearts card and wailed, "No!" He was saved, however, when Patti said, "You can't go back there, honey. You can't move until you get a blue." "Yes!" Jerome was now on the edge of the ice cream floats, and Sally was one space behind Ollie.

Ella barely missed the gumdrop mountain pass; Ollie stood still because he picked an orange; Jerome and Sally advanced a few places.

The next round brought no large moves, but Ollie finally advanced to the next blue. The next round was uneventful, as was the next. In the next round, Ella landed on the blue cherry pitfall; Ollie had to go back to the peppermint stick forest; Jerome drew within hailing distance of home sweet home, and Sally advanced a little bit. She was ahead of Ella and Ollie but had not yet reached the crooked old peanut brittle house.

Ella pulled two reds but couldn't move. Ollie advanced two reds, closing in on the gingerbread plum tree. Jerome pulled two purples but could only move forward one. He was two spaces – one blue card – away from home sweet home.

Ella said, "He has to move back one purple space. He got two, and he needs to move back."

Patti and Jessica looked at one another. Jessica finally said, "Yes, sometimes we play that way. That's the way Mom and I played. But today, since we have two two-year olds playing, I think we'll use the modified rules. Because Jerome is on this last section of road, he won't move until he can go forward."

Ella pouted silently.

Sally moved to the edge of the crooked old peanut brittle house.

Ella said, "The cards are gone." Jessica shuffled them and replaced the pile.

Ella pulled a yellow card and had to stay where she was. Ollie moved a few spaces; Jerome moved to the yellow space before home sweet home – "Just one more, Mommy!" – and Sally advanced a space.

Ella couldn't move; Ollie moved a few spaces; Jerome couldn't move; Sally advanced, just missing the red cherry pitfall.

In the next round, Ella was finally able to move. Ollie moved ahead a few; Jerome stayed where he was; Sally moved forward a few spaces.

Ella moved forward two blue spaces – "I had to wait forever, and now I've had two blue cards in a row!" – Ollie advanced to the ice cream floats; Jerome couldn't move; Sally moved one orange space.

Ella's bad luck continued to hold. She went back to the candy hearts. Ollie moved two spaces; Jerome couldn't move; Sally moved a few spaces ahead.

Ella was able to move ahead to the gumdrop mountains; Ollie moved a little bit; Jerome picked the gingerbread man card. "Mom! Do I have to go back?" "No, dear, you stay right there until you can move forward." Patti threw a glance at Ella, who made a face but held her peace. Sally moved ahead.

Ella moved just one space. Ollie moved a few more toward home sweet home; he was in the middle of the molasses swamp. Jerome couldn't move, and Sally moved past the lollypop woods.

The next round was uneventful. The round that followed would have been uneventful as well, except that Ella once again landed on the blue cherry pitfall.

Jessica sent a silent prayer to whatever gods ruled game boards. She asked for a single blue card for Jerome or a double blue card for Ollie.

Ella couldn't move; Ollie was now four spaces from home sweet home; Jerome couldn't move; Sally landed on the second blue cherry pitfall. "Why me?"

Ella finally advanced one blue space; Ollie advanced as well. Jerome and Sally couldn't move.

Ella advanced a few; Ollie moved forward one; Jerome couldn't move. Sally picked a card and looked to her mother for help. Jessica breathed a sigh of relief. Two blue. From the blue cherry pitfall space, Sally was able to pass Ollie to land at home sweet home.

After the typical "She cheated!" and "I never want to play this game again!" statements, all four suggested, "One more game! Let's play one more game!" Jessica and Patti invented a few things that had to be done right that minute.

Throughout the game, Jessica had tirelessly sounded out and used her finger to point out the letters and the words, willing her two-year-old children to learn to read. Tiger Lily watched the entire time. She thought she had learned everything she could. She trotted to the dining room where her siblings slept beneath the detective table, snack bowls already empty.

She sat down. Little Socks stirred and opened an eye.

"What's up?"

"I think I learned how to read."

When the other cats were awake, Tiger Lily explained her breakthrough. *"I watched while the adults taught the kids to sound out the words, and by the time they got to the lollypop woods, it clicked for me."*

Sassy Pants, like all the others, wore an expression of confusion on her face. *"Wot lollyspots? Wot woods?"*

Tiger Lily sighed. *"I can't explain the whole game to you, but there were several places on the game board, and the lollypop woods were toward the end of the game. Once that clicked, I looked at everything on the board, and I knew how to read."*

"Trill?"

Kali and Ko translated, saying at the same time, *"He thought you could already read." "You read the menus at the Café."*

"I pretend to read them. You know I can't read. Just like you, I never understand clues that involve reading."

"But yu so good at tellin' peoples wot to eat."

"I know where everything is on the menu by now, but mostly, I just get lucky. I'm going to study it now, and see if I can read it on my own."

Tiger Lily told everyone what she knew about the kidnapping, including the story told by Speckles. They marveled at her ninja abilities and agreed there was nothing more the little kitty could have done.

No one had additional information about the drug investigation, but Kali and Ko reminded them of the new guests.

Little Socks asked, *"Is there anything suspicious about them?"*

Kali said, *"The men are handsome."*

Ko, at the same time, said, *"Just two boring couples."*

Tiger Lily and Little Socks looked at one another. Tiger Lily, looking back at the group, said, *"Do you think we ought to take a look in their rooms? Just in case?"*

No one said anything until Little Socks said, *"I'll take a look and see if there is anything useful."*

The cats eventually settled back down to sleep. Before Tiger Lily drifted off, she said, *"By the way, who ate my snack?"* No one answered, but Ko licked her lips.

Angela returned to Marsh Haven after spending an illuminating morning with Geraldine. She learned so much about Chris's precious Annie. She was the worst sort of person. How could Chris be so blind?

She tried to remember everything Geraldine had said. Inspections, filthy businesses, tax fraud, insurance fraud, questionable parentage, possible leanings toward unpopular and outdated racism. That was hard to believe. There were so many people of color – various colors – going into and out of her businesses. And it was hard to square this information with the woman that spent several days in her home. But then again, she would have been on her best behavior.

Still, good behavior was not enough. In order for Chris to secure a position the Senator had in mind for him, his wife would have to have impeccable credentials.

Over a less-than-satisfactory late afternoon dinner at a highly recommended restaurant, she returned to the hotel room and called Austin.

"What do you think I should do?"

"Meet her. Call her this evening and invite her to come to Marsh Haven for breakfast. Or, better yet, ask to meet her in one of her own filthy establishments. You can make your own assessment then."

"But I can't do it alone! Why don't you come here and do it with me?"

"I can't get away just now. What about that new friend of yours? Call her; ask her to join you."

Angela hung up, and before she could change her mind, she called Annie. Then she called Geraldine.

16

That evening, Mem called to invite herself to Annie's apartment. "Please ask Nancy to come. I have something to discuss with both of you. And perhaps it would be fortunate if both Sam and Chris could come, as well."

Annie made the calls to Nancy and Chris and made two more. She called Mo's and asked that they deliver dinner for six – she assumed Frank would be coming – and she asked the Winery to send a bottle of red and a chilled white.

Then she took all of the boxes from her purchases of the other day to the bedroom. Because she had yet to open the boxes and put anything in a location where it could be easily used.

The cats were entranced. They loved Mem but didn't often have an opportunity to see her. She and Frank were surrounded the minute they entered.

Frank put a cat carrier on the floor and Claire walked out. Claire was Frank's blue point Himalayan. She was a beautiful cat and she loved people. Cats, not so much. However, she was in love with Honey Bear. Mo, once the favored one, gave her a long, sad glance. The rest of the cats said a polite hello. Tiger Lily told them they had to. They were, after all, the hosts and hostesses. Within minutes, Nancy, Sam and Honey Bear arrived.

What had looked to be an almost-pleasant evening quickly turned sour for the cats. They would have gone to the bedroom, but it seemed Mem had news to share. They had to stay to listen.

Because there were six adults, they sat in the dining room, the room with a wall of windows that overlooked The Avenue. After the view toward the lake, this was Annie's favorite.

The cats loved it, too. Wide windowsills made for a pleasant place to watch traffic and, tonight, to listen to the humans.

Mem looked at the table, a long wooden table to which leaves could be added to make it shorter or longer. As always, it looked very nice, and placemats dotted the top. Carry-out boxes were in the center of the table, and Annie's dishes – Corelle, pretty, but boring, compared to her new ones – were laid out. "Where is the new stuff?"

"Oh…"

Nancy interjected, "I'll bet if we go into the bedroom, we'll see the boxes."

Annie turned to open a bottle of wine.

Once they were settled and their plates served, Mem started right in. She looked directly at Chris. "Did you know your mother was in town?"

From his expression, and Annie's shocked look in his direction, she knew the answer.

"This is what I know." Mem told the group what she saw and what she heard as she cleaned tables around Geraldine and Angela.

"So I thought I had better insert myself into the conversation. By the way, Annie, I tried to throw Geraldine out, but she informed me the court order had been vacated. I am so sorry. I didn't see the newspaper until later."

The table, even absorbing shocking news, enjoyed a laugh at Geraldine's expense.

"Annie got the conversation back on track. Well, at least I'm not a battered wife or an abused child. Vacated court orders are much more damaging to them."

"Well, you may find that this could be damaging, also. Anyway, as I was saying, I went to their table and introduced myself. Angela, at first, did not tell me that she was your mother, Chris, but of course I had heard it already. I let her get to it in her own way."

"Did she say why she was here?"

"Apparently, she is intent on securing a promotion for you, one that will take you to your home community. She has a Senator prepared to do her bidding."

"Again."

"Again?"

"That promotion was secured for me a while ago, and I turned it down. Because it would take me away from here."

Annie squeezed his hand underneath the table.

Mem looked straight at Chris, then at Annie, then at Nancy. "Well, here's the worst of it. Geraldine has convinced Angela that Annie is the worst sort of 'wife material.' Her parents are questionable, her businesses are filthy and run in a dishonest manner, and, well, she's a 'half breed.'"

"And Mother soaked it up, swallowed it hook, line and sinker, right?"

"Right."

Chris, face grim, rose from the table. He leaned down to kiss Annie on the top of her head, turned to face everyone and said, "I think it's best that I go home and think about this for a while. Annie, I'm going to turn all my phones off. I won't answer the door, either. I'm going to turn out the lights and pretend I'm not there. I need to think."

Chris left, and Mem looked around the table. "I worked Henrie's plan. I smiled at Geraldine until I thought my face would crack. Everytime I saw her I complimented something. Her hair, her clothes, her shoes, her handbag. When I ran out of things to compliment, I delved into her community spirit, the way she always brings people together."

Mem made a face. "It nearly made me gag. But on the upside, I think it was beginning to have the same effect on Geraldine."

"And that," said Annie, "is Henrie's point exactly. We will drive her away with syrupy sweetness."

"From what I saw, it just might work. After a few compliments, they came more easily. And my smile became more genuine, because I saw it created distress."

And then, Annie's telephone rang. She looked around the table. "Dare I answer it?"

"You have to sometime, dear," said Nancy.

Annie answered it. From the look on her face, everyone in the room knew it was Angela. Annie's face went from chagrin to anger to absolute calm.

When she hung up, she said, "I'm going to work Henrie's plan on her, too. I'm going to meet her for breakfast tomorrow at the Café."

"The Café? That filthy place?"

Everyone laughed and Annie said, "Maybe I should take a packet of disinfectant wipes and wipe everything down before we use it."

"And take some rubber gloves, dear. They might come in handy."

"And a small dust broom. You'll probably need to clean around the table before you sit."

"And two copies of this morning's newspaper."

Annie laughed, but inside, her heart was breaking. That woman, his mother, was going to force him to choose.

For a Thursday, it was busy at Mo's. Sure, it was still tourist season, but triathletes were in town as well. Jeff and Mark had to go to the outside garden area to find a seat.

"I thought this was for the winery. It's okay for us to sit here?"

"Yeah. This time of year, they share it. Mo's folks sit on this side and Sassy P's folks sit over there. Or they mix and mingle. The servers figure it out. Hey, look. The two couples from the Inn are over there."

Mark waved at the group of four and the men, facing in their direction, waved back. In a low voice, he said, "I'm going to get to know them a little bit, let them know I'm doing the triathlon, you know. Make an excuse to talk to them."

"They don't look like drug runners."

"Most drug runners don't look like drug runners. Order me a dry red and whatever small plate looks good to you."

At the table of four, Mark introduced himself. Tim made introductions and continued, "Krissie and I are doing the one-hundred mile triathlon."

Melanie joined in. "My husband is the athlete of our family. I plan to conduct a little personal investigation. I hear there are a few wineries around here, at least three on the bike route."

"My friend over there," Mark turned to look at Jeff, who raised a glass in salute, "is planning to exercise at the wineries as well. And me? I'm only doing the fifty. This is my first triathlon." He looked at Randy. "And you? Are you doing the wineries, or…"

Randy gave a brief smile. "I had a boat hired to do a little fishing, but that fell through. Made some calls today, but I haven't found a boat yet that isn't already scheduled. I'll keep trying."

Krissie said, "You never liked to fish anyway. You can always go to the wineries with Mel." She turned her attention to Jeff. "Hey, why don't you invite your friend? We can share the table."

Mark made eye contact to see that they were all in agreement. He turned, waved Jeff over and grabbed two chairs from a table that had just emptied.

At the Inn, Little Socks took advantage of the supper hour to burgle the rooms of the new guests. She went to the lakeside room first, the room of Randy and Krissie.

The couple had unpacked; empty luggage was under the bed and in the closet. On the desk, she found a piece of paper with letters and numbers. She picked that up with her teeth and left the room.

Tiger Lily waited outside the door. She took the piece of paper and waited as Little Socks went into the other room. Once again, the luggage was unpacked. She jumped to the desk. Nothing.

The drawer to a bedside chest was open just a wee bit, enough for Little Socks to get one paw in. It wasn't enough. She trotted to the cat door, looked out to see if the coast was clear, and said, *"I need help. Mr. Bean is strong, and Mo, if he puts his mind to it. We have to open a drawer."*

Tiger Lily ran to the stairs and up. She trotted into the apartment, dropped the piece of paper underneath the dining room table and announced the need. Mo, Mr. Bean and Sassy Pants followed her downstairs.

Little Socks explained the problem, and she from the bed, Mr. Bean and Mo from the top of the chest and Sassy Pants from below put their considerable combined strength to the task.

Soon, the drawer was open. Little Socks jumped in. She used her paws to rearrange the underwear in the drawer. Underneath was an open box of little square packets. She bit into one. The package was flimsy, and her teeth went clear through.

"Ick!" Little Socks spit as much of the liquid as she could out. Then she picked up another one with the same results. It tasted the same. Bad.

Soon, every packet in the box had little cat tooth holes around the edges and in the middle. She grabbed one and flipped it to the floor, then she covered the box with the underwear as best she could.

Mr. Bean looked at the packet on the floor. *"Do you think we should get another one? Just in case? We might have to open one to investigate, and then we'd have one still closed up."*

"Good idea, Mr. Bean." Little Socks dug into the underwear and pulled out another packet. She forgot to straighten the underwear this time. She jumped down, and the four cats pushed the drawer closed. Almost.

Back in the dining room, they examined the burgled articles. Sassy Pants investigated one of the packets. *"Lets me open dis one."*

"Go ahead. Do you need help?"

"Maybe. Lets me try."

She worked on it for several seconds, then looked at Tiger Lily. *"Yes. Help."*

Mr. Bean moved close. *"Why don't I bite this side, and you bite that one, and we pull?"*

They did, and soon, the packet ripped open. Out came a slimy, flimsy rubbery item. *"Wot dis?"*

Tiger Lily and Little Socks came close. Tiger Lily said, *"It looks like one of those balloons. You know, before it gets blown up."*

"But it's slimy."

"Maybe, if you store them for a long time, you have to keep them wet so they don't tear."

"They tear pretty easily," said Little Socks. *"This one is useless now."*

"Did you look at that paper? Can you read it?"

"I didn't learn numbers, only letters. One line says, I think, 'escape stay away.'"

"Stay away? Escape something and stay away?"

"Maybe they meant the boat?"

"Stay away on the Escape?"

"Stay away from the Escape?"

The circle of cats stared at the piece of paper and around at one another. Little Socks asked, "Is there anything else?"

"One other line says 'man in charge race.'"

Kali and Ko, together, said, "It doesn't do you any good to learn how to read." "This is just nonsense."

"They leave out lots of words that help make it clear."

"It's kind of like when Mommy sends a text."

"What?"

"A text. She sends just a few nonsense letters and somehow, on the other end, someone understands it."

"Or not."

"Trill!"

"Mr. Bean saided dat one time Mommy sented sumppin to Chris and he gotted all confused."

"I remember that. He brought that movie with Kevin Costner and the wolves, but she wanted dry white wine."

"I duzn't unnerstand?"

"I think she did something she calls 'abbreviate,' and he abbreviated it to something else."

Little Socks stamped her foot. "This doesn't help us with this situation."

"You're right. So what does 'man in charge race' mean?"

"Maybe they mean the man in charge of the race this weekend."

"That would be Ian."

"Right."

The cats were silent, thinking about the consequences of these new people, possibly drug smugglers, having an interest in Ian.

Later that night, as Tim and Melanie got ready for bed, Melanie noticed the obviously tampered-with drawer. Her first thought was that Henrie, or someone else from the Inn, had invaded her privacy.

She then noticed the underwear, out of place, and the box of condoms. It appeared each packet had been touched and put back into the box.

When Tim went to brush his teeth, she picked up a packet. Then another. And another. Each and every one of them was full of holes. It wasn't Henrie. He wouldn't take pins and needles to her condoms. It was Tim. Or Krissie. When did they find out?

Three people met at Sassy P's for dinner. They shared two bottles of zinfandel and each had a small plate appetizer. By the middle of the second bottle, their voices drew the attention of a little brown mouse. He huddled at the base of a bush in a pot close to their table.

The woman said, "She will get everything she deserves tomorrow morning."

The two men laughed.

The woman again, "Angela is out for bear, and I'm going to help her put Annie in her place. She will never see that Coast Guard officer of hers again. And what's more, she is going to wish she was never born."

One of the men, "Geraldine, are you certain you should do this, so soon after…"

"Don't be a bore, Everett."

"But…"

"Hank, you too? I know what I'm doing."

17

Annie trudged into the kitchen. "Good morning, Henrie."

"Who rose from the wrong side of the bed this morning?"

"Don't start. I have to meet Chris's mother for breakfast."

Henrie turned from his breakfast preparations to stare at Annie. "No."

"Yes. She's been in town for – I don't know – I think she's had a hotel room at Marsh Haven for a couple of nights. And guess who she met?"

Annie leaned against the kitchen counter, a cup of coffee in one hand and the other hugging her body. A defensive stance that did absolutely nothing to help her mood.

Henrie turned from his preparations to lean on the stove, facing her. "From your tone of voice, what I know about Angela, and the dreary tone of this week in general, I would guess she met Geraldine."

"Bingo."

Henrie turned back to the stove. He put the finishing touches on the prosciutto pesto breakfast strata and reached for the warming oven to pull out a pan of what looked to Annie like pancakes or crepes.

"What's that?"

"These are crespelle. They are the Italian version of a crepe."

"What did you put inside?"

"Some have egg, ham and asparagus. Others have spinach and ricotta. Now let us get back to the conversation at hand. What are you going to do?"

"I'm not sure. I know she is going to ask Chris to make a choice, me or her, and I know Chris is caught between a rock and a hard place."

"Chris is an intelligent man."

"He is. Well, the only thing that occurred to me was that I should work the Henrie Plan on Angela as well as Geraldine."

"Ah, yes. The Henrie Plan. Go high, no matter what the issue."

"Sickeningly high."

"Syrup is not as sweet."

Annie sent a text message to Chris. She knew he would not receive it until he turned on his telephone. That could be hours. Or days. He had a radio to stay in contact with the Coast Guard Station; his work would not be affected by a total telephone outage.

She sent a text to Felicity and Trudie as well. Felicity couldn't wait for the conversation to play out over a keyboard. Annie's phone rang at once.

"What? You're meeting Angela? Over here?"

"You know about Angela?"

"Who doesn't? The woman can't stand you. And creepers! She's hooked up with Geraldine! Don't tell me Geraldine is coming with her."

"Oh. I didn't consider that as a possibility. Oh, my. Well, I'll call Mom and see if she and Sam can't just 'happen' to come in for breakfast."

"Call Chris."

"Can't. He turned off his telephones."

"Oh. Well, I've seen Nancy at work. You really can't do better than that."

Henrie greeted Hilly as she arrived. "Hilly, may I please ask a favor?" He detailed what he needed and Hilly agreed. He would leave as soon as it appeared their guests were nearly finished with breakfast.

Henrie and Hilly poured coffee, kept serving trays full and took away dirty dishes as the two couples ate breakfast. Tension crackled and popped.

Krissie broke the silence. "Henrie, is it going to rain all day today, as well?"

"Yes, I am afraid you could use the term 'soggy' to describe the day. I believe even the sand is saturated by now."

"What about tomorrow?" This from Tim. Before getting an answer, he turned to Krissie. "Let's go over to the yoga studio again today. There are a couple of classes that will help us stay in shape."

"Good idea." Krissie cut a look to Randy. "Apparently it would be a good thing for Randy and me to have a break from one another." To Randy, she said, "What is up with you today?"

Henrie, anxious to avoid a scene, answered Tim's question. "The weather prophets predict the rain will end today, but the heat index will rise. As the ground is saturated, the prophets predict tomorrow will be a hot and steamy day."

Krissie groaned. Tim put his head in his hands, shaking it slowly. "I really love triathlons. In the spring. Or fall."

Melanie sniped, "I don't know why you insisted on coming this time of year. What was so gosh darned important that you had to come to Chelsea this weekend? You've never done a triathlon this time of year before."

Jeff and Mark arrived with their breakfast trays from the back porch just as Melanie asked the question. They politely exited to sit in the foyer as the conversation continued. They remained within hearing range.

Tim pointed to Randy. "He insisted. He said Krissie and I needed to try this triathlon. He said it was a great vacation place."

Melanie spat back, "Yes, it's a great vacation place alright. The rooms are a little small, though. Maybe I'll ask about getting a room somewhere else for the rest of the weekend."

Tim said, "What is wrong with you? I've been getting the cold shoulder ever since we went to bed last night."

"As if you don't know."

Krissie said, "You, too? Randy's been a complete jerk since he came up from his morning walk."

Randy said, "A jerk? Who's being a jerk? You're the one that lost that number I needed."

"I didn't know you needed that piece of paper, but I didn't do anything with it. You must have put it somewhere yourself. What was so important about it?"

Tim said, "A piece of paper? That's what you're arguing about? I thought the two of you," motioning to Randy and

Melanie, "were gone for an awfully long time on your walk this morning. That's what concerns me."

Krissie looked at Randy. "You went for a walk with Melanie this morning?"

Tim looked at Melanie. "You did, didn't you? Go on a walk with Randy this morning? You were gone a long time, Mel."

Melanie's expression was guarded. "We didn't go together, but when I got back from the beach, he was just leaving, so, well, I walked a little longer so he wouldn't have to walk alone."

Tim and Krissie looked at one another. Then at their spouses. "Well, this is just great."

Henrie groaned inwardly. The situation was really going to blow up on his watch.

Annie left for the Café, dragging the loaded wagon behind. She waved at Nancy, coming out of the carriage house under an umbrella, and stopped at each place, letting dry cats out onto sidewalks filled with puddles of rainwater. Why bother, she thought.

Nancy followed a discrete distance behind. She was going to enter on her own. Sam, not awake enough for family drama, would have to find breakfast on his own.

When Annie and Tiger Lily reached the Café, Tiger Lily first greeted her "employees" then walked through the dining room to say hello to the guests. Annie went straight to the kitchen.

"What did you make?"

"I made a one-pot dish that will be served to your table only, because frankly, that table could get full fairly quickly."

"You're right about that."

"Anyway, I made an Italian wonder pot with pasta, tomatoes, onions, spinach, beef broth, Italian sausage and spices. To make it appear more breakfast-like, I asked Carlos to send over a plate of Italian breakfast breads. They're already on your table."

"In the back dining room, right?"

"Your table will be just inside the back room, around the corner, out of sight from prying eyes and ears."

"Except Mom."

"Right. Her table – already reserved – is just outside the back dining room."

Annie went to the back room; she smiled at Nancy on her way through. She sat down and waited. To occupy her mind, she read a news feed from her cellphone.

Tiger Lily joined her. She got on top of the table to study the tray of breakfast breads, wondering which would be the best. All of a sudden, the table was rocked by what seemed to be a fifty pound weight. It was Sassy Pants, drenched head to toe, and she landed with one foot on the bread tray. Breads flew in every direction.

"Sassy! What are you doing?"

"*Sorry, Mommy. Ize wet.*" Annie didn't understand what she said, but she understood the shaking. The shaking that drenched the breads, dishes, napkins and water glasses.

Little Socks and Sassy Pants engaged in what appeared to Annie to be an animated conversation. Pity she couldn't understand. But no time to bother with that now. Annie rose to ask someone to help her clean up the table and get another plate of breads.

"Brown Mousie said dat awful Geraldine iz comin' here today and sheze gonna help dat awful Angela give bears to Mommy!"

"What? What does that mean? How did he know?"

"Heze a good tective! He herded Geraldine and dat husband of hers an dat Hank talkin' las nite."

"What did he say, exactly?'

"Zackly, he sez..." Sassy Pants looked down at the table to collect her thoughts. Then she looked up. *"Somebody wants bears. Dey comin' to put Mommy in her place, Dey gonna see to it dat Mommy won't nebber see Chris again, and dat Mommy is gonna whist she nebber borned."*

Tiger Lily sat in deep thought. Sassy Pants finally said, *"Well? Wot we do?"*

"Have you heard Mommy and Henrie talk about going high?"

"Weze gonna get high? On wot?"

"We're going to 'go high.' We are going to be syrupy sweet. First, you need to get dried off. Come on. We'll go to the bathroom and use the hand dryer."

Before they could jump down, several things happened at once. A server appeared with a container for the dirty dishes and ruined breads. Annie and Felicity arrived from the back with a cart containing clean dishes, new glasses of water and condiments. Angela and Geraldine arrived at the table, having come through the front dining room. They surveyed the mess, which included one dry and one wet cat on top of the table and two wet cat paws on two pieces of bread.

"Well. I. Never!" said Angela. Geraldine smirked.

Felicity and the server stared at Annie.

Annie smiled and said, "Angela, Geraldine, so good to see you."

She turned to her mother's table. Nancy sat perfectly still, a glass of water halfway to her wide-open mouth. Annie wondered how long she had held the pose. No time to ponder.

"Mom, would you be so kind as to allow Geraldine and Angela to sit with you?"

Annie took Angela's elbow and turned her toward her mother's table, pulled a chair and seated her. "Angela, this is my mother, Nancy. Mom, this is Chris's mother. Geraldine, please have a seat."

Annie turned to go, then turned back. "Please excuse me. I must dry off a cat. Felicity, we'll eat at Mom's table. We'll just have a plate of bagels and English muffins with the meal."

Annie picked up a frightened Sassy Pants. "Tiger Lily, that table needs a hostess." Tiger Lily didn't move. "Now, sweetheart. Sit next to your grandmother. On your ledge, not on the table, please."

Tiger Lily jumped down, a croissant flew into the air in the process, and Annie left for the bathroom. She was going to put Sassy Pants under the dryer. It would feel good for both of them.

When Annie and Sassy Pants returned to the table, she saw Nancy, chattering about nonsense to Angela; Angela, looking with horror at Tiger Lily; Tiger Lily, on the ledge between Nancy and Angela, calmly licking her front claws while watching Geraldine; and Geraldine, looking like she had just won the lottery. Annie sat next to her mother and put Sassy Pants on the ledge in between the two of them.

Trudie arrived with four glasses of iced macchiato, a thermal pitcher of the same, and a basket of bagels and English muffins. She backed away politely, without wasting a second.

Annie inherited her sweet viper-coming-out-of-the-woodwork voice from Nancy. She recognized her mother's use of it just now, and she turned her own on Geraldine. "I don't know how you do it. You manage to be completely gorgeous even with weather like this."

Geraldine was speechless. For once. Annie moved on to Angela. "Angela. It's so good to see you again. And you've come all the way to Chelsea. Such a nice surprise."

"Are you not going to talk about this?"

Annie's smile stayed in place, but she allowed a question to come to her eyes. "This, what?"

"This disaster. Your cats. On top of the tables in a restaurant. Of all things!"

Sassy Pants gave a low hiss. Tiger Lily shot a glare across the table. Sassy Pants, sometimes clueless, understood and put her hiss on hold. Tiger Lily put a paw on Angela's hand. The hand was snatched away. Tiger Lily purred. She rolled her shoulders and head. She looked at Angela with adoring eyes, purred louder, and put her paw on the table in front of Angela.

Sassy Pants rolled her eyes, but then she purred, very un-Sassy-Pants-like. She climbed onto the table and reached out to Geraldine. In the process, she knocked a half bagel from the basket. Geraldine squeaked and pulled both hands to her breast. She moved her chair closer to Angela. Angela's chair scooted toward her at the same time.

Nancy said, "You know, these cats don't make up to just everybody. You have to be special women to have earned such attention."

Angela looked at Nancy. "What?"

"They don't often give that much attention to people. You're special."

Angela turned from Nancy to look at Annie, who said, "It might have appeared to be a disaster, but the girls were worried about me. They only wanted everything to be perfect, and in the process, well, things happen."

Geraldine turned to Angela. "Didn't I tell you? She talks about these cats as if they're human. She gives them thoughts, feelings. She's nutty as a fruitcake."

"And apparently not everything that she appears, as well," said Angela.

"Please, Angela, let's not hold anything back from one another. What is it that I am?"

"You, and this woman who purports to be your mother…"

"I'm sorry. Excuse me for interrupting, but it is difficult to only purport to be a mother when you've gone through the dreadful hours of labor. Annie, did I ever tell you how badly you wanted to stay in my womb?"

"Later, Mom."

"I'm just saying, you were stubborn from the very first day. Honestly, Angela, you should have known her when…."

"Mother!" Turning to Angela, Annie, smile on her face, said, "Angela, please tell me, what am I?"

Annie's smile felt like a tight rubber band on weak plaster, ready to crack at the slightest provocation. She reached for Sassy Pants and pulled the girl off the table and to her lap. Sassy Pants, realizing she had to snuggle in to help Mommy, did just that. Tiger Lily sat back with a sigh. Sassy Pants was getting Mommy's hugs.

Angela straightened her head, neck and back. Her nose went up. Her head went slightly to the side. Her eyes stayed on Annie. The corners of her mouth drew down. She opened her mouth and out of it spewed some of the vilest insults Annie had ever heard.

Geraldine relished the show. She sat back, smiled in wonder and looked first at Annie, then Angela. Annie, then Angela. Annie, Nancy, then Angela.

Annie's hands tightened on Sassy Pants, but the smile stayed on her face. Tiger Lily jumped to the floor, then up to the platform between Annie and Nancy. She leaned into Annie's shoulder. Nancy's hand went to Annie's leg and pressed.

Annie's smile didn't falter. She kept her gaze on Angela, and a soft gaze it was. Not a hard stare. Not a stare at all. More like an interested and attentive look that didn't waiver.

Annie concentrated. She wanted to remember everything on Angela's list.

Annie was too old to give Angela grandchildren. She didn't come from the right sort of family. Her parentage was in question. Indeed, Annie was some sort of half-breed where her parents were not. And speaking of that, her mother was not fit for proper society and could never be included in family gatherings.

At this point, Nancy said, "As if I would ever want to go to your family gatherings."

Angela, interrupted in her rant, lost a little of her haughtiness as she looked at Nancy. A little less tall in the saddle, she turned back to Annie. She continued. She had it on good authority that Annie ran businesses of questionable repute. Angela heard of failed health department reviews and failed fire marshal reviews. Irregularities with state and federal tax officials, including the failure to pay mandated employment taxes. Issues with the town council and leading citizens, including law suits that Annie could not possibly hope to win.

Nancy, directing her comment to Annie, said, "Don't let that stop you, dear. You just keep right on with those law suits. I'd like a new car, and if you win, you might be able to get one for me."

Angela once again looked at Nancy, then looked at Geraldine as if to say what is the matter with this woman. Even less tall in the saddle, she looked again at Annie. Those cats. Geraldine was correct. Annie must be nuttier than a fruitcake.

Nancy said, "You know, the best fruitcakes have more fruit and rum than nuts. And really, Angela, you should consider getting a cat yourself. They are very soothing. Why, I have one of my own, and if you can disregard the long hairs he leaves in my soup..."

"Shut up!" Angela sighed deeply, leaned into the table, and concluded her rant with the ways in which Annie infected Chris. Annie influenced Chris when he turned down the promotion offered last year. Her outlandish behavior would eventually discredit Chris with the Coast Guard, and he would have no hope of retrieving his good standing. And, finally, Annie's immoral behavior was quite unbecoming. Chris deserved better.

For an insane moment, Annie wondered why her behavior was considered to be immoral when Chris's behavior was apparently not.

When Angela stopped for air, looking less austere than when she started, Annie gave her a few seconds. "Is that all?"

Receiving no answer, Annie turned to waive Trudie over. "Is breakfast ready?"

"Yes."

"Please bring it. Put the crock and bowls close to me and I'll serve."

The crock arrived. Sassy Pants, on the ledge now, stayed out of the way while Annie lifted the lid. A heavenly scent, ripe with Italian spices, filled the air around the table.

As she picked up a ladle and a bowl, she said, "Angela, you're going to love this. It's not really a breakfast dish; we'll consider this brunch. This is an Italian wonder pot. Here you go."

Annie picked up another bowl, filled and passed it. "Geraldine, here's a bowl for you."

She filled and passed the third bowl. "Mom, I know you'll like this."

Annie served herself. She picked up the bread basket, offered it to Geraldine and said, "Please help yourself."

Geraldine, mouth open from surprise with Annie's polite manner, saw something from the corner of her eye. She turned to look into the dining room. Annie followed her gaze.

Trudie and Felicity must have been relentless with text messages. The dining room tables were filled with her friends and family. They sat quietly, some with coffee or tea, some with breakfast. As a whole, their chairs had shifted and they looked at Annie's table. Everyone wore an expression of soft friendliness. Even the other customers, some locals and some tourists, sat quietly and watched.

Apparently, while working Henrie's plan, Annie's brain was able to slow down and savor the moment. She took her time looking around the room.

She saw Henrie first. He must have left the serving of breakfast to Hilly. Her sister Patti with Fritz, Jessica and Paul. Certainly the babysitter – was it Ginger today? – had arrived. Boone and his sons, Daryl and Donnie. They must be having a slow day.

Well, goodness. Terrence & Jerald Timmer-Schmidt were here. It was Friday. They took Fridays off unless their patients had emergencies. Jennifer and Marie sat with them. They must have put themselves on call for the health clinic and left the drug store in the hands of an assistant. Holly and Jolly were here as well. Perhaps JoJo worked the counter at DoubleGood.

Clara was here with Ramon. This must be the weekend his jazz band was off. Annie was glad he would be able to be here for the triathlon. Mem and Frank sat with Sam. Pete and Marco had a table in the corner with Ray and Cheryl.

Cyril and Jock sat at attention in front of the table, vigilant, ready to protect Annie. Ramon's beautiful bergamasco, Fiamma, sat in between them. At their feet sat Tillie and the rest of Annie's cats. Even Kali and Ko. How sweet of them to leave the Inn on her behalf. And the cats that now belonged to Holly and Jolly, Simon Finegan and Oscar McMurphy, sat with them.

Laila sat at a table with Diana, Jerry, Carlos and Isabel. Goodness. Daniela must be watching Mr. Bean's. Jesus and Minnie sat with George and Candice. Pastor Teresa stood at the coffee bar with Trudie and Felicity. Even Jeff and Mark sat at a table in the middle of the room.

By now, Angela and Nancy were staring at the room as well, until Chris materialized from the back dining room. He had come in through the delivery door to the kitchen. As his mother detailed Annie's flaws, Chris had listened, his back to the wall, out of sight. Only Felicity knew he was there.

Chris stood behind the table. He kept his voice low. Only the four at this table could hear what he had to say. "Mother, do you want to have this conversation here, in front of everyone?"

"What conversation is that? Why were you hiding back there?"

"You didn't tell me you were in town, Mother. I had to hear it from other people. Annie let me know she was going to meet you here."

"Well, it's probably a good thing you are here. You must be involved in this decision."

"What decision is that?"

"The decision, obviously, to move on with your life. To align yourself with the proper people, the proper woman. You have to make a choice."

Chris pulled up a chair. Voice still low, he said, "So, I guess we're having this conversation here. Let's start with this. What choice do I have to make?"

Angela, flustered for a second, took a deep breath and recovered. "A choice between the life you deserve and, well, her." An unattractive emphasis was placed on the word 'her.'

"Well, mother, here's the thing. I'm not going to make a choice."

"You would spurn me? Your mother?"

"That's exactly the point. I'm not making a choice. Apparently, you are. Apparently, if Annie is a part of my life, you will choose to distance yourself from me."

As Annie watched, her heart in her mouth, tears began to form in Angela's eyes. "But…"

"Mother, let me put it another way. I love Annie, and I intend to spend the rest of my life with her. I don't know what form the relationship will take, but there is literally no choice for me to make. I love Annie. I love you. However, I no longer recognize you. I don't recognize the woman who said the awful things you just said to a woman who has done no harm to you."

"She's perfectly dreadful! I've heard all about her…"

"You've heard untruthful things from a woman who, for whatever reason, determined years ago to make Annie's life miserable."

Chris did not take his eyes from Angela, but Angela looked at Geraldine, who said, "Really!"

"Mother, look at the people in this Café." Angela looked around the room. "These people are our friends. Our family here in Chelsea. They came here this morning because the Chelsea grapevine heard that someone had come to town to do Annie harm. And Annie's mother. And me."

"You? No one is here to do harm to you."

"If you harm her, you harm me. Look at them. Do you see an unfriendly face in the room?" Chris was working Henrie's program, so he did not mention the one unfriendly face, that of Geraldine. "You are my mother. They will welcome you with open arms. You don't have to do a thing, and they will welcome you. You don't even have to change your mind about Annie. But don't for a minute think that anyone here will support you if you are determined to separate us."

A silence lay at the table. No one in the dining room moved or spoke. Chris finally looked at Annie. "I've got to get to the station. I'll see you tonight." Chris left the way he came in, through the back dining room.

The silence grew until Pete's radio came to life. A female voice in a midwestern drawl said, "Pete, get on back here. The Sheriff's Department at Marsh Haven has that man and the baby. They're pretty tickled. Looks like a cat or somethin' got 'im good. Oh, the baby's just fine."

Pete rose to leave to the cheers of the crowd. Tiger Lily ran to Cyril before they got away. *"You have to get Pete to the Inn today. We have clues for him."*

18

Ian walked in the rain toward the state park. He rarely, if ever, used an umbrella. Umbrellas cramped his style. They prevented quick movement, and they didn't work out well on a run, or on a bicycle, wave runner, paddle board or kayak. Worst of all, they prevented a person from checking personal space.

He looked toward the Inn. Lots of excitement over there. People spilled out onto the porch, town and county police cars. Maybe it had something to do with that kidnapping. He hoped the baby had been found. Ian didn't like having extra police presence around when an event was going on. If the baby had been found, the extra patrol cars would disappear. Yes, he hoped the baby had been found.

Ian entered the state park's office. A man stood just inside the door.

"You're Ian, right?"

"Yes, and you are…I know we've met, but…"

"Don't worry, I know you've met lots of people this week. I'm Randy, staying at the Inn. I'm supposed to get with you."

"About?"

"The plan. The boat I set up fell through. The guy was arrested for some stupid crap. I've been trying to get another one for tomorrow, but they're all rented. They told me to stay away from The Escape, because the owner is a friend to the local cops. But they didn't give me names of other boats or owners I could work with."

"And you thought I could help you, how?"

"I thought you might know of another option, another boat that I could use to make the connection."

Ian was cautious. "I'm responsible for the triathlon; I don't have anything to do with boats."

"I know, I know. Separation of duties and all that. Can you at least point me to the right person? Oh, and I lost your cell phone number."

"I don't remember giving it to you."

"You didn't. Our friends gave it to me."

"Our friends. Yes." Ian paused. "Tell me something that would convince me I'm supposed to talk to you."

Randy thought about it for a moment. "The guy in charge of the race is the key to it all."

Ian looked at Randy for a moment, then gave him the number. He said, "Try Jake's. You'll have to drive there. He doesn't have a telephone. Just go out of town toward Marsh Haven, and you'll see a sign that points to public access points. Turn there, you'll see a shabby tin boat shelter, and if you look closely, you'll see the word 'Jake's' in faded paint."

"Thanks. You can count on me."

Annie got to the Inn after Little Fred. She walked to the library to see Georgia hugging the child with all her might. "Georgia, I'm so happy for you."

In tears, Georgia sobbed, "Annie, she's okay! She's okay! I don't know what to say!"

"Don't say a thing. I saw Martha out there. Go home. Stay there. I'm sure someone can take care of things at Bon Vivant tonight."

"I know. Felicity told me she'd do it. She's already working with Cookie. I think Martha and I will go home as soon as Pete says I can go."

"I'll take care of having lunch and dinner sent over, so you don't have to worry about it."

"Thanks, Annie."

Georgia turned back to Little Fred and Annie went to the foyer to get the menu from the Café. Strange, it wasn't in the rack. As she pulled her phone from her pocket, she noticed Tiger Lily on the floor in the dining room. She stood on and stared down at the Café's menu.

Annie walked in, leaned down and put her hand on the menu to pick it up. Tiger Lily slammed her paw down on the corner that Annie lifted and looked up. *"Oh, it's you, Mommy. You can have it."*

"What were you looking at, sweet girl?"

"I was practicing to read."

"You're precious. I wish I could understand you. I have to take the menu now. I'm going to order something for Georgia and Martha."

"Order the crab and shrimp wraps for lunch and the lemon-cucumber chicken salad croissants for supper."

"What?"

Tiger Lily put her paw on the crab and shrimp wrap, then on the lemon-cucumber chicken salad croissant.

"Thanks. Both of those sound great." Annie dialed the Café and ordered two of each to be delivered to Martha's house. She looked at Tiger Lily. "Did you really mean to suggest those?"

Tiger Lily looked at Annie and sighed.

Tiger Lily looked around. Cyril was still in the foyer with Pete. He looked back as if to say, *"Keep your pants on. I'll bring him as soon as I can."*

Eventually, Pete got up to leave. He walked to the door, but Cyril went to the dining room door and stood there.

Pete said, "Come." Cyril barked.

Pete sighed. "Cyril, I have work to do, come on."

"Bark!"

"Alright. What is it?" Pete walked to the dining room.

Cyril walked to and sat next to the detective table. All of the cats were there, including Honey Bear, Simon Finnegan and Oscar McMurphy. Tillie sat next to Cyril.

Tiger Lily allowed Little Socks and Mr. Bean the honors. Little Socks dropped a piece of paper at Pete's feet, tooth marks and all. Mr. Bean placed the tin foil packet next to it.

Pete picked up the packet first. "Mr. Bean, are you trying to tell me something? Are you in love with somebody?"

Mr. Bean, confused, ran behind Tiger Lily.

Pete smiled. "Don't worry, big guy. Somebody might be looking for this, but I think it's ruined now."

Pete then picked up the piece of paper. The words said, "Escape stay away" and "man in charge race." A telephone number was at the bottom of the note.

Pete considered the information. Could it be related to the drug case? Was it possible that Annie, once again, housed a criminal or criminals? Pete looked at Little Socks. "Did you find this here?"

One blink of the eyes. *"Yes."*

"Did you just agree with me?"

One blink of the eyes. *"Yes."*

Pete rolled his head and looked at the ceiling. "Good gracious. I'm trying to talk to a cat." As he considered his options, he looked around the room. His eyes landed on Cyril. He thought about it for a moment, then he sat on a chair and put his fists on his knees.

"Cyril, do you remember the yes/no?" Pete taught Cyril this game some months ago. If Pete said something that was correct, Cyril was to touch his right fist. Otherwise, the left fist would be touched. It had been quite a while since they had played, but Pete didn't know what else to do.

Cyril rose, walked to Pete and sat in front of him. He took his right paw and touched Pete's right fist.

Henrie appeared at the door to the kitchen. Annie appeared at the door to the foyer. They watched quietly as Pete continued.

"Cyril, do you know what this paper is?" Yes.

"Did the cats find this in one of the rooms?" Yes.

"Was it in a guest room?" Yes.

Pete looked at Henrie. "Who are your guests?"

Henrie said, "Mark." No.

"Jeff." No.

"Tim and Melanie."

Cyril looked at Little Socks. Little Socks turned to Kali and Ko and appeared to get an answer from them. She turned back to Cyril, who replied. No.

"Randy and Krissie." Yes.

Pete and Henrie exchanged a glance. "Is there anything else I need to know about this?"

Cyril looked at the cats. Tiger Lily appeared to talk to him for a couple of seconds. He turned back to Pete, picked up his paw and touched Pete's left hand. No.

"I do not believe this," said Pete. He looked at Henrie, then Annie. "I have just interviewed ten cats and two dogs, and I think I have a lead that will help us on a case."

His phone rang. As he answered it and heard the voice on the other end, he looked at the note and his eyes grew wide. The number on his display case wasn't the same as the one on the paper, but only the last number was off. Like two phones purchased at the same time.

He said, "Why don't we meet somewhere neutral. We can maybe run into one another at CyberHealth. I could use a good cup of tea."

In Marsh Haven, Angela was on the phone again to Austin. "It was dreadful. Perfectly dreadful. There were cats on the table, and she was so rude to me!"

"I can't imagine…"

"She was rude! She kept a smile on her face the entire time, like she was playing a game. And she filled that restaurant with people to pretend they liked her! I wonder how much she had to pay…"

"Angela, really, why would she…"

"And Geraldine! I don't know what to think about her. I just don't."

A silence played out on the line, then Austin asked, "What did you think about the Café? Was it as awful as Geraldine said?"

"Well, to be honest, when we first walked in, I was favorably impressed. The tables were nearly filled, it was bright, and it looked clean. There were fresh flowers at the hostess stand. But then…"

"What happened?"

"We got to the back room, where SHE was, and two cats were on the table, and the bread had gone everywhere. One of the cats was standing on the bread plate! And one was soaking wet. Apparently, she was trying to cover it up. We got there right as someone got there to replace the dishes and bread."

"It was that bad, huh?"

"Well, again, being truthful, we sat at a very nice table, but her dreadful mother was there. She was so…so…stupid! She said the strangest things, about fruitcakes, and giving birth. I just don't know what to think. And Chris…" Angela broke into sobs. Austin waited until she was able to talk again. "Chris was so dreadful. He told me…he said…he's choosing HER!" Angela sobbed again.

Austin finally broke in. "Did you say she invited you to dinner?"

"Yes. To go back to that same place. Apparently it's supposed to be some sort of fancy upper crust place in the evening. I can't imagine…"

"But you'll go?"

"I don't know."

"What time are you supposed to be there?"

"7:00."

"Angela, pull yourself together, put on your best dress and go."

19

Annie, Patti and Nancy sat in the all-season porch. They shared a bottle of crisp, cold white wine. Tiger Lily sat on Annie's lap, lazily watching out the window as her tail twitched back and forth.

Annie did not share Pete's companion interview with them. There were some things that were just too private to share with family. Instead, Annie and Nancy shared their breakfast adventure with Patti.

Annie said, "So, after Pete got his call, everyone in the dining room forgot about us and we finished our conversation. Kind of."

"Kind of?"

"I invited Angela to join Chris and me for dinner at the Bon Vivant tonight and she huffed off. As she left, I said, 'seven o'clock,' but I don't know if she heard me. We'll be there, and we'll have a chair for her. If she doesn't show, we'll enjoy dinner."

"And if she does?"

"I hope we can still enjoy dinner."

"What about Geraldine?"

"She huffed off after Angela. I think – I'm not sure – that Angela was as angry with Geraldine as she was with me."

"Mom, what was your take on it?"

Nancy laughed. "Annie was marvelous. I played the ditzy mother. I provided a little bit of comic relief when it was most needed. And I can take whatever they dish out. I'm a big girl. But I don't have to live near Geraldine and I'm not dating Angela's son."

Annie smiled. "Well, at least we know that he would choose me."

Tiger Lily purred and mewed a few times. *"Mommy, you remembered that butterfly. You let go, and happiness came to you."*

Annie scratched Tiger Lily's cheek, as if to say she understood.

"Oh, Patti, do me a favor and keep the kids away from the guests."

"Have the kids been a problem?"

"Oh, no, nothing like that. I just…have a feeling…I think the kids would be better off if they stayed away. Let Jess know, too. I already said something to the sitters."

The rain appeared to have stopped. Annie was the first to notice the butterfly. Tiger Lily sat up. She jumped off Annie's lap and went out the cat door to the garden. She jumped lightly to a picnic table, getting as close to the butterfly as she could.

Nancy said, "I decided to unlock the cat doors once the rain stopped. I guess I should do that in the morning. It will be hard for me, but Honey Bear will be able to walk around at will."

"Mom, the cat doors have been open at the Inn all week, even when Honey Bear has been here. Henrie told me the first time he forgot, and, well, we've been 'forgetting' ever since."

"That's marvelous, dear. We'll just leave it that way. Honey Bear can visit whenever he wants."

Tiger Lily looked through the screens at Grandmommy, then back at the butterfly. *"Take me with you to Mexico,"* she whispered.

20

Annie put on her best I'm-not-dressed-up-but-I'm-dressed-better-than-normal outfit and went downstairs. "Henrie, I told Chris I'd meet him at Bon Vivant; I need to go early to check in with Cookie."

"I believe all of our guests – with the exception of your family – intend to dine at the Bon Vivant Grille tonight."

"Great." After a pause, Annie asked, "Henrie, do you think we can ever have a month – or even a week – without the possibility of housing a criminal?"

"I certainly hope so. By the way, have you heard from Angela?"

"No. I don't expect to. I expect her to wait until the last minute to decide if she's coming. Oh, I already ordered pizza to be delivered tomorrow night. Ben and James will stay with the kids while the adults have an evening out. Patti and Jessica are looking forward to eating at the Grille. Too bad we couldn't arrange babysitters for tonight."

"Frankly, I believe it will be better for them to dine out after the triathlon rather than before. I do not understand why our guests feel the need to have a large meal tonight."

"I don't, either, but I don't want to discourage the business."

The Bon Vivant Grille was Annie's foray into fine dining. One of her best cooks, Cookie, wanted a better experience than handling the grill at Mo's Tap. Annie wanted to provide him a venue, and because the Café closed every afternoon, she had a facility.

Every Friday and Saturday evening, the casual chic atmosphere of the Café became glamorous casual chic. Table tops were covered in brightly-colored table linens. Linen napkins of every rainbow hue adorned the table tops, adding a burst of color to each table.

The live bouquet of purple flowers at the hostess stand was replaced with a live bouquet of flowers in every color Clara could find. The pendant lights came on, showing off the unique nature of each one.

Cookie, with Georgia's help, managed the farm-to-table menu, which rotated each week. Diners paid a set price and were offered a card, from which they chose an item for each course. Vegetarian and vegan options were available in every course, and carnivores were treated to a choice from each major meat group. Wine and artisan beer were on the menu with separate pricing, as were aperitifs and digestifs.

Jeff and Mark were seated at a window table overlooking The Avenue. Annie and Chris were already seated one table over. Mark noticed the table was set for three.

Mark looked around the room, dazed at the change. Their two-top table had a red cloth with one yellow and one orange linen napkin. The dishes were pure white crockery-style. The same dishes were probably used during the day to offer casual service. Tonight, on colorful linen, they looked expensive.

Jeff nodded at the card on Mark's plate. "What you do is choose something for each course, turn in the card, then sit back and enjoy. We'll take our time. It's a big meal."

Mark looked at the entire list. "They're keeping with the northern Italian theme."

"They try to do that. I think it helps with ordering. All of the businesses do their own thing, but they can reap the benefit of ordering in quantity if they have similar items. And it keeps things exciting."

Mark tried to focus. "How do you choose?"

"We make sure to choose different things that sound interesting to both of us and share."

"Can we order one of everything?"

Jeff looked up from his card and rolled his eyes. "The featured aperitifs are easy. There are only two. Why don't I order one and you order the other."

"Great. I'll take the Nini Bellini. But really, you can have the Campari. I've never liked it. Too bitter."

"You're right. I'll take the Bellini, too. Peaches and Prosecco sound good together."

They were silent as they studied the appetizers. Mark finally said, I think I can knock two off the list, because I don't need too much bread before the triathlon. They sound great, but…."

"I was thinking the same thing, so we can knock off the honey mustard pretzel dip and the Asiago toast. What do you think about the Italian stuffed mushrooms?"

"They sound great, and the pears and bleu cheese on endive sounds good."

"One course down, five to go."

The server brought Bellinis while they continued to look at the menu card. Mark stole a glance at Annie and Chris. They had begun to order, even though the third party had not arrived. He wondered if the third person was supposed to be Chris's mother. She seemed to be a piece of work. That display earlier in the day was, well, in a word, disgusting.

Mark's attention was drawn back to the menu card when Jeff said, "It's hard to share soup, unless we don't mind sharing germs. I think I'm going with the Italian peasant soup. It's made with chicken and two kinds of sausage."

"I think I'll stick with the classic minestrone."

Mark read through the selection of breads that would come to the table in a basket with this course: blueberry lemon banana bread, chive and honey biscuits, and something called Ezekiel bread, a yeast bread made with wheat berries, spelt – that was a new one for him – barley, millet, green lentils and a variety of beans, flavored with honey.

Jeff was talking again. "When we get to the vegetables and starches, we can both choose two. It's still going to be hard to narrow it down to four items."

Mark read through the list. "Can we choose one of everything?"

Jeff rolled his eyes.

They chose citrus sautéed vegetables, grilled corn on the cob covered with Italian seasonings, honey, cheeses and pepper flakes, roasted sweet potatoes, cubed and seasoned with chili powder, garlic and cumin, and spinach and ricotta ravioli.

Mark looked at the entrees. "They have Ossobuco. I love Ossobuco. What are you going to order?"

"I think I'll have the sweet Italian sausage with peppers and onions."

"Good choice. But the baked Italian tilapia looks good…"

"These other items almost make me wish I were a vegan or a vegetarian."

"You can be a carnivore and still order it."

"I know, I know."

Mark glanced at a table of four in the middle of the room, caught the eye of one of the men, smiled and nodded. In a low voice he said, "The four of them are here. Do you think it could be Randy?"

"Possible. We'll find out tomorrow."

For dessert, Mark chose the Semifreddo, a layered fruit loaf and ice cream cake, while Jeff ordered the Stuffoli, fried sweet dough coated with honey. They lingered over their choices, having to give up the pannacotta, the hazelnut chocolate cake and the vegan cheesecake.

Jeff said, "If I were going to get the cheesecake, I'd get the spiced whiskey peaches on top."

"I'd have the pears in pepper glaze."

"How about a digestif? Should we order one now, or wait until later?"

"Let's get it now, while we're looking at the menu."

Jeff marked his card to order a toasted almond, made with Amaretto, coffee liqueur and cream, and topped with shaved dark chocolate. Mark chose the Sgroppino, made with chilled Prosecco, vodka, lemon sorbet and limoncello. It would be topped with mint leaves.

As they turned in their menu cards, Mark once again looked at Annie's table. The shrew had arrived, and it appeared she had come prepared to do battle.

The tension at the table was palpable, but they tried to make the best of it. Their best intentions fell apart during the vegetable and starch course. Tim slammed his fist on the table and stood. "If you want her, Randy, you go ahead and take her. I'm done with this!"

Angela arrived at seven forty. She looked over the dining room and saw Chris and Annie, appetizers in front of them already. By the time she reached the table, her nose was in the air and her voice was tight with anger.

"I see you couldn't be bothered to wait for me."

Annie said nothing. Chris tried to keep his voice calm. "The invitation was for seven, Mother. You didn't accept or decline. We waited as long as we could."

Angela refused to accept responsibility. "You could have waited a few minutes more."

"Mother, as you can see, every table is filled. People are standing in line, and they have reservations to take care of. I took the liberty of ordering for you. They were going to wait to see if you arrived before sending your order to the table."

As he spoke, a plate arrived with a pear, bleu cheese and endive salad, beautifully arranged.

Angela was startled. "Oh. This looks wonderful."

"Would you care for a Bellini, or do you want a glass of wine?"

Chris lifted a bottle from a chiller beside the table. It was a Pinot Grigio from a winery based in Chicago.

"I'll just have a glass of wine, thank you. Did you bring your own bottle in?"

Angela could tell that Chris suppressed a sigh. "No, Mother. Annie's winery, Sassy P's, orders and supplies wine for Bon Vivant."

Angela's head and nose went up just a tick. "Well, I supposed you can't afford to have a wine steward at all of your businesses. Although…"

"Mother, let's not."

"Let's not what, Chris?"

"Let's not make everything that Annie does or says a point for disagreement."

"I would never!"

"Right. So. Let's talk."

"Let me enjoy this salad first."

Angela ate in small, delicate bites while she looked around the Bon Vivant Grille. It was remarkably changed. She had to admit that earlier in the day she found the Café to be an attractive place, and with the exception of those cats on the tables, she could not see anything that was, according to Geraldine, "filthy." Tonight, with the colorful linens and the lighting, the place looked quite remarkable. And those flowers!

She listened with half an ear while Annie and Chris talked in soft tones. Every now and then, one or the other would look up at someone entering with a smile and a wave, or someone would stop by the table to murmur a greeting.

It seemed to Angela that they must know absolutely everyone in town. Well, it was a small town.

Before she knew it, she had finished the appetizer, and the plate was gone. A bread basket appeared on the table and a bowl of minestrone was placed in front of her. The smell of garlic, onion and chicken broth wafted toward her. The chef had used cannellini beans instead of northern, a touch that few would appreciate. The server offered, and Angela accepted a touch of freshly grated parmesan cheese.

Angela couldn't help herself. She took a piece of dark bread, broke and tasted it. Whatever it was, it was marvelous. "What is this?"

"It's Ezekiel bread." Annie explained the ingredients and finished with, "Carlos, from Mr. Bean's Confectionary, made it this afternoon."

"How unique. And tasty. It must be common to this area?"

"No, not really. We like to experiment here."

"Oh. So you aren't known for a specific cuisine, nothing that would draw repeat customers."

Annie didn't answer right away. Chris sat back and looked at his mother. Then he looked around the dining room. Angela followed his gaze.

The tables were full. A few people had risen to leave, and others were ready to fill those tables. Angela looked out the window to see others waiting at the café tables outside.

Chris finally found his voice. She moved her eyes away from the window to look at him. He was saying, "...the

Bon Vivant Grille is known for other things. They are known for the atmosphere, the excellent service, the eclectic farm-to-table menu. As you can see, customers are lined up and waiting to get in."

"Yes. Well. A mark of good service is to have tables ready as guests arrive. Don't you think, Annie?"

Annie smiled. "Whatever you say, Angela."

"There's no need to be snippy."

Angela looked back at her soup as Annie and Chris seemed to have a private, non-verbal discussion. Shortly, she heard, "Ramon and Clara just came in. And look, they brought Fiamma."

Angela looked up to see a dark couple. They would have been a beautiful pair except for the man's dreadlocks. They were followed by a dog. Angela watched, mouth open, soup spoon held somewhere between the bowl and her chin. The dog was huge and had filthy, dirty matted hair. The dog looked just like the man!

She found her voice and turned to Annie. In a loud, carrying whisper, she said, "They both have those horrid dreadlocks! Don't you have a dress code?"

Anne smiled. "Yes, Angela. We require shirts and shoes, except on the dogs and cats, of course. They can come in with nothing at all to cover their private parts. We do frown if they choose to go through a mating ritual under one of the tables."

Annie's smile took on a bit of a dazzle, and she turned to say hello to Clara. She turned back. "Oh, those dreadlocks. You were referring to the man and dog, correct? Because Clara has never had anything like that.

Men and women who are together for a long time do tend
to look alike. At least that's what I've heard. In this case,
it's the dog and man that look alike. Well, they've been
together longer."

Chris stared at Annie. Annie smiled at Angela. Angela
finally shut her mouth and turned back to her soup. Oh!
The bowl was empty! Angela didn't realize she had
emptied her bowl of soup, eaten a slice of Ezekiel bread
and a chive and honey biscuit.

Before she could recover from her shock, the soup bowl
was gone. Placed softly and professionally before her was a
plate of saffron risotto and steamed broccoli with red
peppers.

Angela gathered herself, shutting down any more talk
from this woman, this Annie. She cut and placed a small
piece of broccoli into her mouth. She could taste the
rosemary, basil, thyme and oregano. Indeed, it was easy to
see that the seasonings were not from a tin, but were
freshly chopped and sprinkled lightly onto the broccoli.

After a few more bites of broccoli, Angela tasted the
risotto. Delicious. Parmigiano and Reggiano cheeses
added an earthy flavor. The dish had a light floral
fragrance. Her favorite, very expensive Italian restaurant
could not have done better.

Angela concentrated on her food. Chris and Annie
appeared to concentrate on breathing. In. Out. In. Out.

Angela didn't notice her main course was meatless. The
layered vegetable casserole contained thick slices of
eggplant and zucchini, carrots, mushrooms, tomatoes and
onions. The filling – although Angela again didn't notice –
had a tofu base, and the tomato sauce was rife with

chopped onions and mushrooms that had been sautéed in olive oil.

Angela, concentrating on the last bites of casserole, heard Annie ask that the digestif be served with the dessert. As Annie made her request, Angela heard her say, "You need to turn this table over." What Angela thought was, "Can this evening end any more quickly?"

Angela was served the cheesecake with spiced whiskey peaches. The peaches were obviously ripe, fragrant and freshly sliced. It was almost as if the cook pulled the peach from the tree to put it straight onto the plate. The Sgroppino lent a wonderful lemony finish to the evening.

Angela was determined that Annie not know how favorably impressed she was with the restaurant, the atmosphere, the service and the meal. She finished her dessert, sipped her Sgroppino and held it in her hand as she said, "Chris, why don't you come back to Marsh Haven and have a drink with me at my hotel?"

She was shocked to hear, coming from the mouth of her son, "No, thank you, Mother. I have plans this evening with Annie, and since she was not included in your invitation, I'll have to decline."

Before she could say a word in argument, Chris rose, kissed Annie on the cheek, and said, "I'm going over to talk with Ramon and Clara. If I don't notice, come get me when you're ready to leave. Oh, Mother, I have some items here for you. You may find them interesting."

He pulled a legal-sized envelope from his jacket pocket and placed it beside her table setting. And he was gone.

Angela finished her drink, declined the coffee offered by their server, placed the envelope in her purse, rose, and left without saying a word to Annie.

Saturday was steamy. The heat was oppressive, even early in the morning. Henry closed the windows and turned on the air conditioner. He started two rotating fans on the all-season porch for those who wanted to eat breakfast away from the clamor of excited children.

Henrie served a typical KaliKo Inn breakfast, but in deference to the thriathletes, a crockpot of steel cut oat groats with nothing added – the "nothing added" part was unusual for the Inn – warmed on the side of the buffet. To add to the oats, or to eat separately, were containers of raisins, craisins, walnuts, almonds, honey and peanut butter.

For athletes with nervous stomachs, he added a smaller crockpot of quinoa and a steamer filled with baked sweet potatoes. The fresh fruit bowl contained extra bananas, and a dish of no-sugar added applesauce, homemade, with visible chunks of apple, finished the offering.

Tim and Krissie were the first to arrive. Both were signed up for the one hundred mile event; they were scheduled to take their swims earlier than most.

"Good morning," said Henrie.

"Yeah. Same to ya." Tim seemed a bit, well, off. Henrie did not pry.

Krissie said nothing.

Henrie thought about the behavior of the two couples the night before. They ate at the Bon Vivant Grille, returning earlier than he would have expected. He heard first one come in, probably one of the men, followed shortly by the others. They stomped a bit harder than necessary, even as they knocked water off their shoes.

All went upstairs, but eventually, most came back down. They went in different directions. Henrie did not spy on his guests, but he was aware, for the most part, of their comings and goings. He knew that one man left the house, one man went to the library to watch a movie, one woman went to the beach and the other apparently stayed in her room.

This morning, the tension was palpable. Tim and Krissie barely spoke to one another. On their way out the door, Krissie found a bit of politeness. "Thanks, Henrie, for having what we needed for breakfast. I get nervous before an event, and, well, I forgot to ask about it yesterday. Still, you had just what I needed."

"You are welcome. I am happy to be of service."

Krissie smiled. "Well, thanks again. See you later."

Krissie left the dining room. Henrie could hear Tim. He had waited at the door for her, at least. Perhaps the two of them could come together as a couple once their spouses were out of the way.

Jeff and Mark were next to arrive. Henrie chuckled to himself as Jeff helped his plate to egg casserole, bacon, sausage, a bagel, a cinnamon roll, plenty of butter and cream cheese. Mark didn't chuckle. He glared at Jeff as he got a bowl of oat groats and topped it with craisins, walnuts and a spot of honey. He got a slice of whole wheat toast and added peanut butter.

As they took their trays to the all-season porch, Ben and JoJo arrived, barely in time. The sounds of running little feet followed them in the front door. Ella and Ollie were apparently allowed to leave the carriage house as soon as Patti spied the teen sitters.

Henrie helped Ollie to a toddler's seat while he talked with the teen sitters. "It seems everyone is running late today, but that is normal. I believe Patti wants you to take these two, the twins, and of course Little Fred when she arrives, to the beach to watch as Jessica and Paul start their swim. However, Paul should have left by now. If he actually leaves for the race, I doubt you will see him swim."

JoJo, helping plates, said, "But Jessica is doing the fifty, right? We'll be able to watch her."

Sounds of the twins running came suddenly from the back hallway, followed by the slower footsteps of two parents. Paul stuck his head in the dining room. "Running late, Henrie, have to go."

"No, you do not."

Henrie scooped oat groats into a plastic container. He spooned raisins and almonds on top, added a few drops of honey, closed the container and added it to a bag. Already in the bag were a slice of wheat toast with peanut butter, orange juice and water.

"Walk, do not run, and eat this on the way."

"Thanks." Paul managed a grateful nod and was gone.

Patti arrived to help the little ones with breakfast. "Henrie, I'm sending Fritz and the other kids to the Café for breakfast. I figured the little ones would eat better with less confusion."

Henrie, helping Ella with the chocolate milk, nodded agreement. "Does Fritz plan to spend the day with the older children?"

"Yeah. They're going to follow some of the race, but I think they'll get tired of that pretty quickly. Fritz has a good book and a beach blanket. I think they'll spend most of their day at the beach."

"And you? How do you plan to spend the day?"

"I'm going to help Ben and JoJo."

She got grateful, thankful looks from the teens, both of whom had their hands full with plates and glasses.

Henrie heard the front door open again. Georgia came in. "I thought everyone might want to leave the house early, so I brought Fred. She's had breakfast, but she would probably munch on a bagel or English muffin if you have something like that."

While the women and teens talked about the day, Henrie stepped back into the kitchen, sighed, poured a cup of coffee and walked out the back door.

He loved having a full house, and he loved having the children, but he loved, just as much, getting a little bit of space when both things happened at the same time.

He sat in a chair kept at the kitchen door for moments like this. A small table was handy for coffee or iced tea, perhaps a book. It was rare that he had time this time of day for a book.

Henrie had just leaned back in the chair, eyes closed, when JoJo appeared at the door. "Henrie, you told us to keep the kids away from the guests?"

"Yes. Is there a problem?"

"Not a problem. It's just that one of the women is down here getting breakfast. She's not, you know, doing anything. She's friendly and all. I just, you know, you said…"

"Yes. I will be right there."

Henrie knew this had to be Melanie, who had something going on with Randy, from whose room the incriminating paper had been taken. He rose, moving at a deliberate but unhurried pace. He did not want to appear anxious.

Henrie reached the dining room just as Melanie was standing, two plates and a cup of coffee balanced in her hands, looking for a place to sit.

Henrie reached to the side of the buffet and pulled out a tray. "Allow me to help you, Melanie. I believe you may want to join the other guests on the porch."

As he spoke, Henrie took first the cup of coffee, then a small plate, then the larger one and arranged them on the tray.

"Thanks, Henrie. Yeah, it looks a little, um, busy here."

"Follow me." Henrie carried the tray and Melanie followed, picking up another plate and adding a cinnamon roll on the way. Henrie, not wanting to interrupt an important conversation, raised his voice just a bit as he reached the porch. "I'll introduce you to the other guests, in case you have not met."

If they had been talking, Henrie's voice stopped it. Jeff rose as Henrie entered, Melanie behind. "Hey, Melanie. Join us out here. We decided to let the kids have the dining room."

Henrie set the tray on the table. "You may leave your dishes here when you are finished. I will take care of it later."

"Thanks, Henrie."

"You are welcome. Can we expect to see Randy this morning?"

Melanie sniffed and shook her head. "Who knows? As far as I'm concerned, he could stick his head in a trash can and stay there for a few months."

"Then I should not bother to keep breakfast warm for him?"

"Oh, Henrie, I'm sorry. I should have known you'd have a reason to ask. No, don't bother. I think I heard him leave the room real early, before Tim and Melanie came down."

Jeff sent Henrie a look that said, "Thanks, friend."

Henrie left, wondering to himself if a few months could go by without some kind of criminal investigation going on at the Inn.

When the kitchen, dining room and porch were once again silent, Henrie took his time picking up dirty dishes. On the porch, arranging dirty dishes onto a tray, he felt something at his ankles. Two somethings.

Kali and Ko. Wisely, they stayed in the apartment until the hordes had left. Specifically the horde of children.

Annie came in behind them. "Let me help you, Henrie. How was breakfast?"

"Horrid. How was dinner with Angela?"

"Horrid."

Henrie laughed with the French lilt that Annie loved so well.

"I supposed all our athletes got away on time?"

"Yes."

"Did our erstwhile law enforcement professionals make it out the door?"

"Yes."

"And our criminals?"

"Well, as we do not know for certain that we have criminals, and we do not know for certain who they are, or how many there are, I can say – with absolute certainty – perhaps."

"Well, that's something. How are you going to spend your day?"

By now, the two were in the kitchen. Annie put the tray down, knowing Henrie would not want her to help with the dishes.

"I plan to make a snack that will satisfy our athletes, get breakfast started for tomorrow morning, stay inside and keep the air conditioner on the lowest possible setting, and hope that nothing untoward happens today. And you?"

"I think I'll wander around town for a while. I'll talk Mom and Sam into hitting one or two of the local wineries. We can watch the race, at least some of the bikers."

"Speaking of watching the race…" Henrie picked up the remote and turned the television on to the local news. An onsite reporter was on the beach with a camera.

"If you're just tuning in, this is Dan Tapper, live at the Lakeside Triathlon in Chelsea. Behind me, you can see athletes checking in to start the event. All of the participants of the one hundred-mile event have checked in and are on their way. The people lined up here are checking in for the fifty mile event. Now, Charles, you'll want to see this."

The reporter turned and motioned with his hand as the camera swung. Facing the camera again, he continued. "You'll see the buoy markers are out and swimmers are in the water. There was concern the swim would have to be replaced with a run through the state park, but luckily, there are no rip current warnings today. There are a few swimmers out there right now, doing that heat, and Charles, take a look beyond the swimmers."

The camera took a wider angle. "You'll see some boats out there, just beyond the buoys. One of our local favorites, The Escape, with Captain Ray and his famous Portuguese water dog, Jock, is in close. They're watching for swimmers that get in trouble. If anything happens out there, if a swimmer gets a muscle spasm or just can't make it, Captain Ray will scoop him – or her – right up. I have it on good authority that they don't have to watch for sharks today."

The screen went to a split view, showing the onsite reporter on the left and the news anchor on the right. The anchor said, "No sharks today. Well, that's good news. You'll be back with us throughout the day, right, Dan?"

"Yes, Charles. We'll check in several times during the day. You'll see more swimmers, bikers and, last but not least, the runners. Let me tell you, these athletes are going to wish the lake heat were in the middle of the event. It is hot here today. You could boil an egg…well, let's say you could bake an egg on the sand here today. It's a scorcher. Back to you."

"Thank you, Dan. That was Dan Tapper in Chelsea, covering the Lakeside Triathlon. We're told the event has a record number of entries this year. As he said, it's a scorcher. I understand it's pretty steamy as well. Felix, what do you have for us on weather?"

Henrie turned the television off. Annie laughed. "Dan Tapper was at the Grille last night. He came in as I was leaving. He was with Ian and a couple of his people."

"His people?"

"Yeah, you know. Ian can't do it all. There's a woman that coordinates the lake event, someone that takes care of the state park if they have to use it, a guy that does the run and another guy that does the bicycle thing."

"Man in charge race."

Annie looked at Henrie with wide eyes. "It doesn't have to be Ian."

Out on the lake, Ray and Jock looked toward the open water while Cheryl watched the swimmers. Ray sat in a relaxed position on a deck chair with his feet on the rails. He occasionally raised binoculars to watch boats come and go. Traffic on the lake was heavy today.

Cheryl had an iPad and was able to stream the local news. Her ear caught Dan Tapper's segment, and she turned to watch. When it was over, she turned to look at Ray and Jock. "Jock, guess what. You're famous."

Jock turned with a *"Woof!"*

"I know you already know, but I just heard it on the news. Now everyone knows. That reporter, Dan Tapper, just mentioned Captain Ray and his famous Portuguese water dog, Jock."

"Woof! Woof!"

Cheryl laughed again and turned to keep an eye on the swimmers. So far, no one was in trouble. She kept an eye out for Mark. She was sure that if anyone was not used to an open water swim, it would be him.

Ray didn't turn, but he heard the conversation. He smiled to himself and hoped the news wouldn't give Jock a big head.

Ray picked up a handheld radio. "Chris, come in."

"Yeah, Ray. Do you have something?"

"No, just checking in with you. I don't see you."

"We're out further than you can see. We have a ping on that GPS tracker Jeff set. That boat is probably three miles out by now."

"Can you see him?"

"No, but he can't see us, either. We at least know where he is."

"Stay in touch. How is Pete doing?"

"He's not a sailor. I saw him leaning over the railing a while ago."

Ray heard a chuckle. "How about Cyril?"

"That dog was made for water. He's got the wind in his face and I swear, if there was something to hunt out here, he'd be pointin'."

"Well, it sounds like you're going to have all the action, but I'll stay here for a while."

"Do that. There could be more than one boat involved, and, well, it appears this guy Randy is kind of an idiot. He could be goin' the wrong way."

"Once the swimmers are done, I'll drop Cheryl off and go a little further out, just in case."

"Sounds good. Out."

Chris called to Pete, "Get it together, man. I can see them now."

Pete was on the other side, heaving over the rails. Cyril stood by, whining, unable to help. "I ain't made for boats. I was in the Marine Corps. The land-locked division."

"We should have taken a trial run. You should have said something."

"I didn't know. Oh, well. I'll hold it together."

Pete came close to Chris, and Chris didn't think he would be able to hold much together. "How do you want to do this?"

The Coast Guard speedboat lay still in the water. Chris had positioned themselves between the point that Jake's had apparently made contact with someone else and Chelsea.

"We'll just wave them over, like we're dead in the water and we need help."

"And then what?"

"We talk to them a little bit, then we pull out our, you know, weapons, and take them into custody."

"How many do you think there will be?"

"I don't know. Four or five. But we'll have the drop on them. They won't expect us to be onto them. They don't know we're tracking them. They'll just think we're out here maybe having a little engine trouble."

"I wish I had called this in. We could have used some more guys. Heck, even Marco."

"Too much going on in town to pull any of them in. We'll be fine. Like I say, they don't know we're tracking them. They'll all be on deck, like nothing's wrong. And if I know my maritime law, Jake will know he has to stop, if he thinks we might be in trouble."

"You're right about that."

Pete leaned over the side again and heaved, pulled himself upright and stood next to Chris.

Chris waved as Jake got close. Jake slowed down and circled back. It was a small town. Jake was familiar with both Chris and Pete.

"Hey there, Chief. What are you doing on the water? You're lookin' a little green around the gills, there."

"Oh, I'm fine. Just fine. By the way, Jake, we need you all to come over here now, while we take a look at what you might have."

Pete and Chris raised rifles as Pete spoke. But just then, Pete heaved once more. Chris, momentarily distracted, turned back to see five handguns pointed in his direction.

Ray was happy to be on the water. A small breeze helped keep the sticky, sweltering heat at bay. But not by much. The swimmers were done and Cheryl was back at

The Marina. Ray moved The Escape toward the open lake. While doing so, he tried to raise Chris again. Chris didn't respond. Neither did Pete.

Ray used the radio to contact the Coast Guard Station. They were in the process of sending out another boat. They tried to check in with Chris fifteen minutes before and had been unable to reach him.

22

Annie wished she were with Henrie. He was staying cool at the Inn. She imagined he kept up with the triathlon by watching the news. She was at the Café, helping them through a late breakfast rush and ignorant of anything happening in the world.

Tiger Lily seemed restless. When she was at the hostess stand, she watched through the windows anxiously, ignoring customers completely. Often, she jumped down to visit with other cats.

Honey Bear, on his first day of true freedom from locked cat doors, had followed Nancy and Sam to the Café, and he stayed with Tiger Lily when they left.

Nancy didn't want to leave him. Annie could see the tears in Nancy's eyes as Sam gently pulled her toward the door. Annie sent a silent message of strength to her mother. Honey Bear would be okay. Nancy would have to trust.

The cats from across The Avenue, Simon Finnegan and Oscar McMurphy, were in and out.

Even her own cats, Little Socks, Mo, Mr. Bean and Sassy Pants, were in and out. At least Kali and Ko seemed to stay home at the Inn. Except once. After a particularly busy time, Annie looked up to see what looked to be Kali's tail as it whipped past the window on the way back to the Inn.

Tillie was in and out, weaving through bicycles and legs as she went back and forth across The Avenue.

One just never knew what those cats – and dog – were up to. It almost seemed as they all came in to check in with

Tiger Lily, left to do whatever they did, then came back to check in again. When Tiger Lily was busy, they seemed to pay attention to Honey Bear.

As she finally cleaned up the coffee bar for what seemed to be the hundredth time, Trudie came around to say, "Annie, we're good. Go spend time with your family."

Grateful, Annie waved good-bye and walked to the door. Tiger Lily, Honey Bear and Mo were in deep discussion. Annie leaned against the hostess stand to wait. As she waited, Tillie came in, gave Annie a polite nod, and joined the huddle.

Kali ran in, huffing a bit, and gave a start as she saw Annie. She kept an eye on her Mommy while she continued, more slowly, to walk toward the other companions. When Kali reached the huddle, they all seemed to notice Annie.

Four cats and a dog sat in a circle. They were silent. They looked up at Annie. Annie looked at them with a solemn face. "Go ahead. Finish your conversation. Then we can get on with our day."

They looked at one another, looked back at Annie, then made a decision. They huddled once more to finish their conversation. Three left together, then went in different directions; Tiger Lily and Honey Bear remained behind the hostess stand.

Annie stood looking down at them. After a few seconds, she said, "Tiger Lily, I'm going to meet your Grandmommy at a winery. She's been there a while, so I want to go right away. Do you want to come with me?"

"*Meow!*"

Honey Bear added, *"Meow! Meow!"*

"Okay. Do you need to make arrangements with your siblings before you go? If so, do it quickly."

Honey Bear and Tiger Lily seemed to converse. Tiger Lily started to the door. She stopped to look back at Annie, then continued, going out the door and turning left.

In the minute she waited for Tiger Lily to return, Annie wondered again why she continued to have conversations with her cats. Probably because she knew they could understand her, even though she could not begin to understand them.

Then Tiger Lily was back, Little Socks in tow. Little Socks jumped to the top of the Hostess Stand, as if to take Tiger Lily's place at the Café.

Annie shook her head as she stared at Little Socks. "You're staying here?"

Little Socks lifted her right hind leg and cleaned her nether regions.

Mark thought he was holding his own in the cycling. He hadn't done well in the swim, pulling a fairly long completion time. He made up for some of that in the second part of the race. Biking was his strong suit. He had not been able to ride this week, but his muscles were in good shape following several days of exercise at the yoga studio.

The bicycle route was a forty-one mile loop that meandered along country roads through corn and bean fields, vineyards and livestock. The countryside was what a driver would call "rolling." A walker might use the same term.

Runners and cyclists, however, called it "hilly." Halfway in, Mark's muscles were straining under the uphill pressure. Mark was doing the fifty-mile triathlon and would make this loop one time. Those doing the one hundred-mile were already on their second loop, and still, most of them were passing Mark on the left.

Mark concentrated on the movement in his legs. He needed to remain competitive, so as not to draw attention to himself. He also needed to ride slowly enough at certain points that he could notice unusual patterns of others. He would concentrate on people that gathered at various points along the way to watch the participants. Or not. Chances were that he would see nothing.

Mainly, by entering the competition, he gave Jeff an excuse to mill around. If Jeff and their friends could not make arrests before the end of the event, Mark would have to continue the façade of being a triathlete for another day or two. Just one more athlete chillin' in town after the big race.

Speaking of which, he could use some chilling right now. He pulled the towel off the handlebars and once again wiped sweat from his eyes. Jeff was going to owe him big time for this day.

Mark would pass three vineyards with tasting rooms on this run. He had passed one already. He didn't notice anything unusual, and he didn't see Jeff.

It would be Jeff, not Pete. Based on their conversations in the last few days, the group made a decision. Jeff would not have the filters that Pete would have regarding the locals. He would be able to see people, and their behavior, more clearly.

Over the years, all of the local wineries had developed outdoor seating that allowed customers to watch and cheer on runners and bikers of various events. On this day, the wineries set up outdoor tasting and serving bars; two of them hired catering trucks to provide a variety of food.

When Mark passed the first winery, the smell of burgers and hot dogs cooking almost made him sick. They should move those trucks further to the back.

Mark could see the second winery coming up around the next curve. He positioned himself to be to the furthest left, without getting in the passing lane, so he could see people as clearly as possible. He slowed, just enough.

There was Jeff, at a table with Melanie, who looked a little looped. Jeff gave a huge wave to Mark, letting him know there was nothing going on at this one. Mark could look forward to seeing him at the next one.

Annie got to the Blue Bottle Winery, Tiger Lily and Honey Bear in two carriers, before Nancy and Sam. "Well, kids, they must be at the other place, but don't worry, they'll be here soon. I'll get us a table by the road."

Dan Tapper and his camera crew were setting up at one of the three tables just in front of the road. He turned as Annie claimed the other two.

"Hey, I know you. You're that Annie. Always in trouble. But your places have the best food in the area."

Annie gave him a wan smile. She was used to this. The only time regional media paid any attention to her, the publicity was negative. They didn't bother to interview her when Geraldine hadn't caused some crisis or another.

Annie and the news crew were among the first to arrive at this winery, but already, cars were arriving from the second passing point. The wineries had opened their tractor lanes to vehicles to keep the bikers safe, and cars arrived, pulling out of a vineyard and into the parking lot of the winery from the back.

Annie thought she might see Jeff, or Pete, or someone. She wasn't sure who was doing what, but she knew several people were doing something, and they might need a place here at the winery. Hopefully nothing would happen while the camera was here.

Annie put one of the carriers on a table for herself, Nancy and Sam, and another for…someone.

She addressed the cats in their carriers. "I'm going to get wine. I'll be back, then I'll let you out, Lily Girl. Honey Bear, I'm going to have to put the harness on you."

"*Meow!*"

When Annie got back to the table, a bottle of dry white wine in a tabletop chiller and three glasses, Nancy and Sam were at the table. Sam unpacked a cooler of fruit, nuts, crackers and cheese.

Nancy chatted amiably with Dan Tapper and, apparently, she would be interviewed. A real person-on-the-street interview. How exciting it was to watch the bikers. How wonderful it was for Chelsea to have this event.

"Did you have real food for lunch, Mom? They're serving chicken salad croissants and a couple of other kinds of sandwiches."

"I'm fine, dear. It's too hot to eat much of anything."

"I know. I didn't bring a towel to wipe off. I feel like a leaking sponge."

"You look fine, dear, but here, have a paper towel." Nancy looked at her daughter and added, "Or three. Did you bring the harness?"

"Yes. Do you want to put it on him, or do you want me to?"

"He won't want it, and I don't know if I'm up to a fight with the big guy. I have to keep my makeup intact. I'm going to be on television!"

"I've got it." As Annie opened the carrier and put the harness on a wriggling Honey Bear, long honey-colored strands of cat hair stuck to every part of her wet body. Nothing she did helped. The hair stuck to her chin, neck, chest, arms, and, it appeared, every inch of her clothing.

Annie sighed and gave up. She would wear the hair.

Jeff came up behind them. "I don't suppose you saved this table for me?"

"We did. We won't bother you. We won't even talk to you unless you speak first."

"Why is that, dear?" asked Nancy.

Annie looked at her mother, a little startled that she had spoken so freely in front of her. "Oh, nothing, Mom. I just thought Jeff might be getting tired of being around all of us."

"Then why did you save a table for him?"

Annie busied herself with Tiger Lily's carrier, effectively cutting off the need to reply. Tiger Lily jumped out. No one noticed as she stuck her tongue out at the harnessed Uncle Honey Bear. To rub it in, Tiger Lily danced around the ankles of everyone at the table.

Annie glanced at the news crew, busy with their instruments. She noticed they had a monitor tuned in to the station. Dan would be able to see himself on TV as he spoke. Ducky.

Annie looked back at the winery in time to see Melanie staggering toward them.

"Oh, my. Someone's had a bit much to drink."

Jeff put his face in his hands. "Don't tell me. Melanie is coming."

"Yep. And she is making a kind of a wiggly beeline to your table, Jeff."

"That's okay. I'll deal with it."

Melanie reached Jeff's table and said, "Hey, what happen you? I turn roun and poof! You gone."

Jeff noted the slur and asked, "Did you drive, Melanie?"

"Yesh. How elsh I get here?"

Jeff shook his head and turned to look at the crowd. He saw the people Annie did at the same time. She said, "Oh, hey, there's Ian and one of his folks."

Coming toward them was Ian and a man Annie recognized as Nathan, but she didn't know him.

Dan Tapper saw them, too, just in time for the cameras to roll.

"If you're just tuning in, this is Dan Tapper, live at the Lakeside Triathlon in Chelsea. We're at the Blue Bottle Winery outside Chelsea, watching bikers on their way during the second heat, and look who just dropped in."

The camera swung toward Ian and Nathan. "Two men who are at the heart of it all. Ian Jenkins and Nathan Phillips. Tell us, Ian, how is it going out there?"

Annie watched the monitor. There was only a slight delay in the broadcast. Maybe a second. She continued to watch the interview on the monitor.

Ian must be used to this. In his most smarmy style, he said, "Well, Dan, let me tell you, it's been an exciting day. And a scorcher. Man, it's some steamy weather here today."

"You're right about that, Ian. Tell us, who's in the lead?"

"Well, Dan, you know we can't tell you anything yet. Some of the folks have finished the bicycle event and have moved on to the run, but really, the only completed numbers we have for the meet are the swim times. You know I can't say anything yet."

"Not even to me? I promise not to tell anyone!" Dan gave a big smile, a wink and a nod to the camera.

"I know we can trust you, Dan, but, I have to keep a few secrets for a while."

"Well, thanks, Ian. As always, it's great to talk to you."

Dan Tapper cut the cameras off with a hand, smiled and shook Ian and Nathan's hands and moved off. He gave the crew directions to film the bicyclists for some cutaway film.

Ian shook his head with a smile and moved on toward Annie's tables. He introduced Nathan to everyone at the table but Melanie. He didn't know Melanie.

Melanie gave a bleary wave as Ian said, "Nathan makes sure the bike run goes smoothly, and, well, it's all over for that round but getting the times at the end. He has people to do that, so we're going to enjoy the rest of the day."

Ian counted chairs. "Hey, can we sit with you?"

"Sure. Make yourselves comfortable."

Nathan started to walk away. "I'll, uh, just find a seat closer to the bar. Catch you later."

Ian and Jeff looked at one another. Annie noticed. "You know, I'm going to have a heat stroke if I don't find some shade. I think I'll sit at the bar, too."

Annie made her way there and sat as close to Nathan as she could and still keep eye contact with Jeff. Tiger Lily followed. Annie heard a desperate MEOW from the table as she walked away. She ignored it. She was not going to deal with Honey Bear.

Annie had been at the bar for only a minute when she saw Randy hurry into the outdoor seating area. He looked around in what seemed to her a crazed manner until he spotted Ian.

He hesitated. Annie realized at once what the problem was. Randy was focused on the wrong guy, and that guy was at a table with Randy's drunk lover.

Annie looked over at Nathan. He seemed to be watching for someone, but his gaze didn't linger on Randy. Annie didn't know all the pieces to the puzzle, so this was confusing. He could be watching for anyone. She thought Nathan was up to no good, and she knew Randy was a bad apple, but they didn't seem to know one another.

Randy seemed to gather himself, and he walked to the table. Annie left her wine at the bar and followed him over.

A comedy of errors ensued.

Melanie saw him approach and rose to give him a drunken lecture about his…well, let's just leave it at that. A drunken lecture.

Dan Tapper and his camera crew swung around to film the disturbance at the same time the anchor at the station was saying, "And now, let's go to Dan Tapper, live at the Lakeside Triathlon. Dan, what's happening out there?"

With a slight second delay, the scene played out on live television to the entire region. Melanie continued to give Randy a piece of her mind in a less-than-grammatically correct fashion.

Ian and Jeff turned to see who approached. Annie, coming up from behind, noticed that Ian knew Randy. Well, he must be the one, after all. Ian! Ian was a criminal!

Jeff had a look on his face that said, "Can anything else go wrong?" at the same time Mark sailed by on his bicycle.

Annie waved wildly and called his name. "Mark! Mark!"

The cameras slid in her direction to catch that action, then slid back.

Mark's gaze moved from Jeff to Annie as he heard her call his name. Then Mark was around the curve, continuing on the race.

Well, that didn't do anything worthwhile. What now?

Annie continued to the table. She didn't notice Tiger Lily close on her heels. They arrived at the table in time to hear Randy yell at Melanie, "Get out of the way! I've got stuff to do, and it doesn't involve you!"

"You're right it doesn't involve me! You rat's behind! You son of a garden implement! You...you...you BEAST!"

Melanie was on him now, pounding him on the chest and neck with her forearms. Randy grabbed her to hold her quiet and looked around to Ian. He got his voice under control, but it was still a strangled yelp.

"We got trouble. Real trouble. Come with me."

Jeff stepped in. "Calm down, Randy, everything's okay. What's wrong?"

"I need to talk to him." Randy nodded his head toward Ian.

Nathan appeared from behind them. "Hey, what's happening? You need help, Ian?"

Annie saw everything as if in a haze. Ian. Melanie. Jeff. Randy. Nancy holding Honey Bear. Sam. Then Mark appeared out of nowhere.

Mark grabbed Nathan from behind. One hand was cuffed and the other on the way to being there.

Jeff moved on Randy simultaneously, handcuffing him with what Annie thought was extraordinary efficiency.

After a few seconds of stunned silence, Melanie unleashed her forearms on Jeff. "Stop it! Stop it! What are you doing? Let go of him!"

Ian locked his arms around Melanie from behind. She continued to struggle, turning her curses to Ian over her shoulder.

Honey Bear tried to escape over Nancy's head.

Jeff turned to Dan Tapper. "Turn that thing off, now!" He turned back to Randy. "Randy, what went wrong?"

Dan gave a signal for the cameras to continue to run.

Jeff, realizing the cameras were still on, gave the camera crew a gesture to turn away. They kept rolling.

Mark dropped Nathan to the ground. He moved toward the cameras, badge and a pair of cuffs outstretched.

Tiger Lily moved at the same time. In a blur, she leapt into the air, found Dan Tapper's face and held on for dear life.

The cameraman tried to keep everything in focus, but eventually he stopped on Annie, who stood, mouth open, sweat streaming from every pore, hair soaked and flat to her face, cat hair everywhere.

Jeff's cell phone rang. His hands were full, and all he could do was answer it on speaker. It was Ray.

"Jeff, I'm not sure what happened, but we can't find Chris and Pete."

Annie burst into loud sobs and tears while the camera rolled.

Tiger Lily dropped to the ground and ran to hide behind Sam.

23

Angela extended her stay at the hotel in Marsh Haven. She left several messages for Chris, but he had not yet returned her calls. Heavens. She had made a mess of it.

Over coffee and oatmeal this morning, she opened the manila envelope. The first set of stapled pages carried news items that were very unflattering to Annie. Angela laughed to herself and wondered why Chris had behaved the way he had, only to pass these on.

Apparently, just a few months before, Annie had come under fire for substandard business practices. She had been investigated by the health department, alcohol bureau, the IRS and wage and hour. Angela soaked up every nuance of the articles – newspaper and online – and online versions of television reports.

She moved to the second set of stapled papers. Again, copies of newspaper reports, online reports and television news station reports. While reading these reports, Angela was caught up short. First, by the unflattering photograph of Geraldine and another man at a table, obviously at Annie's restaurant, then by the reports themselves. Statements from the state and federal agencies that conducted investigations, exonerating Annie and her businesses. An interview from the Lieutenant Governor on the loss of the Chief of Staff's job, and an investigation into the role he played, using state resources, to put Annie in the soup. A statement from the Governor himself. A lawsuit to be filed against Geraldine and two men, Hank and Howard. An application for restraining orders. That particular article contained a laundry list of previous grievances against Geraldine and Hank, for criminal acts – actual criminal activity – against Annie.

Angela put that set of pages away slowly and turned to the third. This one was smaller. Two pages, copies of a newspaper article dated this week. Another very unflattering photograph of Geraldine, obviously in a courtroom setting, and what appeared to be the entire speech leveled by the Judge in Geraldine's direction. And the Judge's distaste that he had no choice but to vacate the restraining order.

How could she have been so wrong? How could she have listened to that woman? Why did she not trust her son to do the right thing? Choose the right woman? Why could she not force herself to like that woman? Annie.

In a telephone conversation with Austin, her husband, she decided to wait an additional day and try to repair the relationship with Chris. Even, if it came to it, trying to accept Annie as the woman in his life.

She would try. That was all she could do. But now, what to do with her day? There was nothing to do in Marsh Haven. She had to admit, some of the shops on The Avenue had promise, but…to go there…to that town…that street…so close to "her."

Angela dressed in her best casual clothes: a designer summer shift with slinky high-heeled sandals. She called to make an appointment for a hair and make-up session and a mani pedi at the spa recommended by the concierge. Well, the desk clerk. No one remotely resembled a concierge in this town.

At any rate, she wanted to look perfect when she finally saw Chris. Certainly she would be able to catch up with him by evening. If she had to, she would drive to that town and find him.

Her mani pedi complete and make-up applied, Angela sat patiently in the styling chair. The stylist had touched up her hair with blond highlights to hide the gray. The effect was, well, nice. Now she waited for the "do" to be molded and cemented against the heat.

Angela sipped a glass of chilled champagne – at least the attention to detail in the spa was adequate – and glanced around the room.

The television had been on the entire time, but now, apparently, people in the room were buzzing about it. Angela glanced over and nearly spilled her champagne.

There was a freeze frame of that woman! Annie! Ghastly! Straggly hair, sweat streaming, cat hairs sticking to her chin and chest, and was that…it was…tears!

Behind Annie, Angela could make out a man holding up a badge and…was it handcuffs? Just to the side of Annie was what looked like a man with a cat on his face. The cat was just a blur.

In the far corner of the picture was that other woman, Annie's mother, with a large orange cat. It looked as if the cat was climbing up to or down from the top of her head. The cat must have been digging in with its claws. The woman's face had raw, red marks.

Scrolling text at the bottom of the page read something about a major drug arrest. Annie had been arrested on a drug charge! Hallelujah! She would have to call that station to get a copy of this report to show Austin. And Chris. Two could play this game.

Someone turned the volume up so everyone could hear. The next words chilled Angela to the bone.

"...and still missing are the town's Chief of Police and the Chief of the Coast Guard Station. Details are sketchy, but it appears they were working on the lake end of the drug operation and were perhaps...we have to be clear that this is entirely speculation...taken or otherwise harmed by criminal elements on the water. We understand Coast Guard crews from every station in the near vicinity are looking for them, and all local volunteers have been called in to assist."

Without realizing it, Angela had risen from the chair and moved closer to the television. The view of the anchor was moved to the right of the screen as the left side split to a reporter. His face was covered in bandages, and a few were on either side of his neck as well.

"Dan, what can you tell us?"

"Charles, I'm live in front of the police station in Chelsea. At this moment, two men are in lock-up here, awaiting interviews and possibly a transfer to the county jail in Marsh Haven. Charles, as you know, we were in the right place at the right time and caught, live for everyone to see, an exciting arrest."

The right side of the screen ran the footage from the winery without sound as Dan continued to talk. Angela, mesmerized, watched as Annie came close to the arrest in progress.

"The names of these two men are not being made public at this time, Charles, but we know one to be a Chelsea local, one of the organizers of the Lakeside Triathlon. They were arrested on what we assume were drug trafficking charges. Now, Charles, understand that most of what we say here is speculation. The authorities are not giving us a lot of information."

Charles, once again visible on the right side of the screen, weighed in. "Dan, we understand a woman was arrested as well?"

"Yes, Charles. A woman was arrested for interfering with the police while they attempted to subdue the two men. Police are not releasing her name at this time, but we know that she lives in or is staying at the KaliKo Inn right down the street."

"As for the terrifying news about the Chief of Police and the Chief of the Coast Guard Station, do you know, Dan, what the extent of the involvement is vis a vis those that are being held?"

"Again, this is speculation, Charles, but as you know, we were live, on scene and on camera, during that arrest, the only station to capture it. During that arrest, one of the officers can be heard asking one of the men what went wrong, and we have speculated the questioning to be about the situation on the lake. Back to you...wait, Charles! There's some activity here!"

Dan turned and the cameras followed. The cameras showed activity in the background as Dan talked in an excited tone.

"There's another man, yes, the police are bringing another man into custody. At least that's how it appears. It looks like the man is handcuffed. I just heard someone shout, yes, someone is shouting something like, 'That's Jake.'"

Dan turned to face the cameras and they focused once again on him. "It looks like this situation is still unfolding. We'll stay here and find out what we can. Now, Charles, back to you."

"Thank you, Dan." The screen moved to a full view of Charles, in charge of the anchor desk, with the photograph of Annie behind and to the right on the screen. "What an exciting situation. Again, that was Dan Tapper. He was live at the police station in Chelsea, reporting on the arrests of three, now apparently four individuals in a multi-state, perhaps even international drug bust."

His face turned somber as he stared straight into the camera. The camera moved in for a close-up. "What is this world coming to? They are bringing the scourge of drugs right to our doorstep."

After a beat, Charles turned, looked into another camera and fixed a megawatt smile to his face. "Felix, what's on tap for the weather? It's a scorcher!"

Angela moved back to her chair as if in a dream. The stylist was now behind her, adding product to her hair. Angela didn't protest. She was too numb to move. When she finally started to think, her first thought was that she must look good for whatever was ahead, be it a reunion with Chris or an interview on television.

Cementing done, Angela thanked the stylist and moved to the door, thinking, as she walked, what to do. She had to go to that town. That was all there was to it. Perhaps if she went to the tea room, that cyber place, the woman there could give her information, or direct her to Geraldine, or....certainly not Geraldine...or was she the wronged individual, not Annie? What in the world was she to think…to do…

Angela returned to the hotel, dazed, thoughts of "what to do next" running through her head. As she walked through the lobby, a desk clerk trotted to catch up to her. "Ma'am! Ma'am! We have a telephone call for you. We're told it is quite urgent."

Angela turned, confused. "A call? For me?"

"Yes, please." He led Angela to a chair in a private corner of the lobby. A house phone sat on a table beside it. "Please, sit here. The call will be transferred right away." He made a "go ahead" gesture in the direction of another clerk as he walked away, leaving Angela in private.

The phone rang, and Angela, trembling, picked it up. "Chris? Are you alright?"

The voice on the other end did not belong to Chris. It was a deep voice with some kind of a lilt, perhaps a French accent. The voice was clear, the tone steady, and the diction perfect.

"It appears you are aware there has been an incident. I regret to inform you your son has not yet been found. A search is underway."

"What can you tell me?"

"We know very little. Please, allow me to send a car for you. You can stay here, in Chelsea, and remain informed of all progress. You will be among the first to see him when a rescue is made."

Angela's mind made wild leaps. "That won't be necessary. I can drive. I have a rental car."

"I believe it best that you not drive at this time. Please allow me to…"

"…I must pack…and check out….oh, and call my husband!"

"I will call him and offer accommodation should he choose to come."

"Oh. Yes. Well. That might be best."

"A car will be there within the half hour. Will that give you time to pack and check out?"

"Oh. Yes. I assume so." Angela was still stunned. "I supposed I need to know who is coming."

"Two women, sisters. Their names are Jennifer and Marie. They are on their way as we speak."

"Oh, yes, well, I suppose this is all for the best. Well, I must get ready."

"Certainly. We will be ready to greet you."

Angela hung up and only then realized she didn't know to whom she had spoken or what arrangements would be made. She quickly assumed she had spoken to a police or Coast Guard official. Certainly she would stay in official Coast Guard quarters. That would be fine.

Packed and checked out, she stood at the door to the lobby as an ambulance pulled under the canopy. Two women emerged from the driver and passenger sides. They were blond with medium builds and resembled one another. They came into the lobby. One picked up luggage while the other directed Angela to a chair.

"Angela – may I call you Angela? I'm Jennifer. My sister, Marie, is putting your luggage in the back of the ambulance." As Jennifer spoke, she checked Angela's temperature and pulse and looked into her eyes.

"I'm sorry about the ambulance. We didn't have anything else close at hand. You'll be comfortable in front with Marie. I'll sit in the back."

Apparently satisfied that Angela was functioning properly, Jennifer stood and took Angela by the elbow. "Come on. Everyone's waiting for you."

The first few miles were made in silence. Then Angela asked, "Do you know anything more?"

"I'm sorry, no," answered Marie.

"When we get to the Coast Guard Station, will I be able to speak with someone in charge?"

"We aren't going to the station, Angela. We're going to the KaliKo Inn. The Inn is in constant contact with the station, the police and The Marina."

By the time Marie finished the last sentence, Angela registered the words "KaliKo Inn."

"What?! You're taking me to that place? That woman helped to kidnap my son! Stop! Let me out immediately!" To emphasize the point, Angela pulled on the door handle and had the door open partway.

Marie pulled over as quickly as she could while Jennifer, from the back, tried to calm Angela. "I don't know what you think, Angela, but I assure you, no one at the Inn was responsible for what happened to Chris…"

The ambulance stopped. Angela was halfway out, but Jennifer had jumped down and now stood in front of her. "Angela! What's the matter?"

"That woman! Her! Annie! She's been arrested as a part of this drug ring, and now you are delivering me to her! Are you going to hold me for ransom? Get out of my way!"

Jennifer could do nothing but stare. Marie had already recovered. From behind her, Angela heard an outburst of laughter and a weak, "You have got to be kidding!"

Jennifer stood her ground but found a smile. "Angela, I don't know where you got your information, but Annie has nothing to do with drugs or kidnapping or…well, anything. She's as scared as you. In fact, she's terrified, but she found the strength to think of you. She asked Henrie to call the hotel, to see if you were still there. She knew you would want to stay informed, to be able to see Chris the minute he's found."

"What? But…her picture…on television…"

"That horrid reporter. He probably told the station to use that picture, because it was, well…it is…" Jennifer stopped talking and started to laugh. Once she got started, she couldn't stop.

She laughed so hard that she doubled over. Still on her feet, she weaved back and forth, hands alternately on her stomach, cheeks and forehead, tears rolling down her cheeks. Angela heard much the same coming from behind her. She turned. Sure enough, Marie leaned against the seat, hand on her forehead, tears streaming as she laughed.

Eventually, to the relief of a confused Angela, the sisters got their emotions under control.

Jennifer said, "Come on, Angela. Please get back inside. We'll explain about Annie and her love/hate relationship with the media."

24

Jennifer and Marie escorted Angela into the Inn. Kali and Ko ran to greet her. Politely, they said, *"Welcome to the KaliKo Inn, Angela. It's good to see you again."*

Angela heard, "Meow, ick ick, meow, purrrr," as if from dual speakers.

Angela looked around. The Inn was lovely. Quite unlike some of the kitschy bed and breakfast places she had the distinct displeasure of visiting. This wasn't what she had imagined at all. Although…were those take-out pizza boxes on the hall table?

A teenager, an Indian or Pakistani boy, she could never keep them straight, and another teenaged boy brought several small children from the room on the left. Maybe a library. They were polite enough. The teenagers nodded and smiled, and they took the kids, where? To the second floor? Yes. They had turned on a television set up there. Was this a day care center?

A man approached. This must be Henrie. No. This was not the voice from the telephone.

"I'm Fritz. You must be Angela. My wife and I – my wife Patti is Annie's sister – we got a room ready for you upstairs. We, well, we rearranged the guests a bit. They'll find out when they get in for the night, but they won't mind. Well, I'm babbling. Sorry. I'm nervous. We all are."

Two teen boys, one almost an adult, came from another room. "Dad, do we have to stay here? All our games are at the carriage house."

A girl followed them and said, "Yeah, dad, why do we have to stay here? It's not like Aunt Annie needs our help."

Fritz turned from his children to Angela. "I'm sorry. It's a wonder we parents don't become mass murderers when we have teenagers." Fritz walked the three outside and, apparently, as Angela couldn't hear him after the door was closed, allowed them to go somewhere else. A carriage house? They kept the children in a garage?

As Marie took her luggage upstairs, a woman came from that same room – where the teenagers and small children had been – and approached her.

"Angela, I'm Pastor Teresa. Annie and Henrie asked me to apologize. They aren't here to greet you because the police had some questions for them. Let's go in here and sit. Can I get anything for you? Coffee? Something to eat?"

Angela shook her head as she followed this woman who called herself a pastor. Well, she had heard of such things before. Just not within her social circles.

The room really was a library. Or a kennel. It was filled with books, yes, but also with cats of every color and description. There were the two from the Café, the ones that were on top of the tables. And that orange one that wanted to be a hat. And others. And a little dog.

At least they were quiet. Some of these cats must have been at her home just last week. There were so many of them….

Pastor Teresa directed Angela to a comfortable overstuffed chair. A pretty throw lay across one arm. The pastor picked it up and placed it over Angela's legs.

"You've been through a lot today. You've had a shock. If you fall asleep, I want to make sure you're comfortable."

"I'm sure I won't fall asleep. Not until I know."

A hand-held radio crackled to life. The pastor picked it up. "Teresa here."

A woman's voice was on the other end. "Is Annie there?"

"No, she and Henrie are at the police station. Can I help you?"

"I just wanted to give you an update. Ray called. You know he has a couple of Coast Guard volunteers. George is with him. They've finished covering their quadrant, and they're moving out further."

"Are they sticking to the coastline?"

"Yes. Jake gave the police a good description of the boat, and everyone is bearing down on that description and the harbors they know it uses."

"Other than that, nothing new?"

"No, nothing. I wish I could be there with Annie."

"There are lots of people here, Cheryl. You're helping her more by staying there."

"I know. Oh, did you know Mem and Frank are staying with Janet and the kids?"

"Yes, I heard. We sent food over."

"Good. Well, I'll let you know if I hear anything else."

A woman in Indian or Pakistani dress came in carrying a tray with appetizers. She was followed by a Hispanic woman with a tray of breads and cookies.

The Hispanic woman spoke. "Angela, I'm Isabel. This is Laila. We'll be here as long as we're needed, so feel free to ask us if you need anything. We'll be in the kitchen."

They left, and Angela looked at Teresa with the unspoken question. Teresa answered. "Laila owns the grocery store across The Avenue. She and Annie are good friends. Isabel is married to Carlos. He manages Annie's bakery and candy shop up the street."

"But they aren't from here."

"They are. They live right here in Chelsea."

"But they weren't born here."

Teresa's answer took on "a tone."

"No. Laila is from Pakistan. She has the appropriate documentation to live and work in this country. She owns a business and pays taxes. A lot of taxes. Her children were born in the United States. Isabel is from Mexico. She is married to a citizen and is in the process of becoming one herself. She works here and pays taxes."

Angela sat back. Well, they were kind to her. The help is supposed to be kind, after all.

As if she could read Angela's mind, Teresa said, "They are friends. They are not 'the help.'"

Angela heard the front door open to a subdued flurry of activity. In swept that couple and their dog, the dreadlocks people.

The dog came straight to the library. She sniffed Angela from a polite distance, then headed for the corner where most of the cats and the little dog lay. She made room for herself among the rest and lay down with a sigh, head on her paws.

The dreadlocked man went in another direction but soon, the woman was in the library. "Angela, I'm Clara. I own the flower and gift shop across The Avenue. Let me say how sorry I am you're having to deal with this. I'll be in the kitchen if you need anything."

As Clara left, Angela looked again at Teresa. "Haiti. She's a citizen. Taxes. Lots."

Angela helped herself to a small plate of appetizers and a slice of what looked like banana bread. It wasn't banana. Pear, maybe, with notes of Roquefort and plenty of walnuts. The appetizers were interesting. The spices indicated they were from the Indian and Pakistani region of the world.

Laila came back with a tray laden with thermal pitchers and drink condiments. "I have coffee, two kinds of tea, and everything you might need."

She left, and Angela noted the cups were ceramic, heavy, and made for comfort drinking.

She could hear talking and laughter from the kitchen. Everyone had friends here. She didn't. She didn't even have friends at home. She had social intimates. She had political contacts. She had attorneys, accountants and money managers. She did not have friends.

Angela pulled the throw up just a little bit, so it reached her chest. How long would she have to sit here with this pastor…this pastor who seemed so cavalier about people? She, Angela, was the most important person in this room. When was someone going to pay attention to her?

It was as if that cat could read her mind. The tiger cat – was it Tiger Lily? – moved from her place in the pile and jumped softly to the arm of Angela's chair. The cat placed a paw on Angela's arm, then another on her leg, and finally, ever so carefully, she sat in Angela's lap. She curled up, leaning her back into Angela's stomach. She closed her eyes and purred herself to sleep.

Angela didn't know what to do with her hands. She finally placed one on Tiger Lily's side and left it there, watching as it went up and down, up and down, with the soft cat's breathing.

Angela leaned her head into the pillowy headrest of the overstuffed chair, closed her eyes, sighed, and fell asleep.

25

When Angela woke, the long summer day had finally turned to night. A soft glow came from a lamp in the corner. Her legs had been lifted to a velvety ottoman; a duvet had been drawn over her. Her shoes were on the floor beside the chair. And she was surrounded by cats.

Tiger Lily was no longer on her lap, but a hefty gray kitten stretched full length across her upper legs. A long-haired gray cat curled on top of her ankles. Wasn't that the one that pulled up her prize roses? Apparently he didn't remember how she had screamed at him. One of the cats that had greeted her when she arrived at the Inn stretched out on the arm of the chair.

Angela looked around the room. The pastor was gone. Sitting in chairs to her left and a little behind her were Annie and a tall black man. She listened. She couldn't understand the words, but the voice was familiar. This had to be Henrie. Apparently one of Annie's confidants. A black man with a French accent. Did this woman know any Americans?

Angela caught herself up short. She had determined, after hearing the story of the reporter's ambush from Jennifer and Marie, to be more open-minded about Annie. They were American. Certainly. They were blond and spoke with midwestern accents.

Angela needed something to drink, but she didn't know how to extricate herself from the cats. Annie noticed.

"Kids, wake up. Let Angela get up."

One drowsy face lifted from Angela's lap. One eye opened down at her ankles. One cat sprung nimbly from the arm of the chair.

"Come on, Mo. Mr. Bean, get up." Annie moved close and picked up the kitten. The big gray cat rolled off.

"I'm sorry, Angela. I didn't know which was best, to let them settle in or accidently wake you up by keeping them off."

"It's okay. It was…nice, actually."

"Let me get something for you. Water? Coffee? Wine? Something stronger?"

"I could do with a martini."

"Gin or vodka?"

"Vodka, please."

"Flavor? Henrie makes an outstanding lemon drop, or…?"

"A lemon drop sounds wonderful." Henrie nodded and moved out of the room. Angela raised her legs, and Annie helped her move the ottoman away.

"Have you heard anything? Have they found Chris?"

"Not yet. Let's get settled with drinks and I'll tell you what I know."

The rest of the house was silent. "Has everyone left? The house was so full."

"All of the guests, well, most of the guests are in bed for the night. Even my family. Everyone else, the folks that came over to help Henrie and I with everything, they've gone home."

"Oh. I see." Actually, Angela did not see. She didn't understand why people thought highly enough of Annie that they would come in the first place.

Henrie returned. He carried a small tray with three lemon drop martinis. He put the tray on a table and pulled two overstuffed chairs to make a small circle with Angela's chair.

Angela, eyes wide, observed the process. Certainly he didn't intend to sit with them! But he did! Intend to sit!

Annie seemed impervious to the situation. She was asking a question. Angela tore her eyes away from Henrie as she heard, "Have you met Henrie? I know you've spoken on the telephone…"

Angela found a polite answer. "No, we haven't met. How do you do?"

"Very well, thank you." Before sitting, he asked, "Can I get anything else for you? It has been quite some time since you have eaten."

"No, thank you. Not at the moment." Then Angela remembered. "Were you able to reach my husband?"

Henrie sat down. "Yes. He is on his way. His flight will land shortly, and he will go to the hotel for your rental car. I made arrangements for the agency to drop an extra set of keys at the hotel desk for him."

Angela was impressed. "Thank you."

"Not at all. I was happy to be of service."

"So, what do you know? What can you tell me?"

Annie took a sip. "The boat Chris was on was located by the Coast Guard. It had a GPS tracker. It was abandoned, and…some blood was found."

Angela was shocked. She couldn't stop her mouth from gaping and her hand from coming to her mouth. "Was it Chris?"

"We don't know. There wasn't a lot, I mean, it wasn't enough to indicate arterial flow, so that's good. They're doing everything they can, even in the dark, to look for him. And Pete and Cyril."

"Who are Pete and Cyril?"

"Pete is the Chief of Police. He was on the boat with Chris. Cyril is his dog. A special dog. A kind of police dog."

Angela's muddled mind could only think, a dog? They're wasting time looking for a dog? Annie was still talking.

"Anyway, this is what we have been able to piece together. First of all, two guests here at the Inn are federal agents. Jeff works with the FBI and Mark with the DEA."

The names and acronyms swam around Angela's mind. Law enforcement of some type she was sure. Annie was still talking, but the sentences were a blur.

"...on their own time ... agencies weren't interested ... information that a drug ring...."

Annie stopped to take another sip. Henrie started to talk. Angela turned to look at him, but the words still seemed to swim just out of grip.

"A 'connection,' I believe is the correct term, wanted to sell drugs ... thought he could erect a 'pipeline' here ... triathlon weekend ... additional tourist traffic...."

Annie took the story over. Angela was beginning to feel like a ping pong ball, eyes going to first one, then the other.

"The plan was to get someone here that could connect the land and lake ends."

"Excuse me? Land and lake ends?"

"Someone would bring drugs, I don't think they know what kind yet, across the lake. They would meet a local boat a few miles out, someone that we all know and wouldn't suspect, and then, that local boat would bring the drugs here."

Henrie continued. Angela "pinged" to look at him.

"The boat would deliver the drugs to someone here who would distribute the drugs. The drugs were to go to someone we already know, again, so no one would suspect."

Annie again. Angela "ponged."

"Someone we didn't know, someone we thought was a tourist, was to connect the distributors with the locals. Then he would leave, having secured the connection, and no one would suspect people they've known for years."

Henrie – Angela "pinged" – said, "An arrest was made...."

Angela interrupted. This was a salient point. "Who was arrested?"

Annie – Angela "ponged" – said, "A local boat owner. He's kind of an idiot. He told the police everything he knows."

"And?"

Henrie (ping), "A local man, someone we all know. He coordinates the bicycle portion of the triathlon. Apparently, he has had some financial difficulty."

"Who else?"

Annie (pong). "One of our guests was involved. He was the outsider brought in to connect the locals."

"One. Of. Your. Guests."

Henrie (ping). "It happens. On occasion."

"On occasion."

Annie (pong). "Yes." Annie's tone seemed to harden. "On occasion, a guest of the Inn has other than innocent motives for being in town."

Henrie (ping). "We have not found the correct filter to assure all of our guests are law abiding citizens."

Angela didn't know what to say. Then she remembered the woman. "A woman was arrested. Who was she?"

Annie (pong). "She was a guest. I think she was only having an affair with him. We don't think she knew about the drugs."

"An affair?"

Henrie (ping). "It happens. On occasion."

"What?"

Annie (pong). "They were here with their spouses. There was some kind of affair going on, and she got in the middle of the arrest."

Angela braced herself as all of the bad feelings toward Annie returned.

"I cannot understand Chris's attraction for you. Your businesses are despicable! And a danger to the community!"

Annie rose, forcing Angela to look up at her. "I'm going to bed, Angela. My niece will stay up to make sure Austin finds you. Henrie will show you to your room."

Annie's tone seemed to soften. "Chris will be found, Angela. Everything's going to be okay."

The cats ran ahead of Annie as she walked out of the room. Angela noticed that her step was heavy and her shoulders stooped.

She didn't' see the tears that suddenly freed themselves and fell down Annie's cheeks.

26

The air conditioner was already running as Annie and the cats got to the kitchen Sunday morning. It was early. Five o'clock.

Mr. Bean was first to enter. He reached up as tall as he could to pat Henrie's behind as he bent over the oven. Henrie knew who it was without looking.

"Mr. Bean, you will make me spill this breakfast bowl. That would not be helpful."

Mr. Bean, mostly silent to the human world due to damaged vocal chords, gave Henrie a purr and another pat.

Kali and Ko danced around his legs crying for *"Bacon, please!"* Henrie understood. "You are up very early. Your bacon will be ready in a few minutes. I will start it now."

Annie, looking a little sleep deprived and a lot sad and distressed, poured a cup of coffee. "How can I help you, Henrie?"

"Sit. Talk to me. Do not touch anything."

"Can I at least make bacon for the cats?"

"No. But thank you."

Henrie started the bacon in two large skillets. He always ran out of bacon. He didn't understand the fascination. But, according to Annie, bacon was a food group of its own. As were dark chocolate and dry red wine.

Henrie sighed.

The smell of bacon mixed with the aroma from the oven, a cheesy Italian breakfast bowl with eggs, sweet

Italian sausage, purple onion, red bell pepper, and mozzarella and parmesan cheeses.

The cats prowled the kitchen, but finally settled in to wait. Little Socks jumped to the top of the refrigerator. Sassy Pants and Mr. Bean sat on the window ledge, looking out rather than in. Tiger Lily and Mo sat out of the way under the kitchen table; Kali and Ko stayed underfoot. Henrie knew to look down before moving his feet.

While the bacon cooked, Henrie opened three airtight containers. He took a piece from each container and placed them on a small plate for Annie.

"An Italian breakfast scone, bacon cheddar beer bread, and maple bacon pull-apart bread."

She bit into the scone. "Yum. I taste sun-dried tomatoes. And basil. I taste basil. Did Carlos make this?"

"Yes."

She tasted the beer bread and swooned. "Outstanding."

"This last one, what did you say it was?"

Henrie looked at the bread she was ready to taste. "Maple bacon pull-apart bread."

"Is this Italian?"

"I do not believe it is."

Annie tasted it. "Heaven! Buttery, sweet and bacon-y. When did he bring them over?"

"He brought them yesterday."

"I didn't see them when I was digging around for something to eat last night."

"He put them in my apartment so no one," he gave a meaningful glance to Annie, "would eat them before this morning."

"Oh. Oops. Does everyone know my habits?"

Henrie chuckled. "Not just you. There were many people in the kitchen last night."

From the refrigerator, on a shelf marked "For Sunday Breakfast: Do Not Touch," Henrie pulled out a breakfast cake, ready for the oven, and ingredients for a breakfast skillet.

The cake went into the oven. Soon, cubed French bread, mozzarella, parmesan and chevre cheeses, hot Italian sausage, apples, sage and pesto added to the kitchen's aroma.

Henrie took a few slices of cooked bacon from the first skillet and crumbled them into seven dishes. He carried the dishes to the detective agency. Seven cats followed, not sedately, meowing and purring their thanks. After they ate.

Henrie figured they were too greedy to acknowledge the gesture before eating. Or perhaps, they were each afraid that someone would eat from more than one dish. Someone like Ko.

Annie walked to the stove and took three slices of bacon for herself. "You're too good to us, Henrie. But thanks."

Henrie nodded and added other breakfast meats to the skillet, then started another large pan for the last dish of the morning.

While he sautéed red bell pepper and onions, he asked, "So, tell me, how do you really feel this morning?"

"You know. I didn't sleep. Not much, anyway. My thoughts go from knowing he's safe to knowing he's hurt to knowing he's…you know."

Henrie added Italian sausage to the skillet, along with some garlic, basil and crushed red pepper.

"We have to believe he is well and that he will be returned to us. Pete and Cyril are with him. Certainly they are keeping one another safe."

Henrie scrambled eggs, then added salt, pepper and crumbled bacon to the bowl. He poured the mixture into the skillet. Steam rose, allowing the smells of all the ingredients to blend together.

He looked at Annie, who had said nothing.

She looked up at him to say, "That's my prayer, Henrie. That's my prayer."

Jeff and Mark came down early. Annie looked at the clock. It was just past six o'clock. Their faces were haggard. Annie thought she noticed a combination of sleep deprivation and angst over the situation.

She helped them fix trays to take to the porch and made one for herself. Annie put her tray on the table and went to the corner to turn on the fans. As she sat down, she asked, "Is there any news?"

"No," said Jeff. "Nothing, except that they continue to look at ports where these men do business."

"Won't they know you'll be looking there? The description of the boat, their photos…certainly they know you're hunting."

"I agree. We're going out with Ray this morning, and we'll look at ports where they aren't known."

Silence reigned as the three ate breakfast. Jeff, after a few minutes, looked up. "Annie, I can't tell you how sorry I am, for so many things. But I think the most important thing is that Mark and I are off the reservation, and we convinced Chris to help us without going through channels. I can't tell you…"

"Jeff, I appreciate your apology, but you know us. You know Chris – and Pete, too – would have helped no matter what. We love this town."

Jeff's cellphone rang. He checked the screen and answered. "We're leaving in five minutes, Ray. Should we bring anything?" He listened. "That's covered." He listened again and looked up at Annie. "She's right here. She can tell me where to find him. We'll see you soon."

As he hung up, he asked, "Does George live above Mo's? We're supposed to pick him up."

A commotion made them look up. It was George. "I'm here." He looked at the plates. "I'll bet Henrie will let me take breakfast to go."

Later, as Annie helped Jessica with the twins, Patti, Fritz and the rest of the children arrived. Fritz had two large baker's boxes.

"It's Sunday. We have to have those sugary donuts you find in every town in America. Except here. I had to go to Marsh Haven for these!"

"Fritz, we could have picked some up at Mr. Bean's yesterday."

"The top box is from there. Mr. Bean's donuts are tasty." Fritz nodded his head at Annie.

"But…"

"But, they're not as sweet as…well, as sweet as we're used to. I'm sharing. I have enough for everyone."

Fritz moved some of Henrie's serving dishes around, putting the bread basket on top of the detective table. The boxes were opened. Annie could see classic glazed donuts, glazed donuts iced in white and chocolate (with alternating drizzles), some chocolate iced donuts with what was probably a jelly filling, others that were filled with custard or lemon, and some covered with cinnamon sugar.

In the box from Mr. Bean's, Annie saw a selection of potato donuts probably flavored with bacon, cheddar and tart cherry. She saw some of her favorites, bourbon salted caramel, maple bacon, chocolate chipotle, and her personal favorite, orange ginger cream. In the corner of the box, she saw a Turkish coffee donut and one made with chocolate peanut butter.

Children pushed and shoved. "Mine!" "I called dibs!' "Mom, I called dibs!" "Dat me!" "I got it first!" "MOOOOOMMMM!"

Fritz and Paul, together, yelled, "SHARE!"

Annie waited for everyone else to choose and then moved toward the box. She was going to get that orange ginger cream. Her hand had almost touched it when she heard guests enter.

She turned. Krissie and Tim. Both were downcast. Krissie's eyes were red and swollen. The wrinkles around Tim's eyes made him look eighty years old. Annie said a polite good morning and said nothing more, waiting for them to speak if they chose.

Henrie was of the same mind. He said nothing as he motioned them to a small table for two away from the madding crowd. Henrie poured coffee for Krissie and Tim while other adults quieted children into a more polite dull roar.

Krissie nodded her thanks to Henrie. "We'll be leaving as soon as we've eaten. We're packed. We packed everything that belongs to, um, our spouses. If you have a place to store those bags, we plan to leave them. They may have need of clean clothes, other things."

After taking a sip of coffee, Krissie moved to the buffet. She helped her plate to a little of everything and the one orange ginger cream donut.

Annie sighed.

Tim filled a plate as well. Back at the table, he spoke to Henrie again. "If Melanie asks, tell her the house locks will be changed by tomorrow morning. Anything else she wants, she'll have to call our attorney."

Henrie looked at Annie. Annie nodded. He turned back to Tim and Krissie. "I will be happy to tell her. If she asks. The charges against her are minimal. She will probably be released on her own recognizance tomorrow."

"If she wants to get home or find a place to stay, here in Chelsea, I mean, she'll have to figure out how to pay for it. I've already cancelled our credit cards and I'll lock her out of our joint bank account tomorrow morning."

Krissie huffed. "I doubt Randy will be out tomorrow. I doubt he'll be let out before ten to twenty. But, if he calls, I suppose you can tell him to…"

Tim silenced her with a hand on her arm.

Krissie sighed. "Well, perhaps you can ask the police department to send someone for his things. Just in case. He won't be needing anything from home, but if he asks, I've cancelled our cards, and I'm going to the bank first thing in the morning, too."

Annie realized they had made plans together. It was good they had one another to lean on. They would be okay.

Angela and Austin appeared in the dining room door. They were followed shortly by Nancy and Sam, dressed and ready for church. Angela and Austin gaped at Nancy. Her face was streaked with bright red scratch marks, not infected, but certainly not healed.

Nancy, chatty as usual, said nothing about the marks. She had probably forgotten about them the minute she turned away from her mirror this morning.

Nancy smiled and chirped, "Angela, it's so good to see you. Of course, I am devastated about the circumstances. We so love Chris. And you must be Austin. I'm Nancy, Annie's mother. Sam, come say hello. Sam is my husband. If there is anything we can do for you, please let us know."

Austin held his nose until Nancy moved from them to the doughnut box. His gaze followed. Nancy's chatter seemed to run down. She looked at Fritz. "Didn't I ask you to get an orange ginger cream for me?"

Little Sally looked at Austin and said, "Mommy, who dat? Mommy?"

"Shhh."

"But Mommy, who dat?"

Annie stifled a smile and moved to greet Austin with a handshake.

"I'm glad you could come. So sorry you had to make the trip. I hope the room is comfortable."

She stopped herself from babbling by turning to focus on Henrie. Henrie nodded at her, coffee pot in hand, filling cups as he encouraged her – silently – to push forward.

"Please, sit and have breakfast. We'll be going to church in about a half hour. It's just up the street. You're welcome to come."

Krissie stood. "You can have this table. We're done. Thanks, Annie, for everything. I'm sorry for…well, I'm sorry for so much I don't know what to say. Anyway, here, folks, have this table."

Krissie and Tim left the room. Austin finally pulled his eyes away from Nancy and moved to the table for two. Henrie took dirty dishes from the table and added two clean coffee cups. "Are you Henrie? Is there any news?"

"I am sorry. I can only report that many organizations and individuals are involved in the search."

Austin seemed not to listen. Annie knew he was concerned, but also tired, scared and, face it, put out that he was dependent on her for hospitality.

And apparently he was "taken" by Nancy's face, now adorned with Honey Bear's scratches. The poor thing must have been frightened nearly to death to have caused such damage.

Annie sighed and turned to go upstairs. As she reached the stairway, she saw the cats. She hadn't noticed before, but now she realized they had not been in evidence since their morning bacon.

Tiger Lily cleaned herself after eating Henrie's bacon. She worried about Cyril, but there was nothing she could do to help him. She stretched out on a pillow underneath the detective table and was about to go to sleep when The Dreaded Uncle Honey Bear stuck his head under the tablecloth.

Tiger Lily was startled. She wasn't used to Honey Bear having the run of The Avenue. She would no longer have a heads up to his presence by hearing Grandmommy come in.

Honey Bear said, *"I've been thinking."*

"Wot?" "Trill!" "You?" "Didn't know you knew how."

Tiger Lily yelled, *"Quiet!"* Then to Honey Bear, she said, *"Tell us."*

"You say you have a mouse."

"Brown Mousie," offered Sassy Pants.

"Yes. That one. Perhaps he heard something last night that could be helpful. All sorts of people drink at night, and, well, he's in the right place."

"Good idea!" "Let's go see Brown Mousie!" "Wow!" "Trill!"

Eight cats, led by Honey Bear and Tiger Lily, ran through the foyer and out the door. Outside, they didn't even bother to use the sidewalk. They cut across the lawn in front of the carriage house and barreled into Sassy P's.

Everyone wanted to be the first to get in and find Brown Mousie. Cats tripped over one another, vying for the cat door. Mr. Bean and Mo, going through at the same time, had to stop to bat one another in the face. Neither would back out to let the other enter until Sassy Pants, from behind, caught both of them in the haunches with her front claws.

They ran through Sassy P's, looking under every piece of furniture. Finding nothing, they went to the back dining area and did the same. Most of them called out, over and over. *"Brown Mousie! Brown Mousie!"* They got nothing in reply.

Finally, exhausted from the search, they sat underneath a potted bush and breathed heavily.

Sassy Pants, younger than most and not as winded, said, *"Lets me calls him. We probly scairt him bad."*

"Good idea."

"Brown Mousie! Itz me, Sassy Pants. We's not gonna hurts you. We wants to talk to you. Iz you here?"

A little brown nose poked out from a hyacinth. Sassy Pants saw it and trotted up.

"Hey! We's not gonna hurts you. We wants to no if you sees or hears sumpin las nite bout bad men."

Brown Mousie looked at the large group of his natural enemies. He quivered and shook, but reminded himself these cats were supposed to be his friends. He finally looked at Sassy Pants and gave a quick nod.

"Cool! Wot you hear?"

The little brown mouse chittered and Sassy Pants translated.

"She hears some mens tawkin' bout some guys."

"Dey has a boat."

"Dey sells drugs."

"Dey awmose gotted cotched by a cose gard."

"Dey tinks dey no who it is. Mus be dose idiots fwom cross da lake, dose wons dat gotted rested las year."

"Da one guy say he seen dem rite afore dey rested las year in Treaty. Is dat wot you say, Brown Mousie? Treaty?"

"Yes, Treaty. Da one guy gots a girlfren in Treaty."

"She has a house on da lake."

"Day probly go dere."

"Lease dat's wot da guy sayz."

Sassy Pants sat back and looked at the cats. *"I tink dat's all."*

"So," said Little Socks. *"Now we have a town. How do we tell Mommy?"*

Eight cats and a little mouse looked around at one another. No one had an idea.

Finally, Mr. Bean, in his whispery voice, said, *"Tiger Lily, did you learn how to write?"*

"No. But I guess I can figure it out. I would have to make the words on something. I can try."

Little Socks jumped up. *"I'm going to the office. We can find paper there."*

They scrambled up and toward the office. Sassy Pants stayed back for a bit. *"You better nots come. Dey excited an mite forget youse a fren."*

Brown Mousie nodded and slipped back into the hyacinth stems.

In the office, the desk, computer table and bookcases were filled with cats looking for paper. In their haste, they knocked down books, pens, inventory sheets and a few bottle openers.

Kali finally yelled, *"Here! This is the printer. There's paper here."*

Kali grabbed a piece of paper with her teeth. Ko got another, and Mr. Bean, anxious to help, ripped one up in his excitement. Then another. And another. Dismayed, he looked at the half sheets of paper on the floor and the other half sheets still in the printer.

Little Socks huffed and grabbed two in her teeth. She pulled. The two in her mouth and the half sheets came loose, half sheets slowly falling to the floor.

On top of the desk, Tiger Lily looked with dismay at the pens and pencils. *"I can't hold these things. How am I going to write?"*

Honey Bear called from the wine room. *"Come in here. You can paint with your paw. We just need to find something that will work."*

The cats ran out of the office, leaving a clutter.

Mo prowled the top shelf of a jelly and jam rack. He found a raspberry jam with just the right amount of color.

He stood to get a better grip and tipped the jar over. Too late, he called, *"Trill!"* There wasn't time for anyone to translate that into "Look out below."

The jar landed with a loud crash. Shards of glass and clumps of jam spread out over the floor. The cats received splotches of red raspberry jam on various body parts, but the glass missed anything important.

Kali dropped a piece of paper by the largest clump of jam. *"Here. Use this."*

Tiger Lily stood, paw poised over the jam, then she sat. She looked at Little Socks. *"How do you spell Treaty?"*

"You expect me to know?"

"Well...."

Tiger Lily thought about it. There were two sounds. Tree and dee. She closed her eyes and visualized the game board, sounding out the words in her mind. The first word was "candyland." There was a dee sound in there! She reached for the jam, then stopped herself. No, that was the second sound.

There was a tree in the middle of the board. What were the words? She concentrated as hard as she could, and the words finally swam into focus. "Gingerbread plum tree." That was it! That last part!

She dipped her paw into the jam, and with an unpracticed talent that could be likened to a toddler's first attempts, she drew a letter for the first time. She made a passable "T" that used up half the page. She sat back to look at it. *"I think that's right, but it's too big. I'll have to make the letters smaller."*

She used part of her paw, just the front corner, to get jam for the second letter, a hard one.

Sassy Pants could barely breathe. She got closer and closer, until, after Tiger Lily made the stick then dipped again to make a curly piece, Sassy's nose was on the page.

Tiger Lily bopped her on the nose, leaving a red, sticky mark on the little girl's nose.

Tiger Lily dipped again and made the rest of the "R."

"The next two are the same."

By now, Tiger Lily had just a corner of a page left. She put the smallest tip of her paw in the jam, made a line, then an approximation of three little lines. She tried to do the same again, but only had room for the first line.

"I need another sheet of paper."

Ko brought her sheet over. Tiger Lily made the three lines for the second "E," then sat down to think again. What letters made the dee sound?

Oh, right. She dipped her paw again and made another stick, then curved a line around to make a "D."

"I'm on the last letter," she said, as she dipped and made a short stick. She dipped two more times and made little lines for the top of the letter.

She sat back to look at the two pages. *"I think Mommy can read it."*

They all looked at the pages, proud of their accomplishment, until Honey Bear said, *"So, you're going to tell them to go to Treaty, but what are they going to look for?"*

Mr. Bean was the first to come up with an answer. *"Girlfriend!"*

Mo said, *"Trill!"*

Kali and Ko translated at the same time. *"Can you spell that?" "That's a hard word!"*

Dejected, they looked at the completed papers. Little Socks jumped up. *"I know! Make a picture!"*

"Yes!" "Trill!" "Draw a picture!" "You can do that!"

"I need another piece of paper."

Little Socks brought one to her. Tiger Lily stared at the page, then looked around at solemn faces. *"Does anyone know how to draw?"*

No one answered in the affirmative.

Mr. Bean suggested, *"You need a head."*

Tiger Lily put her entire paw into the jam, then smashed her paw onto the paper, making a blurry paw print.

"Then a body," offered Ko.

Tiger Lily dipped her whole paw again and drew a line from the head to almost the bottom of the page. The line and the head were the same width. *"How do I make the head bigger?"*

"Make more prints on top of it."

Tiger Lily did that, adding two more paw prints to the head.

"You needs leggies."

Tiger Lily thought about it, then put just the tip of her paw into the jam. She made one skinny line on one side of the body, then dipped again to make a second.

She sat back. Everyone looked at the picture with a critical eye.

"I don't think she'll understand."

"She might."

"It's too much for her to have to figure out. Mommy's nice and stuff, but is she that smart?"

"Mommy's really smart."

"Well, I'm just sayin'…"

Tiger Lily roused herself. *"We have to do this. Who's carrying the pages?"*

Kali, Ko and Mr. Bean grabbed pages and followed Tiger Lily home. They did the best job they could to keep the pages out of the dirt on their way across the yard to the Inn.

Annie stared. All of the cats were there. Honey Bear sat in front of the group, side-by-side with Tiger Lily.

Annie could never help herself. She talked to them as if they could answer her. "What have you been up to?"

Most cleaned themselves. Annie noticed red stuff on some of them, and she reached down to pick a piece of broken glass from Mo's long hair. Mo had a history with broken glass, and it wasn't pretty.

Annie picked him up to examine him closely. She didn't see any more glass, but she wiped a red spot from his tail. She brought her finger to her nose. Raspberry?

Tiger Lily sat behind three pieces of paper with lots of tooth marks, splotches and lines in something red, and dirty paw prints. She looked up at Annie and touched the papers with her paw, one after the other.

"Is there an order to this? Is that what you're saying?"

Tiger Lily again touched first one sheet, then the second, then the third.

Annie reached down to put Mo on the floor. She picked up the papers, careful to do it in the order Tiger Lily instructed.

Confused, she looked at the splotches and lines. She sniffed the pages. She looked at them some more.

Suddenly, she ran through the dining room to the kitchen. She grabbed the telephone and dialed. When the phone was answered on the other end, she cried, "Cheryl, call Ray! Tell him to go across the lake to Treaty."

"Why, Annie? That's nowhere near the search area."

"I don't have time to explain. Just tell him! And tell him there's a friend or a girlfriend…well, someone lives there."

Tiger Lily had followed Annie into the kitchen. After she hung up, Annie reached down to scoop her up into a hug. "My precious girl. I don't know how you did it, but…I love you."

Tiger Lily would have purred, but the hug was way too tight.

27

Henrie had followed Annie into the kitchen. He now looked at the pages, spread out on the kitchen counter. They were a raspberry mess.

Nancy and Sam came to the kitchen. Henrie turned his back to them to shield the pages. He scooped them up and took them to the pantry, closing the door after depositing them on a shelf.

"Annie, I've just been trying to explain your odd behavior to Austin and Angela. I'm afraid my explanations are not making much sense. What got into you?"

"I just had an idea, Mom, where Ray could go to look for Chris, and, well, I wanted to share it as soon as it came to me."

"What kind of an idea?"

"Oh, I remember hearing about…um…"

Henrie broke in. "She remembered hearing about some drug traffickers in a town across the lake."

"Where would you hear about that, Annie?"

Henrie answered. "One hears things at Mo's and Sassy P's. In fact, it is difficult to go anywhere in town without hearing gossip. Putting the gossip into the proper perspective is the trick."

"Henrie's right, Mom. I heard about this, oh, weeks ago, and it just now came to me."

"Well, be that as it may, if we don't leave now we will be late for church."

Henrie and Annie followed, holding back as the rest of the family left for Soul's Harbor. As they walked out the door, Annie heard Austin ask, "What happened to your face? And, if I may be so bold, what is that smell?" She didn't listen to the reply. She counted heads to make sure all her cats were present and moved closer to Henrie.

Henrie asked, "Are you sure you interpreted the pages correctly? We have never known them to do this before."

"Henrie, I swear Tiger Lily has been learning how to read. This is the logical next step. She's learning to write."

"How do you know she is learning to read?"

"She's paying more attention to the menus."

Henrie looked down at Annie. "Really?" It sounded more like a dissing statement.

"Really."

Henrie pressed on. "Then why, if she is learning to write, would she point you toward Treaty?"

"Who knows? They heard something. They sensed something. They have spies out in the community. I don't know. Henrie, I just hope I didn't send them on a wild goose chase."

"Let us hope your wild geese are flying toward Chris."

"It will take them forever to get across the lake. Hopefully they can call the state police over there while they're on the way."

By the time they reached the church, Annie was wiping her face with a tissue. She looked at the kids and wondered how they could remain so cool with all that fur.

Inside the church, Annie and her group sat in the back three pews. The cats jumped up and claimed lap space on or pew space beside Henrie, Annie and Nancy. Honey Bear, of course, claimed Nancy mostly for himself, bopping cats on the nose if they dared to come close. Most of the adults held fans like the ones that used to be handed out by funeral homes for use in church. Funeral homes didn't make them anymore. Annie had commissioned them from a local printer the summer before, when the church's air conditioner went out. At the back of the room, Annie could feel a bit of a breeze from all the fans in front of her.

Teresa based her sermon on the text from Ecclesiastes Three. She read from the New King James Version of the Bible.

To everything there is a season, a time for every purpose under heaven: a time to be born, and a time to die; a time to plant, and a time to pluck what is planted; a time to kill, and a time to heal; a time to break down, and a time to build up; a time to weep, and a time to laugh; a time to mourn, and a time to dance; a time to cast away stones, and a time to gather stones; a time to embrace, and a time to refrain from embracing; a time to gain, and a time to lose; a time to keep, and a time to throw away; a time to tear, and a time to sew; a time to keep silence, and a time to speak; a time to love, and a time to hate; a time of war, and a time of peace.

As she moved from text to sermon, Teresa directed her comments in large part to Annie, in the back on Teresa's left, and to Janet, in the middle on her right.

Annie didn't remember all of it, but she remembered these lines. "It is not yet time to dance, because we wait to hear. It is not yet time to mourn, because we wait to hear. We must trust that before the sun sets, it will be time to dance."

As Teresa released the congregation, she said, "Annie and Henrie asked me to say that, even though we are in a period of crisis, the community picnic will still go on. This is Sunday in Chelsea. We wouldn't know how to act if we couldn't have our picnic on the beach."

Annie heard voices in the kitchen. She and Henrie followed the voices and found Trudie, Felicity and Candice. Candice filled a large picnic basket with containers.

"Hi. We thought we'd get the picnic ready so you didn't have to."

Henrie started to protest but Annie put a hand to his arm. Instead, he said, "Thank you. That was thoughtful."

Annie took stock of the picnic basket. "Are you taking this to Cheryl?"

"Yep. I'm going to sit at the radios with her until we get word from someone. Anyone."

"I should go with you."

"You should not should upon yourself. But that being said, allow me to should upon you. You should stay here with your family...and with Chris's family."

"Do I have to?"

Candice laughed, the full-throated, head-thrown-back-to-show-off-that-gorgeous-hair laugh.

Henrie moved among the dishes of food, covered and ready to be packed for the beach. Annie joined him.

There was fried chicken. How could you have a picnic without fried chicken? Annie couldn't smell evidence it had been cooked here, so Trudie and Felicity must have opened up the kitchen at the Café early this morning.

They made sandwiches as well. Annie opened the lid of the first container and sniffed. She picked up a corner of pumpernickel bread. Corned beef and hot pickle mustard. The next container held herbed chicken and hot peppers on pita bread.

Then they reached the salads. Annie looked at Henrie and he looked back. Henrie reached into a drawer and brought out several forks, a handful for her and a handful for him.

Red potato salad with a light oil dressing and scallions. Annie tasted dill. Corn and chickpea salad in an oil dressing. In this salad, Annie tasted both lime and cilantro. Last, she tried the tomato and pasta salad made with penne and red onion. She forked a piece of fresh basil before closing the container.

Two large round trays were on the end of the counter. One contained vegetables, the other fruit. Strawberries, blueberries, apple slices, grapefruit and orange sections, kiwi and mango.

Trudie put the trays on the bottom shelf of a rolling cart, then loaded other dishes on the middle and top shelves. Henrie pulled out paper plates and napkins. Felicity added pitchers of iced tea and lemonade.

Rather than be a fifth wheel, Annie said, "I'm going to check on Austin and Angela." She went to the second floor and knocked on a guestroom door. It was answered by Austin.

"We're having a picnic on the beach. Please come down and join us."

"I believe we would rather not."

"I'm sorry to hear that." Annie turned to walk away, then turned back. "We'll just be outside. You get to our private beach through the back porch. You haven't had a tour. Just take a left at the bottom of the stairs, instead of going to the dining room."

"It's a private beach?"

"Yes. It's part of the Inn's property."

"Well, in that case, we may come. Who is attending?"

"Almost everyone that lives on The Avenue, and a few additional folks. Friends. It's open to anyone, including guests of the Inn. Right now, the only guests that will be here for lunch are my family."

"We'll think about it. Thank you."

Austin closed the door with a little force. Annie stood for a few seconds, then turned to go downstairs.

On the beach, Nancy and Sam played at the edge of the water with their grand and great-grandchildren. And the cats. Annie watched them wistfully. They had a good life. They had the time and money needed to maintain a home and to vacation with family. With a few ups and downs, they had their health.

Tiger Lily and Mr. Bean stayed close to the picnic tables as Annie arranged food. Annie absent mindedly touched and petted them as she wondered what life had in store for her in her later years. Hopefully, she would share her life with Chris. Probably here, in this house and on this beach.

They would frolic at the edge of the water with cats. Twenty cats. More. Perhaps they would open a shelter for homeless cats, and all the neglected cats of Chelsea would make their way to the Inn.

They would all be healthy. Friendly. Not prone to accidents in the house. Nurturing of other cats and dogs, and well, why not, the mice of the community.

As she thought about it, gazing out at the lake, head moving this way and that, eyes a bit glazed over, she was startled at Henrie's touch.

"A penny?"

"Oh! Henrie. Sorry. I got lost in a little daydream."

"Care to share?"

"Um…I think not. Oh, people are starting to come."

Indeed, people were starting to come. Annie and Henrie moved into host and hostess mode and greeted everyone as they arrived, taking plastic containers, crock pots and glass dishes to arrange on the table. Meats and main dishes closest to the plates, then salads and side dishes. Half of the second table was eventually filled with desserts of every variety.

Rolls of paper towels were handy – for dirty hands and sweaty faces – at the ends and in the middle of the tables. Annie reached for a towel and then turned when she heard the hum of an electric wheelchair.

Holly, Jolly and a young, handsome coffee-skinned man made their way along the bricked walk that followed all of the well-traveled areas of the beach. They were preceded by two large cats, who lunged forward when they saw the other cats at the water's edge.

"Jet, I'm glad you made it. Did you get moved in?"

"Yeah, kinda."

"Kinda?"

Holly laughed. "We're going to have to figure out what's mine, what's his, what's ours, and what's way too much."

Jolly added, "And some of that, in the common rooms, will be what's mine! I'm glad we made those separate suites, though. It's going to be nice to have a man around the house, and a place to go by myself."

A sharp voice from behind said, "Well, this seems like a big event."

Annie turned to Angela. "Not really. Everyone who can come does, and, well, the food just happens. Angela, let me introduce you."

As the young adults greeted Angela, Annie said, "Holly and Jolly own the hardware and electronics store across The Avenue, and Jet has just moved in with them. Next week he's going to start work at Sassy P's." After a second, she added, "My winery. Next door."

"Oh. I see."

Holly widened her eyes just a bit and said, "We're going to dabble our toes in the water."

As they left, Annie turned back to Angela. "I'm so glad you decided to come. You'll have a chance to meet our friends."

"You certainly don't waste any time, do you?"

"Excuse me?"

"Chris is out there, somewhere, he could be hurt, or...or dead...and here you are, throwing a party."

Annie found her spine. "I am not throwing a party. Everyone who can be looking for Chris is looking. I'm doing what I can to hold myself together, and this is how I do it. I have friends. I count on them. They count on me. We do this for one another. We make life go on, no matter what."

"And you're all such good friends. I know. I'm sick of hearing about all your friends. And what is it with all of you? You mix everything up. Just look at that couple!" Angela motioned toward Jet and Holly.

Annie turned to look. Jet picked Holly up from the wheelchair and set her gently on the sand at the water's edge. He crouched beside her as Jolly walked along the edge, picking up and bringing something, probably shells, to Holly.

"Jet and Holly? What's wrong with them?"

"They need to stick with their own kind!"

Annie was confused. "You mean Holly should only have a boyfriend that lives in a wheelchair?"

"No! You know what I mean! He's a Mexican!"

"What? Jet? He's Puerto Rican, and he grew up in Chicago." Annie leaned over to busy herself by taking off lids and putting serving utensils into the dishes.

"So okay, he's not Mexican. I'm not familiar with all those groups. How many Puerto Ricans are in the United States?"

Annie stood up straight and turned to look Angela square in the face. "Is that a trick question?"

"What?"

"Forget it." Annie turned from the table to walk away. Instead, she stood still. She looked at Carlos, Isabel, Daniela, Rosa and Valeria. They must have been standing there for a few moments. Among the five of them, they held seven trays of breads, cookies, pies and one of Daniela's amazing Mexican meat dishes.

Without a word, they moved past Annie to set the dishes on the picnic table. Carlos nodded. Isabel and Daniela moved toward Annie to give her a hug and murmur words of encouragement. As they left, moving toward a stash of chairs halfway to the water, both Rosa and Valeria touched Annie's hand.

Annie looked at Angela. "Well, you are making yourself very welcome here." Annie turned on her heel and stormed down to the water.

Annie stayed to herself. Well, almost. Tiger Lily stuck to her like glue. Annie kindly brushed off suggestions from several people that she join them at this set of chairs or that, or at this game or that. She accepted a glass of chilled white wine from Jesus, but otherwise stayed to herself. With Tiger Lily.

Until Janet came up to her.

"Annie, how are you doing?"

"Oh, you know. How are you doing, Janet?"

"The girls and I are fine. Well. Not really. But we haven't hit pure panic mode yet. I see you have in-laws to deal with."

"More like outlaws. I've tried to hold it together for them, but that woman doesn't make it easy."

"I can tell. People are talking about it. Wondering what they can do to help."

"I don't know if there is anything they can do."

"Well, they're trying. Look."

Annie turned around. Henrie sat with Angela and Austin at a round table close to the garden. Martha had come; she sat with them.

Laila joined Janet and Annie. "Henrie's got them under control, Annie. Look. Mem and Frank are going to join them."

Three cats were on top of the table, poking around the plates. Sassy Pants, Mo and Speckles. The cats were teaching the little kitten bad manners. Still, Annie hoped one – or even all three – would step in Angela's plate.

Henrie looked up and caught Annie's eye. He excused himself and walked to the water to join the small group.

"Are you ready to resume life among the living?"

Annie smiled. "Only you are allowed to say such things to me. And Laila. And Janet."

Annie's eyes were drawn to the path leading around the side of the Inn. A lone man approached.

"Look, Ian's here."

Mo saw him as well. Mo leapt from the round table, accidently snagging Austin's plate with his hind claws. Mo went one way; the plate went another.

Annie laughed. Mo could never get enough of Ian and his two-handed kitty caresses. Poor Austin. No. Not poor Austin. Welcome to my world, Austin, and like it or leave it.

Annie turned back to the water, praying silently that Chris was out there, and that he would be home soon. Then she heard it. The commotion that always accompanied a press group.

She turned.

Dan Tapper, face and neck marred with yesterday's cat scratches, was on her private property. He led a camera crew to her private garden area and looked everywhere for…for her! Darn that man! Annie had taken all she was going to take.

She thrust her wine glass into Henrie's hand and stomped through the sand to the garden area, hands in power-walk mode. When she reached the news crew, she squared off nose-to-nose with Dan.

"This is private property. You have no right to be here. Get out!"

The cameras rolled, catching her sweaty face.

Annie stood her ground. She had time to register the marks on Dan's face left by Tiger Lily the day before.

Dan Tapper backed up just a bit, enough to face the cameras and say, "We're here on the private beach behind Annie Mack's KaliKo Inn. She's here, with, well, it looks like a lot of people. Looks like they're having a party to celebrate the homecoming."

Annie grabbed Dan by the elbow and pulled him around. "What? What do you know? Did you hear something?"

Around the beach, cell phones came out of pockets and backpacks. Annie glanced around. Did anyone have anything yet? Jet glanced up at her and came at a fast trot. He showed her the local news, streaming live.

Dan Tapper wasn't on screen yet. The anchor spoke, but with the natural noise going on, Annie couldn't make out what he was saying. Scrolling at the bottom of the screen were the words, "State Police report men found in Treaty."

Annie turned to Dan and grabbed him by the lapels with both hands. "Talk to me! Did they find Chris? Is he alright?"

Annie registered a large number of people behind and around her. She heard her mother, somewhere by the camera. Nancy screamed, "You terrified my cat! You ambushed us on camera! Give me that thing!"

She heard Angela and Austin. They were yelling almost in unison, "Tell us what you know!" "What do you know?"

Henrie came up behind her and leaned down to whisper something.

"What, Henrie? What?"

"Cheryl is on the phone. Chris is safe. They are all safe."

Annie collapsed back into Henrie's arms, then she rebounded. Before Henrie could stop her, Annie's fist, in a sharp right cross, connected with Dan Tapper's nose. Annie heard a gratifying crack. Her blouse shone with red, wet spots.

The cameras rolled on.

28

Annie sat in the shade of the garden outside the all-season porch. Her right hand was alternately in a pan of ice water and on her lap in a towel.

Jennifer got to her quickly. The bruising would be minimal. Unfortunately, Marie got to Dan Tapper quickly, too. Annie wished he had to suffer more before pain killer was administered.

Annie watched Martha. She stayed behind to clear up the mess so Annie and Henrie could tend to other things. She was a great friend.

Annie sighed. She looked at Tiger Lily.

Tiger Lily sat on the table. She seemed to talk to some butterflies. Only for a bit, though. A group of them, dozens, seemed to rise as one. Tiger Lily and Annie watched as they rose on the breeze and turned south. Soon, they were gone.

Annie turned to look at Tiger Lily. The cat watched the horizon, perhaps willing the butterflies to return. Or to take her with them. Annie couldn't tell. Tiger Lily finally lowered her face to look at Annie.

"They'll come back next year, darlin' girl. Come here. I'll give you a hug if you give one to me."

Tiger lily jumped to her lap, careful to avoid the injured hand.

Annie could hear Jenny, her attorney, on the porch. Jenny talked in a low tone to Nancy, Sam and Henrie. Annie heard snatches of Jenny's side of the conversation. "...saw the tape ... clearly told them to leave ... Tapper obstructive ... pushed you, Nancy ... neither of you will be charged."

Annie looked at the water. So calm. There were times she wished she had a sailboat. She could go out anytime she wanted. Put out, leave the world behind. Maybe she would take the cats. Surely she could teach them to swim.

Austin appeared in her line of sight. He had been walking on the beach. Now he walked toward the Inn. Toward her. He would walk right past her and might be forced to speak.

Annie sighed again.

Tiger Lily sat up and put a paw on her cheek. Annie turned to look at her. Tiger Lily said something.

"What is it, darlin' girl?"

Again, Tiger Lily said, *"Remember the butterflies, Mommy. Let them go, and happiness will come to you."*

Annie hugged her tight. "I wish I could understand you. I think you're smarter than all of us humans put together."

Tiger Lily purred.

Austin reached her and actually pulled up a chair. He sat heavily, reached over and took Annie's hand. The uninjured one.

She was so shocked, she let him do it.

"Annie, Angela and I had a talk a while ago. I've just been walking, thinking things through."

Annie said nothing.

"Angela has...we both have been pretty rough on you. Parents gets ideas about what their son should do, what he should be, and, to be honest, we wanted something different. Something different than what he chose."

"You mean me."

"No. I mean everything. He chose the Coast Guard when he could have been an officer in the Navy. He chose this town when he could have lived near us."

Austin continued to hold Annie's hand. He looked at the lake, where the sun started to hang low in the sky. The long August day was not yet finished.

He continued, "And yes, he chose you, but you aren't the issue. You live here. You have a life here. You would never push him to go further. To go higher. I don't think you would ever hold him back, but, in our world, a wife pushes her husband to be all that he can be. Not just what he wants to be."

"So you aren't going to ask him to choose? Me or you?"

"I was never going to do that, Annie. Angela has had a hard time with this, and it looks like that was what she was doing. I don't think, deep in her heart, she really meant to do that, but I can see how it looked. From your perspective."

Annie said nothing more. Tiger Lily reached up again to touch her cheek. She looked down at her first kitty. Her first kitty looked back as if to say, "See, Mommy? I told you."

Henrie brought a phone to Annie. "I think you will want to take this call."

Chris. Annie almost started to cry. She held onto Tiger Lily so tightly with one arm that the cat struggled to get free.

Henrie took Tiger Lily from Annie and walked back to the porch. As Annie spoke into the phone, she noticed Henrie seemed to whisper into Tiger Lily's ear.

To Chris, she said, "Are you okay? Will you be home soon?"

On the other end of the line she heard, "I'm fine, Annie. I'll be there in a few hours. The police just finished with us and Ray has The Escape ready to go."

"How long will it take?"

"I'll be there before you know it. I love you, Annie."

"I love you, too."

The two let a silence drift, then Chris said, "My parents are there?"

"Yes. Your dad's right here. I'll give him the phone."

Austin, Annie realized, had struggled against taking the telephone from her, but now, he took it slowly, nodding his thanks.

"Son, we're...I'm so happy you're not hurt, that you're on your way home. I just...we were just so afraid. .... I know, son. .... Yes, we've made arrangements to stay a couple of nights. .... Yes. Here at the Inn. This is a great place. Nice people. Good people. .... I can tell you she has a great right cross...." With a chuckle, he said, "I'll tell you that story later, son. .... I'll let you talk to her."

Annie took the phone with a smile. "Chris, don't believe everything your father tells you."

In the library, a pile of cats and one little dog settled in for story-telling.

Honey Bear told Tillie, Fat Cat and Scaredy Cat about their morning adventure.

Tillie, Fat Cat and Scaredy Cat were dumbfounded. Tiger Lily could write?

Little Socks, Kali, Ko, Mo, Sassy Pants and Mr. Bean were dumbfounded. The Dreaded Uncle Honey Bear was telling a story?

Speckles soaked it up. She was impressed to be a part of this great gathering. All of the detectives in one place! And then, they invited her to tell them about Little Fred and her Great Adventure!

"She can't talk, not like us, so she couldn't tell me what happened. But I think she's okay. She looks alright, and she still eats and poops and pees. For a little while, she cried a lot. I think that's settled down, though."

"What about that man? What happened to him?"

Speckles giggled. *"I scratched him all up, and he got really infected. They had to take him to the hospital."*

Everyone laughed with appreciation. Mr. Bean asked, *"What will happen to him?"*

"Mom and Martha talked about it a couple of times. It sounds like he said he would sign something away, I'm not sure what, but when he does, he won't be able to say he's Little Fred's dad."

"That sounds good."

"Yeah. And he's going to go to prison for a while, and then he has to stay away."

"Far away?"

"He can't come to this town."

"*Well, that's good news. Hey, has anyone heard what's happening with Cyril?*"

Tiger Lily walked in, head and tail held high. "*They'll be home in a few hours.*"

"*Really?*"

"*Chris was just on the phone with Mommy. Henrie said everybody was okay, Cyril, too.*"

"*I'll bet he and Jock will be able to tell us stories for a long time, now.*"

"*Yeah. Jock will have to tell Cyril that news guy called him famous!*"

"*He'll rub it in real good.*"

"*Just like when that dog like him was going to win the dog show.*"

"*Trill!*"

"*No! Dat wasznt a good time. Dey wuz mad.*"

"*Oh, surely it won't be that bad.*"

"*I don't know. I think Jock better keep that to himself.*"

"*Jock isn't made that way. But maybe he'll wait until Cyril is all rested up.*"

"*Hey, Scaredy Cat, who's that guy with Holly?*"

"*That's her boyfriend. His name is Jet. He's going to work at Sassy P's.*"

"*I tot I seed him afore. He wuz in da wine-ry a cupple times. He toks to Jesus an Minnie bout a job.*"

"*Yeah. Sounds like he's going to help Jesus with the wines and help manage the place.*"

"*He smells nice.*"

"He's nice to Holly."

"Jolly likes him, too."

Kali got a dreamy look on her face. *"He's handsome."*

The room lapsed into silence until Mr. Bean asked, *"So did it work, Tiger Lily? Did they catch the guys in Treaty?"*

Tiger Lily purred and stretched to her entire length. She took her time with the stretch and finally curled into a comfortable stance. She smiled and looked around at the group of companions.

"Henrie said we're heroes again. He said Ray went across the lake after getting our message. He said they found out where the bad men might be – he didn't explain that part – but they found them. In Treaty."

Tiger Lily downplayed the extraordinary role she played in this adventure. Before she dropped off to sleep, she said, *"We'll have to thank Brown Mousie for the tip."*

Tiger Lily woke up when Annie left the house. She was talking to Henrie. "Janet's here. We'll drive to The Marina, but Chris and I will walk back."

Annie's family was in the television room when they arrived. Everyone. From Nancy and Sam to the twins. There was too much excitement in the air for two-year-olds to sleep. Annie went upstairs to get Angela and Austin while Chris took the time to hug everyone, starting with Nancy. "You're getting some battle scars, Nancy."

"They'll clear up. Marie gave me something that – she promised me – will clear it right up."

"Is that what I smell?"

"Yes. It's got a dreadful odor."

Everyone had to say something, but by the time he got to the twins, the hugs had run out. Jessica laughed. "They'll get to know you one of these days, but not yet."

Chris heard his mother come into the room. He turned just in time to brace for the rush and the arms that wrapped around him.

They stood for a while, rocking back and forth, while Chris said, "It's alright, Mom. I'm fine. I'm fine."

Austin reached over to shake Chris's hand while Angela continued to hold him close.

Annie and Henrie came into the room with trays of drinks and snacks. Chris heard Annie say, "Turn it on. Let's see how bad it is."

The large screen television was turned on and the nightly news started to scroll. Annie led Chris to a comfortable seat in front of the television.

"Good evening. Welcome to the Lake Region's best nightly news cast. I'm Charles Veritone, and this is WQVX, Channel Two news. Tonight we have footage of an earlier report from Dan Tapper. Once again, he was in Chelsea for breaking news. Dan, it's been quite an exciting couple of days there. What do you have for us?"

The camera cut to Dan Tapper. He stood in front of a countertop desk. His face and neck were covered in red streaks. His nose was wrapped in gauze. Behind him was the photo of Annie at the Blue Bottle Winery.

Chris would have laughed, but his ribs hurt too much. Instead, he croaked, "You've got to be kidding!"

Dan Tapper was talking. It was the voice of a man with a nose stuffed with wadding. Neither his appearance nor his voice kept him from speaking in his most officious manner.

"Once again we were live in Chelsea with breaking news. Two men, believed kidnapped or even, possibly, killed, in a major drug incident, were found today in the town of Treaty, on the other side of the lake."

Dan turned to look toward Charles, and the screen split. Dan was now on the right and Charles on the left. Dan talked; Charles nodded somberly at each important point.

"Charles, as you know, we were the only station to capture live, on camera, a major drug arrest at the Blue Bottle Winery. We continued that coverage, and once again, we were the first to get the news that the men, now known to have been kidnapped, were rescued. Yes, rescued from the private home of a drug moll – I believe that is a term we can use here, Charles – and returned to Chelsea."

Now Dan turned to look straight into the camera. "I was live at the home of this woman." Dan turned to indicate the photo of Annie, then turned back. "I wanted to give you, our loyal viewers, additional information on the rescue. We were there, doing the job that we newsmen do every day," he looked back at Charles, who nodded on cue, "because, Charles, you know we are the front line. We are the ones that put our lives on the line to keep you informed."

Dan looked back at the camera. Gravely, he said, "Let's just roll this for you." The full screen dissolved to the video.

The footage appeared to be unedited. It was a jumbled montage of people and body parts with voices overlaying voices.

Chris saw Annie. He saw and heard Annie tell the news crew to leave the premises, then he saw her grab Dan by the elbow to ask him what he knew.

Dan didn't answer Annie. He tried to keep the camera focused on his face. In the background, Chris saw several cellphones come out. Soon, a man Chris didn't know handed Annie a phone and she watched something streaming on it. Annie then grabbed Dan by the lapels and yelled into his face. The only clear words were, "Chris? Is he alright?"

The next voice belonged to Nancy. She wasn't on camera, but she was angry about something. The camera was no longer focused on Dan, or on anything around him. It jumped up and down, left and right. Chris heard someone from behind the camera say, "She won't let go! Help me!" Then in a few seconds, "Get this (bleep) away from me!"

Chris recognized the voices of both his parents. They wanted to know what the news crew knew.

Chris saw feet approaching Annie from behind. He recognized Henrie's shoes and pants legs. The camera rolled up in a wild arc, and Chris saw Annie. It looked as if she had fainted.

No. She just had a moment. All of a sudden Annie was all motion. A hard right cross left her body and connected to Dan Tapper's nose. The video stopped.

Dan was on screen again. The freeze frame behind him showed Annie's fist as it connected with his nose. Dan's head was tilted well over his right shoulder. A spray of blood, frozen in time, reached toward the camera.

A self-righteous Dan looked into the camera and said, "The safety of our citizens is at stake if the media is not allowed to report the news. We report. You decide. This is Dan Tapper, reporting to you live, from the front lines. Charles, back to you."

The camera was now on Charles, who looked as if he were stifling a laugh. He recovered quickly, though. He smiled at the camera, said, "Thank you, Dan. And now, Felix, what's up with the weather?"

The library was silent as a tomb as Henrie, remote in hand, turned the television off. No one moved. No one breathed.

Finally, Annie's almost-adult nephew, Allen, started to laugh. Then Percy. Then someone else. Then the entire room burst into laughter.

Cellphones started to chirp with tweets, Facebook links, messages, texts and calls. Annie turned on a computer and brought up her Facebook account. Message after message, post after post. The newscast was trending.

Before going to sleep, Chris turned to Facebook on his cellphone. He chuckled, leaned over to kiss Annie on the cheek and said, "He reported. The world decided he was an idiot."

Chris wanted to hold Annie as they slept, but seven cats surrounding and covering them made that impossible.

29

Henrie leaned against the doorway between the kitchen and dining room. The summer morning had dawned clear, but over the lake, clouds threatened another storm. It couldn't come too soon. The rain would break the heat.

Henrie considered Jeff and Mark. They were gone. They had taken breakfast to go and were on the road. They needed to explain their behavior of the past week to their respective superiors. Thankfully, a new drug supply line was nipped in the bud and, in the end, no great harm came to any citizen. Still....

Henrie turned his thoughts to the guests that remained. He watched the controlled chaos.

Patti and Fritz stood at the kitchen counter, filling thermal mugs with coffee. The modified school bus was packed and ready to go.

Allen and Percy filled plates, grabbed juice boxes and went to the library to play a video game.

Gracie ran to Henrie, gave him a hug and yelled, over her shoulder because she was already running to the library, "I'm not eating. I'm on a diet!"

Ella and Ollie stood at the buffet and argued over who should get the larger cinnamon roll.

Jessica and Paul, just in from putting their bags in the bus, ran to the back room to the sound of screams. It sounded as if the twins had fallen into a blender. They had not. Thankfully.

Nancy and Sam, of course staying on for another few weeks, stood above the fray but close enough to grab a hug or kiss from a soon-to-be-departing grandchild.

Austin and Angela now seemed to be a part of the family. They sat at the main dining table and helped with drinks and fallen utensils.

Chris moved around the room, talking to adults and children, one at a time. He moved slowly, carefully. Henrie knew his ribs were wrapped and that cuts and bruises were – for the most part – hidden beneath a polo shirt and khakis. One eye was black and a contusion was visible on the other cheek.

Annie sat at the kitchen table. She talked to Patti and Fritz as they prepared to leave.

All in all, thought Henrie, it was a good morning. He loved the children, but he would be glad when the house was quiet once again.

The phone rang. Annie answered. Henrie heard her half of the conversation.

"Good morning, Jesus … What?" At this point a look of chagrin came over her face and she looked at Henrie. She rolled her eyes. "A break-in? …. What was stolen? …. Nothing. Well, what makes you … Oh. A mess, huh? …. Raspberry? …. Cat prints? …. Do you think … Well, look, before you call the police, try to figure out if anything was stolen, and then …. Okay. No, I don't think we need to lock the cat doors. We might have mice. … The prints were only in that one place, right? …. Thanks, Jesus. I'm sorry you have to deal with that. Let's not call the police unless you find out something was taken."

Annie hung up. She and Henrie continued to look at one another, then both burst into laughter.

"I should have known, Henrie. I should have checked."

"We had no idea, Annie. What is that phrase of yours? No hurt, no foul ball?"

Patti said, "What? What are you guys…"

"Never mind, Patti. It's just…it's just a thing."

Hilly arrived by mid-morning. She looked carefully as she walked through the foyer, library, all-season porch and dining room. As usual, she found Henrie in the kitchen. "Not as bad as I thought it would be, but the rooms may be a different story. They're all empty now, right?"

"We have unexpected guests in the room facing The Avenue. I believe they stepped out to do some sightseeing. Perhaps you should start there."

Hilly poured a cup of coffee and leaned against the counter. "So. You had some excitement here. Care to share?"

"Please have a seat. I will regale you."

After several minutes of "regaling," Hilly gave a final bark of laughter. "I'm going to talk to Annie about giving me some boxing lessons. I have a couple of clients…."

Henrie laughed. Then he stood. "I would assist you today, but I must restock the kitchen larders before our next guests arrive."

Kali and Ko stood at attention in the dining room. Hilly gave them a half salute and said, "Come on, girls. We've work to do. I could use your help."

At Babar Foods, Annie and Nancy argued about groceries. And about cooking.

"Mom, I know what I'm doing. You taught me how to bake a pie. I'm going to bake two different kinds."

"Why don't you leave the baking to Carlos? Or Felicity? Or Henrie? Why ruin any hope of a relationship with Angela by doing the baking yourself?"

"Mom, I'm not completely inept in a kitchen."

Laila came out from the back room. "Only mostly inept. What are you going to make?"

"I'm going to make a main dish, a tomato tart, probably without a pie crust, soup, and dessert."

"What kind of pie for dessert?"

"Pear, bleu cheese and walnut."

Nancy turned on Annie. "Okay. Tell me about the pear pie. What recipe are you going to use?"

"I don't have a recipe, Mom. I learned to cook by watching you. You just throw stuff in."

"Well, what are you going to throw in?"

"Sliced pears, big chunks, I like big chunks, some crumbled bleu cheese, walnuts, a little bit of flour, a very little bit of brown sugar, and lemon juice."

"How will you make the crust?"

"Make a crust? Mom, I've never made a pie crust. I'll get it here. Laila carries the best kind."

Nancy's eyes rolled to the back of her head.

Laila said, "Tell us about the soup."

"Groundnut stew. I told Felicity about it, and she uses it sometimes at the Café."

"I've had it there. Sometimes it's creamy and sometimes it's more like a stew with vegetables. What will you do?"

"Creamy."

"Ingredients?"

"Oh, good gravy! Alright. I cheat. I'm going to start with a box of your roasted red pepper tomato soup, and I'll cook it with peanut butter, hot sauce, and cubed firm tofu, diced tomatoes, sautéed onion and garlic, and I'll probably throw some peppers in with the onions, and, well, whatever spices seem to fit at the moment."

"That's what Felicity makes?"

"Yes. I gave her the idea."

"Okay, I believe you. Tell us about the tomato tart."

"I like to use yellow tomatoes. The recipe I read years ago called for Roma tomatoes, but I slice yellow ones and let them drain. Then I use, let's see, sautéed onion and garlic with some mozzarella cheese – that's supposed to go on the bottom of the pie crust, but I can just put it on the bottom of a pan – and basil, and…I'll have to think about it. Cheese on top. Oh, and an egg scrambled with a little milk, poured on top before it goes into the oven."

Nancy asked, "What are you forgetting?"

"Hot sauce. I put hot sauce in the egg and milk."

"Not that, dear. What else are you forgetting?"

"Nothing, Mom. Unless you want me to say the words."

"Say the words."

Annie, in a sing-song voice while her head went back and forth in rhythm, said, "Always bake your pie on the bottom rack of the oven."

"Okay. Well. They might turn out just fine."

"They will. You'll see. I've got this."

Felicity leaned over the service counter to peer into the dining room. The Café was hoppin' today. Servers were busy, but Felicity had trained them how not to handle a rush. Don't run. Don't slam. Don't yell. Don't get excited. Keep a steady pace. Her crew took and delivered orders, bussed tables and managed the latest gossip about Annie.

She glanced at the hostess stand. Tiger Lily stood tall and proud, accepting pets and well wishes from customers going and coming.

Trudie appeared from around the corner. "I've been listening. Everyone is telling the same story. They're getting the gossip straight."

"Any flack from Geraldine and her crew?"

"They've been in and out, trying to spread a different story, but our folks are straightening everyone out. Geraldine is spreading it around that Annie was arrested Saturday, then again Sunday."

"Well, we knew that would happen. Did you see Cookie's numbers from Saturday night?"

"Wow. Eye popping. Everyone wanted to see 'the place that woman owns,' huh?"

"Looks like it. Hey, I have to get busy."

"Me, too."

Little Socks hopped from student to student, assisting as they worked on their yoga poses. To one woman, she yowled an admonition that her leg was not yet high enough. To another, she patted an ankle, clearly telling the student to put a bit more oomph into the pose.

Diana, watching the class rather than leading it, had to laugh.

All morning, people had been in and out, wanting to hear the latest. Diana tried to keep the gossip straight, but some people, mostly women, wanted to believe that Annie had gotten herself into the soup again.

It appeared to Diana that Little Socks gave her worst judgement to those women.

Pete and Cyril had lunch at Mo's. Pete hoped to escape the Monday morning gossip. He wasn't so lucky. He had to take a stool at the end of the bar because the tables were full.

Georgia appeared in front of him.

"It's good to see you, Pete." She leaned over the bar. "Hey, Cyril. It's good to see you, too!" Cyril answered with a bark and a wave of his tail.

Georgia tossed a piece of jerky to Cyril. He barked a thank you, picked it up and trotted off to find Mo.

"Pretty busy in here today."

"Yep. This is one of those all-hands-on-deck days. We knew it would happen. George called us last night."

"How's that little girl doin'?"

"Perfect, thanks to you and everyone else. It's good to have that chapter in the rear view mirror."

"What's George doing out on the floor?"

"We're just that busy. When the kitchen is overloaded, I go back to help Cookie and George comes behind the bar. When the floor is busting at the seams, George goes out there. There aren't enough people to go around."

"What are people saying?"

"About you, nothing much, except that you were, you know, held and all. How are you, by the way?"

"Fine. A few bumps and bruises."

"And Cyril?"

"He was too quick for 'em. Whenever they reached out to give him a kick, he materialized somewhere else."

"Good for him. I hear Chris was beaten up a bit."

"A bit. Not too bad. No broken bones."

"That's good. Oh, and you asked….mostly, people are just laughing about Annie again. Geraldine and her friends have been pumping up the gossip mill. We've been working overtime putting people on the right path."

Pete chuckled and ordered a burger and sweet potato fries.

Isabel sighed inwardly. It wouldn't do for anyone to notice her distress.

She worked the counter at Mo's. They were busier than she had ever seen since moving to Chelsea. Jerry couldn't turn out truffles quickly enough, and Carlos and Daniela together were hard pressed to stay ahead on cookies and pies.

The woman Isabel knew to be Geraldine stood at the counter, at least ten people behind her, and took a painfully long time to order. Mr. Bean and Tillie turned cartwheels, preened, asked for pets, rubbed ankles and, in general, made themselves loveable.

"I'll have two of those and, no, make that just one. No, I'll have three."

"Are you sure?"

"Yes…Oh, take one of those out. I was right the first time at two. Now, let me see, I want…one of those. No, that one to the back. Yes."

"Only one?"

"Yes. And I'll take…oh, give me another one of those."

And on and on and on and on.

Isabel finally turned and made eye contact with Carlos. He hurried to the counter.

"Sorry, Isabel. I didn't see how busy the counter was."

"It's okay, Carlos, but if you could please help this gentleman?"

Before Geraldine finished, Isabel watched as Carlos took care of everyone that had been in line behind her and a few more.

Geraldine finally left the store, having purchased a grand total of eight items.

Isabel reached into the dog and cat treat section. She picked out a piece for Mr. Bean and a piece for Tillie. She leaned over the counter and beckoned for them to come close.

"You worked hard to keep the guests happy while that woman took up counter space. Thank you."

At Sassy P's Wine & Cheese, another strong day was at hand. Jet stood behind the tasting counter. Today was to have been a training day, but with the number of customers, Jet was thrown to the wolves. Literally.

The first thing he learned at the morning briefing was how to handle gossip. Today would be a gossip day. This is the story. Stick to it. Do not deviate. When customers try to move you from the story, pull them back.

Today, Jet learned, keeping the gossip straight would be more important than knowing the differences between a Cabernet and a Merlot, or knowing the nuances of one Pinot Grigio versus another.

At one end of the counter, a customer said, "I'll have another taste of that Cab, Jet."

"Your taste card is filled. Can I get you another card, or would you prefer a glass?"

"I'll take the glass. Say, tell me about that reporter. What was it he did to make Annie throw a punch?"

At the other end, two young women pointed their cellphones at him and clicked away. Jet walked to that end and asked, "How can I help you?"

"You were on TV last night!"

"Yes. For just a second."

"We saw you. Cool. What was it like?"

"It all happened fairly quickly. Would you like to try a tasting today? Or can I get a glass of something for you?"

In the middle, an elderly man ordered three glasses in succession, each time asking yet another question about the incident the day before.

And on it went.

Sassy Pants was in kitty heaven. Customers were delighted to have her on the bar in front of them, "stummy" exposed for a tickle, while they filled themselves with tales of Annie.

Customers prowled the other side of The Avenue as well.

People on their lunch break stopped into The Clinic to ask about nonsense health issues. And to gossip. Jennifer called Marie to ask if they could please switch places for the day. To her chagrin, at The Drug Store, she sold an amazing amount of small items. Bandages. Iodine. Antiseptic ointment. Floss sticks. At the counter, questions about Annie and the weekend abounded.

At Bloomin' Crazy, Clara sold dozens of single flowers of all varieties. Customers stood at the refrigerated case and took inordinate amounts of times to make their selections. While they considered their flower options, they asked questions. And more questions. A few made sizeable orders.

Jolly actually sold a computer at DoubleGood. A man who came in only to gossip saw a display and said, "Oh, you sell computers? I've been needin' to get me one-a them. I want to watch the news online, ya know."

At Babar Foods, both before and after Annie and Nancy were in to shop, Laila fielded dozens of questions about "that woman" and her crazy friends. Laila didn't bother to tell them that she was one of the crazy friends.

Mem sold tea and scones at CyberHealth to people who wanted to sit and gossip and kitchen gadgets to those who wanted to stand while they got their information. A group of young adults came in to play online games in the back. For some odd reason, they needed a great deal of attention. Each time Mem responded to a request, she fielded still more questions.

Teresa was sorry that she didn't have a volunteer. Mondays were typically slow at Soul's Harbor's charity gift shop. Today, as usual, she handled it on her own. Today, most of her stock was depleted before noon. That was good for local charities, but not so good for Teresa, whose legs, feet and back ached from walking, reaching, stretching, lifting and carrying.

People who never shopped for antiques stepped into Antiques On Main. They poked around, looked at furniture, browsed Gema's jewelry counter, and talked. Some even made a purchase. Or two.

All in all, it was a good day for Chelsea small business owners.

It was a good night at the Inn. Henrie, happy to have an evening off, absented himself from the evening's festivities. He sent a prayer to the gods of…well, whatever gods would help Annie tonight.

In the upstairs apartment, Sam paced the kitchen while dinner was prepared. Nancy finally sent him to the dining room.

"Go set the table, Sam. Make yourself useful."

Sam walked to the dining room and saw – for the first time – the table draped in a linen rainbow. He took a closer look. Tablecloths that were made for smaller tables were layered together. It was pretty. Colorful linen napkins were already folded into swans at six places.

On top of the buffet, he found six sets of vibrant dinner plates and soup bowls, six funky looking wine glasses and six colorful water glasses. The silverware was a riot of color as well. Sam noticed Annie had placed six dessert plates and forks to the side, with six more napkins and a fancy pie server. A hand-painted pitcher sat on an acrylic table saver; it held iced water. As Sam placed the plates and silver around the table, he noticed table savers that would probably serve as trivets in the center, another fancy pie server, an upright soup ladle, orange, and several serving utensils. Colorful. Of course.

Sam not only set dishes around, he poured ice water into the glasses and filled the pitcher again. He set out two bottles of zinfandel and put two bottles of pinot gris into two chillers. The chillers were a boring silver color.

Finally, the witching hour arrived. Sam opened the door to Chris, himself a bundle of nerves, and poured two healthy glasses of wine. He realized he was going to have to hold the glass by the bowl, rather than the curvy, funky stem. Chris seemed to do alright with the stem.

Austin and Angela arrived, fashionably late by ten minutes, by which time Sam needed to replenish the wine for himself and Chris, plus pour a glass for "the parents."

Sam's toes were popping out of his shoes. His fingers couldn't stay still. His stomach did flip flops.

Then dinner was served. Sam watched as Nancy put her dishes on the table. Sam wasn't nervous at all about them. She made a mixed green salad, served in a purple ceramic pie pan, of all things, steamed green beans with almonds, served in a yellow pie pan, and buttery biscuits, in an orange pie pan. What was it with the pie pans?

As everyone sat at the table, Sam closed his eyes tight. He'd been smelling the savory goodness of this supposed tomato tart and the groundnut stew for an hour, but smelling wasn't seeing. Smelling wasn't tasting.

Annie brought an orange soup pot to the table, opened the lid and allowed the steam to circulate. It smelled wonderful. Like peanut butter. She placed the ladle in the tureen and said, "We serve family style here. I'll probably stand to serve the soup, but everything else will be passed."

Angela nodded her approval, although, Sam thought, she could hardly do anything else.

Finally, Annie brought a cherry red pie pan, fluted, to the table. It held a delectable-smelling dish. Sam could smell basil, cheese, onions and garlic. He sighed in relief and thought he saw Chris do the same.

Sam began to relax. He had a third glass of wine.

After dinner, Nancy and Annie cleared the table, and Sam poured coffee. Into colorful mugs that matched the dishes. He began his deep breathing exercises.

He'd been smelling this pear pie also, but once again....

The pie was a hit. It came out in a green pie plate and was served warm with scoops of vanilla bean ice cream. Angela marveled at the idea that bleu cheese, walnuts and pears could be combined into a delicious pie.

As they got up from the table, Sam walked over to Chris. They engaged in a long, heartfelt handshake of congratulations.

Annie didn't burn down the kitchen, and she actually made one heck of a meal.

30

Annie sat on the ground in the clothing tent. She sorted gently-used clothing for the back-to-school block party. The August party was always held in her private park on the last day of the month. While the beach would be perfect in August, the sand was not conducive for distributing clothes, shoes, food pantry items and school supplies.

Hair stylists preferred the park also. The breeze was relatively calm between her long building and the trees of the state park, while the breeze off the lake could be an issue. Kids enjoyed getting a new "do" at the start of the school year. Well, it wasn't actually the real start. These days, they were back in school by the middle of August. Things changed faster than Annie could keep track.

Annie heard someone call her name. She popped her head outside the tent. "What? Did someone call me?"

"I did." The booming voice belonged to Harry. Harry worked for the rental company that supplied – free of charge – tents, tables, chairs, cookers, and anything else needed by the block party committee.

"Where do you want this here thing?"

Annie took a look at the piñata set. The committee chose Angry Birds. Red, yellow and blue birds in a variety of shapes and sizes would hang from a tall shepherd's hook. Before they were smashed to pieces, that is.

Then she turned to survey the available space. This grassy area was privately owned but used by the community as a sort of long, narrow pocket park. Maybe it could be called a deep pocket park.

Throughout the space were groupings of furniture that remained year-round: picnic tables, benches, arm chairs, Adirondack chairs and rocking chairs. The park was set for the block party now. With the additional tents and activity areas, the area was a little congested.

Tents were in place for the food and drinks, shoes and clothing, school supplies and food pantry. A large-ish area was set aside for lawn scrabble, and another area, a little smaller, was painted with large, colorful round dots for lawn twister.

A plastic fence lined an area near the park. Large buckets of water stood on each end. Sponge Bob sponges soaked in preparation for a game of round robin dodge ball.

Other games dotted the park: colorful horseshoes, a bean bag toss with monster-painted goals, and a ring toss game using anchored wine bottles.

Annie pointed to an area behind Sassy P's, close to the back side of the KaliKo Inn. "I think we can find room for it over there."

"Won't that be too close to the water balloon dart board?"

They walked over to survey the property. "No, I think if we put the piñata over here, no one will be near the darts."

"What's goin' on this table? The paper here said 'no chairs,' so I didn't put any."

"Jesus and Jet painted some blocks of wood to make a jenga game. Kids will stand around the table to play." Annie juggled the table as they walked by. "It feels secure enough. I don't think table movement will knock the blocks over."

"Yep. I think it's solid. Well, I'll just set those birds up, then I'm done. I'm gonna get me one of them root beer sandwiches."

Annie laughed. The "root beer" sandwiches were actually made with root beer-soaked pulled pork. "We thought it would be a hit with the kids."

The park was beginning to fill up. Toddlers, grade school aged children, pre-teens and teens found the game areas of their choice. Cats and dogs ran freely, or were present on leashes or in carriers. Annie saw a hamster in a cage and a ferret and a rabbit on leashes.

Volunteers made sure everyone had food, drinks, and an opportunity to "shop" in the tents. Everything was provided at no charge, but decorated buckets were in good supply to receive cash donations.

Annie checked in at the food tent. Trudie was up front at a give-away table. A deep urn filled with soapy water was surrounded by bubble wands that ranged from three inches to over a foot long.

"Are these for kids only?'

"Nope. They're for the young at heart."

Annie picked up a long wand with several different sizes of holes at the end. She dipped her wand into the bubble bowl and waved her way to the front of the park. Bubbles floated in her wake. Three of her cats ran behind her and tried to catch them.

Under the shade created by the deck on the second floor of the Café, she found Chris. This was the outdoor dining area of the Café. Today, tables and chairs were moved to the side to make way for easels.

Chris dabbled in a few modes of art. He called it his stress-relieving hobby. A few pieces were given as gifts, and he kept a few for himself. Most, however, were sold for charity. Several pieces hung at the charity gift shop of Soul's Harbor, and he set up a display at most of the town's block parties. The items sold benefited the charity picked for that particular party.

This year, the committee decided to give the proceeds to the trust fund set up by the public school. This fund provided coats, boots, scarves and gloves to children who otherwise would go without in the cold winter.

Annie looked at the pieces on display. There were watercolors of sailboats on the lake, sunsets over the lake, local lighthouses at various times of day, and The Escape in its new rainbow colors.

Chris had a relatively new style: charcoals with a pop of color. He had several from which to choose. Among them were a sketch of Ramon and Fiamma from the back, looking very much alike. They sat on a park bench facing the lake; a bright rose glow indicated the sunset.

In another, a baby in a carrier held tight to the tail of a tortoiseshell cat. The cat looked up at the baby with adoring eyes. A bright yellow rattle was in the baby's other hand.

Recalling a scene from a recent block party, two long-haired cats looking very much like Honey Bear and Claire ran toward the lighthouse, the beginning streaks of an orange sunset in the distance. The faces on the cats gleamed with excitement. Annie leaned in close. The cats were running to the right. In the lower left corner, nearly invisible, was the figure of a woman, running, arms in the air.

"I'll buy this one, Chris, and give it to Mom. I don't know whether to tell her she's in it or let her figure it out on her own."

"Let her find it. If she doesn't mention it, then you can point it out to her."

Annie looked at the back corner. "Did you put those out?" She indicated a pile of pillows and cushions arranged haphazardly, but with thought. The cushions were stacked so that the ones in the corner were higher than the ones on the end. There appeared to be room for several cats and dogs.

"Yeah. You know, they play so hard while the party goes on, then they have to wait around for us to clean up. They're always zonked out somewhere, together in a pile. I just thought I would make it easy for them."

"Thanks." Annie turned to look at the other charity sale item in the front corner of the dining area.

The backdrop was a life-sized watercolor of a white sand beach on the lake. The lighthouse was visible in the distance on the right, and on the left, also in the distance, was the rainbow-colored Escape. A deep blue sky melted into the greenish blue water. A few whitecaps were visible. Birds flew overhead, one in the foreground with lots of detail.

"This is great, Chris. There is so much detail. It's so…so…lifelike."

In one box to the side were painted cardboard cut-outs. Annie had already looked at these. She knew they were life-sized pictures of each of her cats, Kali and Ko back-to-back together, and three dogs, Cyril, Jock, and Tillie. Velcro was on the back of each cut-out, to allow them to be mounted on the white sand beach.

In another box to the side were large picture frames. They were simple and ornate. They were made of rugged wood, gold, silver or brass-toned plaster, and wood or plastic painted in various colors. They were square, rectangular and oval. Some were over-large, to allow for large groupings in a portrait or painting.

Individuals, families or groups could choose their picture frame, choose cut-out companions if they wanted, hold the frame in front of them and have a portrait snapped by the resident photographer. Chris.

They could purchase a digital photo or order a print.

"Let's do ours before it gets busy." Annie waved Henrie over.

Henrie took the camera with a bit of trepidation. "Please, show me how to operate this contraption while Annie prepares the scene."

Annie knelt to put cut-outs of each of her cats on the beach, arranging them so they would be behind and surrounding Chris and her. While she worked, she felt a paw on her back.

She didn't have to turn to see who it was. "What is it, Mr. Bean?" He pawed her again. She turned. All of her cats were there. Tiger Lily looked at her with reproach. Really?

Annie sighed. She should have known they would want to pose. She dragged a bench over – one that was there for just such a thing, but the organizers had envisioned children on the bench, not cats – and asked them to get on. "Come on. It doesn't matter where you sit, as long as you leave room for Chris and me to stand in front."

Most of the cats were on the bench. Tiger Lily stood by Henrie and wouldn't move.

"What?"

Tiger Lily pawed Henrie's leg twice.

"Really? Well, you're right, you know."

Annie turned and saw Jet walk by. "Jet, can you come help us, please?"

With Jet behind the camera, Annie, Chris and Henrie posed, foregoing any frame. None would be large enough.

On the background, in the sand, were seven cats. All of them behaved as the photograph was taken. Except, of course, for Sassy Pants, who had turned to paw at a seashell painted into the sand.

As she left to do a walk-around, Annie gave Chris a kiss on the cheek. "You know I kind of consider this block party to be our anniversary."

"You do?"

"Yeah. This time last year is the first time we really, you know, took an interest in one another."

Chris laughed. "You mean it's the first time you took an interest in me."

"You didn't pay any attention to me before then."

"I did. You tried to ignore it."

"I can't imagine ignoring you."

"But you did. That's okay. I liked the chase."

Annie laughed as she walked away. She didn't want to admit that she, too, had enjoyed the chase.

Sassy Pants sunk onto the top cushion. It had been a very long day. First, she had to help at the Winery, then she had to help set up for the party. When the guests started to arrive, she directed them to various tents. Then she helped at several of the games. It was expected, you know, of famous kitty cats. That they help at the games.

Now the crowd was thinning. Mommy and her friends were cleaning up. It was time to rest.

She was joined shortly by cats and dogs from all over The Avenue. And beyond. The big dogs took up all the bottom cushions.

Cyril, Jock and Fiamma were now good friends. Fiamma had given up flirting with them, pitting one against the other. She still had a flirty attitude, but she didn't try to use it with these two big boys. Well, not often, anyway.

Sassy Pants thought back a couple of weeks, when they all worried so much about Cyril. Thank goodness he was found, and he wasn't hurt. Well, not bad. His paws were bruised up a bit, and he had a bump on the head. But he was okay now.

The best part was being able to tell him how he was saved. How if it hadn't been for her, Sassy Pants, who befriended a mouse, they would never have learned where he was.

So, okay, Honey Bear had to have the idea to talk to Brown Mousie. And Kali, Ko and Little Socks got the paper. And Mo found the ink. And Mr. Bean had some good ideas about drawing. And Tiger Lily, well, she did something absolutely amazing. Still, it all started with her, Sassy Pants, who made a friend of Brown Mousie.

Then Jock had to screw it up and tell Cyril that the news guy called him, Jock, famous. But when the big boys watched those news casts, over and over and over, it was laughable that anything intelligent could have come from that reporter's mouth. So Jock dropped it.

Now the cushions were filled with companions, yawning, stretching and getting comfortable for a nap. Tiger Lily was the last to arrive. She jumped over Jock, then settled down on a cushion with her feet on Cyril's back.

"We're getting to be so many, there's hardly room anymore."

"Chris maded enuff pillows for all of us, soze we be comfy."

"He did a pretty good job."

Cyril lifted his head to look at Tiger Lily. *"Tell me again how you can write."* Truth be told, Cyril was a little jealous.

"Mommy and Henrie are teaching me. Well, they have stuff that all of us can use."

The big dogs sat up and looked at Tiger Lily, thoughts of a nap long gone. *"Really?"*

"Yeah. In the basement, in that room we were in the night our humans got kidnapped. There's a stack of paper, and Mommy taped up all the letters in the alphabet. She told me to practice. So I did. Henrie takes those practice papers and puts

them in another pile, so we can all look back at them if we want."

"What do you use to write with?"

"Henrie makes an ink stuff. It tastes good. Usually it tastes like tuna, but sometimes it tastes like salmon. Anyway, as long as I can keep everyone from eating it," she darted a look at Ko, *"there's plenty to use. He puts more in every day."*

"So knowing how to make the letters is all there is to it?"

"No, you have to know how to spell, too. Mommy and Henrie are helping me with that, too."

"How?"

"Well, they realized, after I practiced letters for several days, that I needed to know more. So they've been hanging pictures up. Pictures of something with the name of it underneath."

"Like what?"

"Well, like chair, boat, dog, cat, man, woman, phone, paper, goose, cow. You know."

"But…"

"It's just the beginning. Like yesterday, she put pictures of all of us up, and our names."

"All of us?"

"Yeah, and Speckles, too. But you're there, Fat Cat, and you, Scaredy Cat. She uses the names the humans gave you. Even you, Claire. She put your picture there."

"Me? I don't ever help you with your work."

"But you and Honey Bear are, well, friends." Claire and Honey Bear, sitting close to one another, smiled sweetly at one another. Mo gagged. Sassy Pants had to force herself to not mention how gross it was.

"*So you can write our names now?*"

"*I'm practicing. And Mommy made it easy. Underneath our names, she put what she calls abbreviations.*"

"*Wots dat?*"

"*We've talked about this before. It's just one or two letters instead of several. This is an example. My name, Tiger Lily, is really two words. So I can abbreviate it to the first two letters of each word. Some of us are named like that. Others aren't. Like Kali and Ko. I can't use just the first letter for them, because it's the same first letter. So I have to use two letters for one word for them.*"

"*That's confusing.*"

"*It is. But I practice every day.*"

"*Is that the last of it, or will she put up more pictures?*"

"*She said she was going to put up pictures of humans, like her, Chris, Henrie, Pete…you know…all our friends.*"

Mr. Bean had a thought. "*Isn't abbreviations the thing that Mommy sometimes gets in trouble with? When she sends text things to Chris? And they get confused?*"

Tiger Lily considered this. "*Yes. I'll have to be careful how I use them.*"

Little Socks asked, "*What about numbers? You didn't know what the numbers were.*"

"*Mommy said after a while she'll put numbers up, too. But not now. She said it would be too much.*"

Tiger Lily's brain was tired, just thinking about all of this. Apparently, the conversation wore everyone else out also, because soon, the corner was filled with nothing but breathing and light snoring sounds.

Annie sat in a chair underneath the deck of the Café. She waited as Chris finished with the last of his customers. He had done a brisk business all evening, taking photographs, selling paintings and charcoals, and taking commissions to do special portraits in charcoal or watercolor.

She gazed at the pile of cats and dogs. To a certain extent, some pairing up was going on. Honey Bear canoodled with Claire; Kali curled up with Simon Finnegan; Oscar McMurphy made time with Mo.

Annie mused that Mr. Bean was the only boy kitty without a girl. Maybe she should write a poem about that. Ha!

Tiger Lily startled Annie when she jumped to her lap. "Darlin' Girl, I didn't see you."

Tiger Lily kneaded her way into a comfortable place on Annie's legs, turned around three times and curled up with a purr. Annie leaned back and closed her eyes. She lapsed into a dream of Chris and scores of cats on the beach.

Tiger Lily dreamed about flying. Not quite flying. She soared as she chased the beautiful late summer monarchs to the mountain ranges of central Mexico.

Thank You For Reading!

The family of cats and the author hope you enjoyed reading this book as much as we enjoyed writing it!

About The Author

Kathleen Thompson was raised on a small family farm in Indiana. She has an undergraduate degree in Sociology from Manchester College (now Manchester University) and an MBA from Indiana University South Bend.

In a variety of towns and circumstances, she served as a probation officer, parole agent and juvenile residential counselor before moving into administrative, marketing and fund raising positions in human service organizations. Ms. Thompson took a break from human services for seven years to own and operate a bar and restaurant. Let's be honest; that's another type of human service.

While making plans to return to her rural roots, Kathi and her mother discovered an injured kitten at the family farm. The kitten, whose face was a mass of injuries, decided to make Kathi her guardian. She wrapped herself around an ankle, purred like a V8 engine, and wouldn't let go.

Against the advice of her mother, Kathi took the kitten home and to a veterinarian. The vet diagnosed road burn serious enough to take all the fur from the left side of her face, and the kitten – Tiger Lily – eventually healed and took a huge piece of Kathi's heart.

Tiger Lily was joined by the rest, rescue kitties, all: Little Socks (thank you, Aunt Mary); Kali, Ko and Mo (thank you, Connie); Sassy Pants (thank you, Ant Sherwy); and Mr. Bean (thank you, Pulaski Animal Center). Recent arrivals Speckles (thank you, Tennille) and Moriah (thank you again, Pulaski Animal Center) have joined the cast but will not live at the Inn.

Tiger Lily's Café rattled around in Kathi's brain – there isn't much else up there – for all of the years since, sometimes as an actual café and sometimes as a book. It was less expensive to write the book.

Connect with Kathi and her family of cats at their website: www.tigerlilyscafe.com, or find them on Facebook: www.facebook.com/tigerlilyscafemysteries.

Find us on the web: www.tigerlilyscafe.com

Find us on Facebook: Tiger Lily's Café, A Mystery Series by Kathleen Thompson

Text to join: Emails are sent every two weeks. You can opt out at any time. LILYSCAFE to 22828 (You may also sign up for the emails from the website.)

www.ingramcontent.com/pod-product-compliance
Lightning Source LLC
Chambersburg PA
CBHW062109170626
46813CB00002B/377